55

FOR BETTER, FOR WORSE

LEAH LAIMAN

POCKET BOOKS

New York   London   Toronto   Sydney   Tokyo   Singapore

This book is a work of fiction. Names, characters, places and
incidents are products of the author's imagination or are used
fictitiously. Any resemblance to actual events or locales or persons,
living or dead, is entirely coincidental.

An *Original* Publication of POCKET BOOKS

 POCKET BOOKS, a division of Simon & Schuster Inc.
1230 Avenue of the Americas, New York, NY 10020

Copyright © 1994 by Xyrallea Productions, Inc.

ISBN: 0-671-86483-1

First Pocket Books printing July 1994

10 9 8 7 6 5 4 3 2 1

POCKET and colophon are registered trademarks of
Simon & Schuster Inc.

Cover art by Punz Wolff
Stepback art by Diane Sivavec

Printed in the U.S.A.

FOR BETTER, FOR WORSE

❧ 1 ❧

It was to be the wedding to end all weddings. A huge snow-white tent, its poles wrapped in white satin, had been set up on the estate grounds. Knots of white freesia tied with satin bows trimmed the seams and perfumed the air with a heavenly scent that could have been the essence of paradise itself. More freesia, purple this time, surrounded a profusion of white and purple orchids that rose from silver chalices in the center of each table. The guests were just beginning to arrive, and the caterers had finished laying out crystal and silver, linen napkins, and plates of the finest china. Each table had its own champagne fountain, and an oversized bowl of beluga caviar cushioned in a silver tureen of cracked ice, with a tiny long-handled spoon nestled in its inky center. No expense had been spared, but then, why should it have been? This was to be the wedding of Andrew Symington, heir to the D'Uberville Motor Company fortune, and he was marrying the woman of his dreams.

The fact that Samantha Myles, his bride-to-be, came from a working-class family—so far below the D'Uberville-Symington station at the apex of Woodland Cliffs' society as to give some of the dowagers headaches just thinking about the change in altitude—made no difference to Drew. Sam was beautiful, with copper hair, green eyes, creamy skin, and a gorgeous figure that belied her appetite. And she was smart. A natural-born automotive genius, Sam had invented a device that could change the production of automobiles and result in a more cost-conscious, environmentally sound industry. Though everyone knew it was a love match, the merger of her genius with the fortunes of the scion of DMC could also prove to be profitable all around.

When she'd accepted Drew's proposal, Sam hadn't even considered her fiancé's family business. It had been his patrician face, with his straight black hair and startlingly blue eyes, rather than his formidable lineage, that had attracted her at first. In fact, knowing he was a Symington had only made her more determined to forget all about him after their first inauspicious meeting at the Millpond. He had been in the company of his then-fiancée, an idiotic social climber named Bethany Havenhurst, when he found Sam, naked and shivering behind a tree, after an interrupted skinny-dip. If ever Cupid's arrow had played havoc with the lives of inappropriate targets, this was such a case.

But the more determined they had become to splinter the instantaneous link that had been forged between them, the tighter the bond had become. Until, unable to fight Eros's charge, they had finally accepted what they had known from that first moment: They loved each other. They could not live without each other. They would marry.

There had been complications. Ugly personal business between Sam's sister and Drew's father when Melinda Myles had worked for Forrest Symington as his executive assistant. The antagonism of Drew's mother, the formidable Mathilde D'Uberville Symington, whose family fortune and aristocratic lineage had made possible the Symingtons' financial and social positions. But the particulars of the wedding reception made it clear that all objections had been laid aside. Everything was being handled with the kind of elegance and good taste that only lots and lots of money— D'Uberville money—could buy.

It would have been understandable if the Myles family had felt out of their element. They were simple people who had lived in Oakdale all their lives. At one time or another all of them had worked for the Symingtons at the D'Uberville Motor Company. Their friends were the men and women who worked on the line, who came to the wedding in their Sunday best but with car grease permanently embedded under their fingernails and in the creases of their hands. They were an odd mix with the elite of neighboring Woodland Cliffs' society, who sported designer gowns they would wear just this once, that cost more than the bride's father, Harvey Myles, made in six months. Yet, somehow, it worked. The warmth of simplicity mingling with the air of elegance created an atmosphere both genial and gracious, so that everyone felt welcomed and welcoming. The bride's guests marveled at how down-to-earth the boss could be. The groom's guests couldn't get over how interesting the workers were. And both sides agreed that inasmuch as it was the wedding of the year, it was, after all, going to be a lot of fun.

For the bride, it was all too good to be true. Samantha Myles looked at herself in the mirror and couldn't believe the image that confronted her. She felt like Cinderella in her white gown. Made by the House of Chanel of the finest peau de soie with tiny swirls of seed pearls at the hem and on little cap sleeves, it hugged her body before bursting into a full cascade of train in back. Her hair had been swept up into a crown of copper curls by Alexandre, flown in from Paris by her future mother-in-law, especially for the occasion. A sheer veil fell from an ingenious cluster of pearl-studded silk and fresh flowers all the way to the floor. And even Sam, modest about her appearance and dismissive of her beauty, had to acknowledge her radiance, ascribing it to inner joy rather than to the plain fact that she was absolutely gorgeous.

Stepping onto the terrace of the guest wing at Belvedere, the Symingtons' estate, Sam gazed down at the white tent that covered the lush green-grass carpet of the grounds. The sun was shining, and the air was cool and fragrant. She searched the throng for a glimpse of Drew, desperate to see him, but hoping she wouldn't. Things were too good to give the fates any excuse to administer a portion of bad luck.

"Don't worry, he's here," said her sister, Melinda, joining her.

"Have you seen him?"

"Yup. He looks good in tails."

"He looks good in anything. Even better without anything."

"I don't think I need to hear this," Melinda said, laughing.

Sam looked at her maid of honor. No puffed-sleeve, Empire-waisted special, Melinda's gown was a sophisticated swirl of chiffon, that fell like a Grecian column from an embroidered bodice that accentuated her full breasts and narrow waist and hips. A spray of tiny purple orchids, the same color as her gown, was pinned into her chestnut hair, which tumbled loose over her shoulders.

"You look beautiful," Sam told her sister.

"Look who's talking." Melinda smiled back.

They hugged each other then, careful not to mess themselves, but needing to feel the closeness, to know that no matter what fate befell them, they'd still be the Myles Militia, standing together against the world.

"Am I dreaming?" asked Sam, closing her eyes.

"Yes," said Melinda simply.

"Pinch me."

Melinda did as she was told.

"Ouch," said Sam, opening her eyes, rubbing her arm. "What did you pinch me for?"

"You told me to," said Melinda, sitting on the edge of the bed.

"No, I didn't. I was sleeping."

"Well, you must have been dreaming, because I distinctly heard you say, 'Pinch me.'"

Sam sat up and looked around. She was in her old bed in her old room at her parents' house on Thayer Street.

"Oh, God," she groaned. "I *was* dreaming."

"It couldn't have been that bad a dream. I've been trying to wake you up for ten minutes, but you just kept turning over and smiling a lot."

"I dreamed I was getting married today."

"You *are* getting married today. If you get out of bed, that is."

Sam hoisted herself out of the bed and went to the open window. The sun was shining, and the air was cool and fragrant. An awning had been raised over part of the backyard where folding chairs had been set around a dozen bridge tables. Since Drew's friends and family were not expected to show up, they had figured they wouldn't need much more. Diane Myles, Sam and Melinda's mother, had gathered pansies and anemones from the garden and was bunching them into little vases in the center of each table. Sam smiled. It wasn't elegant, but it was sweet.

"How are you feeling?" Sam asked her sister.

Melinda patted her tummy. "A little sick when I got up, but I'm okay now. Let's hope the little monster stays quiet today."

"How's your dress?"

"It's fine. Don't worry. Mom let it out enough so

no one will know your maid of honor is five months pregnant."

"Everybody here probably knows already."

"That's true," Melinda admitted. "Does it bother you?"

"Of course not. At least it doesn't bother me what other people think. The question is, does it bother you?"

"Not as much as it should. I mean, I wish things weren't so complicated, for your sake as well as mine."

"Well, don't worry about it," Sam said. "Since Drew has been disowned and I'm obviously never going to have anything to do with my father-in-law, I'm free to hate him for what he did to you."

"You don't have to hate him, you know. I don't. I should have known better. And I really want this baby."

"I know. We all do."

"Good. Because I'm going to need all the help I can get."

"Drew and I can practice on your baby until we get one of our own."

"Okay. But first we've got to get you married. So how about getting dressed?"

Sam walked over to the bedroom door, where her wedding gown hung on a wire hanger, still in its plastic dry-cleaner's bag. She had borrowed the dress from a friend at the plant who had gotten married the year before. It was a classic white gown, full and lacy, not necessarily a style she would have chosen for herself, but it fit. Her mother had helped her open the bodice into a sweetheart neckline that showed off Sam's elegant long neck and smooth bosom, reaffirming the old adage that all brides are beautiful. This wasn't going to be the wedding of her dreams, but it was going to be her dream come true. Andrew Symington had chosen Samantha Myles over his family and his fortune. They loved each other. They could not live without each other. They would marry.

The doorbell rang, startling them both.

"Oh, God, it's Drew already. He's way too early. I want to see him. Do you think it's okay? I'm not in my wedding gown. But I don't want bad luck. Maybe I'd better not."

"Calm down," Melinda chided her overeager sister. "How do you know it's him? Maybe it's a delivery or something."

They didn't have to speculate long, as Diane opened the door to the bedroom. She hesitated for a moment, looking at her daughters, each beautiful in her own way, each setting out on a course that Diane knew would be filled with hazards. She wondered what she could have done to make things come out differently. Things happen, she told herself, to you, to your children. Lives change and there's nothing you can do about it, except hope that everyone gets through the crises unscathed.

"What is it, Mom?" Melinda spoke first.

"There's someone to see Sam."

"See, I told you it was him." Sam was grinning in spite of herself as she pulled on her robe. "I probably shouldn't see him, but I'm going to anyway." She started heading out the door.

"It's not Drew," Diane said, stopping her.

Sam looked at her mother and, for the first time, noticed the concern on her face.

"Who is it?"

"His mother."

"Shit," said Melinda.

Sam looked at her. "She's my future mother-in-law. If she's come to apologize and wants to come to the wedding, I have to tell her she's welcome."

"What about the fact that I'm pregnant with her husband's child? Doesn't that strike you as being a little awkward?"

"Yeah. *Very* awkward," Sam said. "But she didn't have anything to do with that, and neither did I. Drew has already chosen me over his family once. I'm not going to make him do it again. He's—"

"She's waiting," Diane interrupted, hating to see her daughters squabble on what was supposed to be a happy day.

Sam looked at her sister.

"Go on," Melinda said, her hand involuntarily moving to her belly. She knew Sam was right: none of this was anyone's fault but her own. If anyone didn't belong here, it was her, not Sam, not Drew, not even his mother. As if reading her thoughts, Sam put an arm around her shoulders and gave her a quick kiss on the cheek.

"You're still my maid of honor, no matter what. So put the time to good use and make yourself beautiful. You've got a lot of hard work to do," she teased, even though they were all aware that the famed glow of pregnancy, cliché though it was, had magically appeared on Melinda's cheeks and made her natural beauty even more radiant.

Walking past Melinda, Sam caught a glimpse of herself in the mirror. Her face was scrubbed clean, and her long copper hair hung loose over her shoulders. The flannel robe she had put on over the T-shirt she wore to bed was perfectly respectable. But somehow, seeing herself like that, she felt vulnerable, unprotected, and just a little inappropriate.

"Mom, can you stall her? I can't go out like this. Just give me a minute to throw something on. Please."

Diane had no great desire to spend any more time than necessary with the doyenne of the family that seemed to be ravaging her own, but she understood how Sam must feel.

"Okay. But hurry it up."

Waiting for her son's . . . She couldn't even bring herself to think the word. Waiting for *that girl* to appear, Mathilde D'Uberville Symington surveyed the living room where she had been placed after the hasty removal of a plastic cover from the sofa. The room was clean, but it was decidedly tacky, and she wondered what had happened to Drew's vaunted good taste. The very thought of linking the D'Uberville dynasty, descended from generations of French nobility, to this clan—the essence of proletarianism—made her stomach churn. Even her own marriage to Forrest Symington, who was viewed as beneath her, had been frowned upon, but at least Forrest, crass and nouveau as he might have been, was already keeping company with the Ford and Bouvier girls, and he was assured of a niche in the upper echelons of the American aristocracy, such as it was. Even so, it had taken a vast infusion of D'Uberville funds and a move away from the closed ranks of the established gentry to the small arena of Woodland Cliffs to really gain them a sure foothold at the summit of society. And as though the family hadn't enough strikes against it, Drew's chosen had to be the sister of some little tart whom Forrest had managed to get into trouble. Naturally, Mathilde had known about Forrest's dalliances for years, but as long as his infidelity had kept him out of her bed, she'd thought it a reasonable price to pay. But now, after she had worked so hard to maintain a life of refined and elegant beauty, several ugly possibilities had suddenly converged here in this ugliest of living rooms.

"Samantha will just be a few minutes," Diane said, appearing in the doorway. "Would you like some coffee? It's just instant, but—"

"Non, merci. No, thank you," Mathilde translated, unaware that the disdain on her face made her meaning all too clear.

The two women stared at each other for a moment. Diane saw Mathilde's style, her polish, her sophistication. Everything she wore, everything she was, screamed of money and power. But there was tension in the hands that twisted a Belgian lace handkerchief, and Diane saw a weariness in the corners of her eyes that even the best surgical adjustments had been unable to obliterate. In an instant all thought of envy had passed from her mind and been replaced by a contemptuous pity. From her own bitter experience, Diane knew that this woman had lost the affection of her husband many years ago and had endured his philandering in order to maintain a sham marriage in a sham life. And now she was about to lose her only son because he had somehow managed to see through the distortion of his parents' existence and refused to participate in it. This woman was sitting in her living room, feeling superior, certain that she had all the advantages. But Diane Myles knew with a certainty that Mathilde D'Uberville Symington had nothing, and she had probably brought the situation on herself. Diane excused herself when she saw Sam approaching.

"I'm sorry I've kept you waiting, Mrs. Symington," Sam said, quietly entering the room. She had slipped on a simple pale yellow sundress that complemented the blaze of her hair. She still wore no makeup, but nervousness had touched her cheeks with a hint of rose, and her perfect white teeth shone through cherry lips as she offered a slight, sweet smile.

So much for her son having lost his taste, Mathilde thought. The creature was exquisite. But life was about a lot more than aesthetics, lust, and even, for that matter, love.

"This is difficult for me," Mathilde began.

Sam was surprised at the thickness of her accent. She knew that Mathilde D'Uberville Symington was French; everybody did. But somehow she had not expected her to sound so foreign. Suddenly Sam saw her as Mathilde must have seen herself, as a cultivated stranger in a brash new world, trying desperately to maintain her Continental elegance in an atmosphere whose denizens found her pretensions more amusing than admirable. Sam felt sorry for her. It was hard to think of her as the enemy.

"I know how you must feel about me," said Sam, kindly getting to the point for her. "But I love your son and I will make him a good wife."

"I don't doubt that," said Mathilde.

Sam breathed a sigh of relief. She had always believed that Drew's mother, if not his father, would come around. A mother wouldn't give up her only son so easily.

"I'm so glad we have your blessing." Sam moved toward her, ready for a tentative embrace. But Mathilde stiffened, and Sam felt the barrier between them as surely as if it had been a brick wall.

"Mais non. You misunderstand."

"I . . . I guess I do. You said—"

"I said I believed you would make Andrew a good wife. But not the right wife. They are very different things."

"I don't understand." Sam's heart was sinking. She didn't like the course of this conversation. She was beginning to wish she had refused to come out of her bedroom.

"Let me be clear. My son is not just any ordinary young man. He stands to inherit not just money but position as well. You know that—"

"I love Drew for himself. I don't give a damn about his money or his position." Sam felt her stomach inching its way up to her throat and tried to will it back down.

"Precisely my point. You don't care because you can't understand. Drew does care. Maybe he denies it now, *en plein amour.* But wealth and position are his legacy. If you take that away from him, he will not be happy. Not for long."

Sam told herself she would not cry, she would not raise her voice. "I am not taking anything away from Drew. You are doing that. I am offering him my eternal love and devotion. He seems to feel that is enough. I have enough faith in him, and in what we have together, to agree with him."

Mathilde saw that her task would not be easy. This girl, with her soft measured tones, was either a clever gambler or completely sure of herself. Either way, Mathilde had to do something to shake her confidence.

"From the day he was born, Drew has lived a privileged life. When he was ten, and home from boarding school on *un jour de vacances,* his father took him to the plant to show him how the cars were built. It so happened that one of the workers had his son there that day also, and Drew made friends with him. When he came home, he announced he wanted to be 'normal' like other children. He told us that his new friend had asked him to come and live with his family. At first his papa and I, we just laughed. But when Drew kept insisting, we decided to let him try. There was nothing wrong with the family. They were nice people. We, of course, checked. But they were ordinary. They lived in an ordinary house, in fact, quite close to here, I think. After one day, Drew called us and asked us to send the chauffeur to drive him home. He found his new friend's home nasty, he said. Except when he has been in Europe, Drew has lived at Belvedere ever since. Do you think that just because he's no longer ten, he's any different?"

"As a matter of fact, I do," said Samantha, sounding more certain than she was feeling at the moment.

"That is only because you've never lived in luxury."

"Maybe."

"I can change that."

"What?"

"Do not be offended. I do this only because I know you love Drew and it was never his money you were after. But if you do love him, you must see that making him break with his family could only cause him pain. And for us to accept you into our home would be impossible. *Especially* you . . . with *your* family."

Sam looked at Mathilde, who met her eyes. She knew about Melinda. In spite of herself, Sam felt mortified. In the financial arrangement made with Forrest Symington, Melinda had agreed not to name him as the father of their child, but it was clear that Mathilde knew. Sam wondered if Mathilde knew that her husband had also had an affair with their mother. No wonder she didn't consider Sam an appropriate mate for her son. Sam couldn't blame her. She probably would have felt the same way if she had been in Mathilde's position. Yet Sam still loved Drew and wanted to marry him. But suddenly, somehow, she felt as though she were doing something wrong.

"I don't ask you to give up Drew and stay here stuck with nothing," Mathilde said. "A million dollars will give you a whole new life. You are young and beautiful. You will meet someone else, and you will be free to do what you want, go where you want. This way no one will lose."

Sam's shame receded. Mathilde should have stopped while she was ahead, she thought to herself. She almost had me feeling guilty.

"Are you offering me a million dollars to leave Drew?" she asked quietly, in control again.

"Only because you love him, and because you would both benefit from the arrangement."

"Because I love him," Sam said, "and because I know that, in spite of everything, he loves you, I'm not going to hurt him by telling him you were here today. Now, if you'll excuse me, I have to get dressed for my wedding."

"Oh, God, I look so fat. This dress was a big mistake," said Melinda as her mother zipped up her gown, a cloud of peach chiffon that flowed from an empire waist.

"You don't look fat," Diane told her. "In fact, you look pretty darn good for someone who's five months pregnant."

"I wish I looked more pregnant; then at least people would know for sure. This way they're just going to think I'm fat."

"Honey, I don't want to disillusion you, but I don't think they're going to be looking at you all that much. This is supposed to be the bride's day."

Melinda pursed her lips, studying herself in the mirror, turning sideways and sucking in her breath.

"It's this color. It makes me look huge. I should have gotten the black."

"You can't wear black to your sister's wedding."

"Why? You just said nobody would be looking at me anyway."

The door opened quietly. Unnoticed, Sam stood in the doorway of the room she and Melinda used to share and watched her sister bickering with their mother. Suddenly she felt bereft.

"Mom, am I doing the wrong thing?"

"Oh, dear," said Diane, turning her attention to her other daughter. "What happened?"

"Nothing much. Basically, she said I was ruining her son's life, and then she left. That's all."

"Bitch!" interjected Melinda. "But it could have been worse. She could have stayed."

"Thank you very much, Melinda," Sam said. "That's really helpful."

"Well, it's true. That whole family sucks. They're a bunch of stuck-up pigs who use people—"

"Will you please shut up," Sam cried, losing her temper. "You're talking about my fiancé's parents."

"I'm talking about the bastard who got me pregnant and then tried to talk me into having an unsafe abortion because I was an embarrassment to him."

"Let's face it, you still are." Sam heard her mother gasp and was instantly sorry.

"I don't need this!" Melinda said. "Mom, undo the zipper."

"Girls, calm down."

"No. Undo my zipper. I hate this goddamn dress

17

anyway." Since Diane was clearly making no move to help her, Melinda reached behind her back, opened the zipper, and wriggled out of the gown herself, letting it fall to the floor as she continued.

"And, since you asked, yeah, I think you're doing the wrong thing. It's going to take your Prince Charming about a week and a half in your cozy walk-up in Oakdale before he realizes he's in the wrong part of town and scurries home to Woodland Cliffs."

Now it was Sam's turn to be shocked. She felt tears smarting her eyes.

"Stop it, both of you." Diane could see that immediate intervention was necessary. "You're both a little tense, and you're saying things you don't mean. Samantha, you're marrying Drew, not his family, and you know better than anyone what kind of a man he is. Do you love him?"

Sam nodded, shaking the tears loose from the corners of her eyes.

"Do you trust him?"

More vigorous nods, more tears.

"Then you're not making a mistake. Now come into my room and let's get you dressed." As she pushed her elder daughter out the door, Diane turned back to her younger child.

"Melinda, the dress looks fine. All it needs is a smiling face above it. Put it on and cheer up. This is your sister's wedding day. Let's not spoil it, okay?"

"Me? I'm not the one who . . ." Melinda began to protest. But they were already gone.

She stopped shouting as her eyes caught her own image in the mirror, standing in her underwear, a pool of chiffon at her feet. As usual she could not resist studying her image. Even though her pregnancy hardly showed, her body had already changed a lot. She looked at her breasts, rising above the peach lace of her bra. Fuller than before, they had become a centerfold's dream. Her hands moved to her belly, swelling slightly over the top of the matching lace panties. She had always prided herself on her flat tummy, but now, when she wasn't desperately trying to zip herself into clothes she could no longer wear, she found something delectable about its new roundness.

She let her hands move in small circles over her stomach, pressing in places, feeling for an answering nudge. Before she could control it, a wave of worry swept over her, until she reminded herself that the doctor had said she probably wouldn't feel the baby kick for another week or two. She wanted this child. She hadn't at first; she'd been so scared. She was still scared, but she wanted it now.

She stepped out of the gown, leaving it crumpled on the floor, and sat down on the bed. Fairy tales don't come true she thought, scowling. Her sister was marrying the man of her dreams, but Sam and Drew were going to start their life together in a dump. Drew had no job and no money; he'd been disowned, with no chance of ever being reconciled with his wealthy and prominent family. Cinderella had won the heart of the prince, but instead of moving into the palace, she would still be Cinderella and he would move in with her—not exactly a formula for a lifetime of happiness. Meanwhile here was Melinda, having had a taste of luxury and the limousine life, back in her blue-collar home, abandoned by the wealthy and prominent man who knocked her up. Her life was more like a bad country song than a fairy tale: "I'm my sister's maid of honor even though she knows I'm wild, and now the bridegroom's father is the father of my child."

"Life sucks," she said out loud, and picked up her dress and hurled it in the general direction of the door, managing to hit the total stranger who opened it at that inopportune moment.

"Get out!" screamed Melinda, assuming that one of the deliverymen had made a wrong turn. They'd been underfoot for the past few days, and they were damned annoying.

"I'd like to," he said, sounding just as irritated as she was, "but this thing you threw at me is stuck to me somehow."

"That thing happens to be my bridesmaid's gown, and stop pulling at it. You're going to rip it."

"The zipper is caught in my sweater, and I can't get it out. Do you want to come over here and help me, instead of just shouting at me?"

Furious at this intruder for presenting her with another problem, and at herself for causing the problem in the first place, Melinda marched across the room. Cursing under her breath, she found the spot where the zipper had lodged between the threads of his pullover and started to extricate it.

"Just leave it alone, damn it. I'll do it," she scolded as he tried to help. "You're just making a mess of it."

"Why'd you throw it at me if it's so precious to

you?" he demanded, dropping his hands and letting her work alone.

Melinda tugged hard, freeing the gown but leaving a visible hole in the sweater.

"Okay, you're free. Now get the hell out of my room!"

"Are you always this hostile, or just on happy days?"

"Fuck off, mister," she said, as she slammed the door behind him.

"You're sure he's here?" Sam nervously asked her mother.

"Of course I am." Diane laughed, hugging her anxious daughter. "He's at the back door waiting for his cue." They were in the kitchen, getting lined up for the procession. Mrs. Voskovic, their next-door neighbor, had offered to be the wedding coordinator, but her constant chatter got on Diane's nerves, and with fuses already short, she'd sent her out into the backyard to sit under the awning and watch with the other guests. A string quartet from the music department of the community college had agreed to play for twenty-five bucks a head.

"He doesn't look sorry, does he?" Sam pursued her fears.

"Not a bit. He's a little nervous . . ."

"Nervous? Why?"

". . . Like you. But he seems happy."

"I should have seen him."

"You said you didn't want to. It's bad luck."

"I know. But then I could tell—"

"What's the holdup?" asked Melinda. She looked beautiful in the peach dress she hated. A single peach rose, large and in full blossom, was nestled in her chestnut hair. Anyone who didn't know would not have thought she was pregnant, or even overweight.

"We're waiting for Jack. He had to wait for the rest of us to get done so he could change," said Diane.

Sam had grown to trust and admire Jack Bader since he'd successfully represented the Save the Millpond project for Sam, but she still had some misgivings. "Do you think it was wrong for me to ask Jack to be best man? I mean, I've got Melinda, but Drew didn't have anybody. . . . I've done that to him, haven't I? Made it so he couldn't even have his own best man."

Melinda looked at Sam's apprehensive face. She felt guilty for the things she'd said before. Clearly Sam would have a lifetime of doubt to contend with; she didn't need to be racked with qualms on her wedding day. She hugged her sister, careful to leave some space between them to keep their dresses from crushing.

"Hey, what happened to the girl whose motto was 'I think; therefore I'm right'?"

Sam shrugged. "You always said I was wrong."

"Since when have you listened to anything I had to say? Come on, Sam. You're my big sister. You're not supposed to get scared."

"Well, I am."

"Don't be. This marriage is right for you and you

know it. I'm sorry about what I said before. I didn't mean it. I don't know what got into me."

"Maybe you're getting your period."

"Very funny." But she was laughing. They both were.

Diane gave Melinda a grateful look. When they wanted to, the sisters knew how to take care of each other. Everything was going to be fine. Suddenly Melinda's face clouded. Diane sighed, praying silently for a reprieve.

"Who's that man?" Melinda was glowering.

Diane and Sam both turned. "Jack!" Sam sang out, opening her arms. "Just in time. I was getting ready to call the whole thing off, but since you've already got your tux on, we might as well go ahead."

"You're Jack?" Melinda asked, incredulous. He looked better now, shaved and cleaned up, wearing a tuxedo instead of the jeans and ratty sweater she had torn, but he was definitely the intruder. For the first time, she noticed the long blond hair, which he had tied into an inconspicuous ponytail for the occasion.

"And you must be the lovely Melinda," he said, with a trace of irony so faint that only Melinda could hear it.

"I forgot you two have never met. You're both such a big part of my life, it seems as if you should know each other."

"In a way, I feel as if we do," said Jack, grinning broadly.

"Come on, kids," said Diane, as she signaled the

quartet to start the processional. "It's time to do it."

Jack offered his arm to Melinda. She almost refused it, but she saw Sam's face, happy and hopeful again. She placed her hand on his arm, but there was no warmth in the gesture.

"Have you no sense of decency?" she whispered, as, still smiling, he locked her hand in his and forced it into the crook of his arm.

"Have you no sense of humor?" he whispered in return, as he led her down the makeshift aisle to the strains of the Pachelbel canon.

Sam wasn't quite sure how she got there, but suddenly it was her turn. For a moment she stood and surveyed the scene. Folding chairs had been arranged in rows, with an aisle down the middle, before an improvised altar. In them sat about sixty guests, all dressed in their Sunday best. She saw Drew standing, his back toward her, and she wondered if he was thinking of the grounds of Belvedere, so far removed from her parents' backyard. But when the strings began their sweet rendition of the Wedding March from Wagner's *Lohengrin,* he turned toward her, and all her questions and fears became irrelevant.

Everything Sam needed to know, she saw in Drew's face. He did not see the crowded yard with its patches of brown grass. He didn't even notice the rickety chairs or, in the background, the haphazard reception tables. He paid no attention to the guests, dressed by K mart instead of a couturier. His entire focus was on his bride as she moved slowly and deliberately toward him, and his eyes told her that there could be no mistake.

As Sam smiled, a cloud moved away from the sun and lit them all with a heavenly glow. Anyone who saw knew that it was right. Sam and Drew loved each other; they belonged together. And in a radiant light that transformed a shabby backyard into a Shangri-la, they became husband and wife.

2

"Good morning, Mrs. Symington."

He was propped up on his elbow watching her when she woke up.

"Good morning, Mr. Symington. What are you doing up so early?"

"I'm glad you asked. Certain parts of my body got up before me and just refused to rest until you woke up."

She laughed and moved into his arms. "Well, I'm awake now, and anything I can do to help . . ."

They had been married a week, and it had been a variation of the same theme every morning as well as every night, with a few afternoons thrown in for good measure. They had decided not to go anywhere on a honeymoon, preferring to save the money until they had time to assess their financial position and figure out what they were going to do next. But, holed up in Sam's small apartment, which they had reconfigured for the two of them, they were definitely having a honeymoon.

"You know," Sam said a few minutes later, "making love to you is different since we've been married." She was sitting up, straddling him, and he was still inside her.

"Really?" He smiled. "Better or worse?"

"Just different. Maybe better." He moved a little, and she sighed. "Better, definitely better."

"Why?"

"Because we're just making love. I'm not taking a political position."

"I like the position you're taking, whatever it is."

"And I don't have to worry about the ramifications."

"I wouldn't say that," he said, putting his hands on her breasts and moving a little more. She moved with him.

"It's different for me, too, you know," Drew went on.

She was surprised. "How?"

"I'm not afraid."

She stopped. "Were you afraid before? Of what?"

"Don't stop. I was afraid you'd leave me. You were always bolting. I was never sure if I was going to see you again. I was always thinking that maybe if I did everything right, I could make you really love me, and then you wouldn't leave me."

He was sitting up now, too, and they were rocking together, closer and faster.

"It worked," Sam said between gasps. "Just keep doing this, and I'll never even leave this bed."

"Can we stop talking now?" Drew whispered as he wrapped his legs around her, pulling her even closer.

A moan from deep in her throat was her only answer, and they rolled back down onto the bed, lips pressed together, bodies fused, hearts beating in syncopated rhythm with the intensity of their all-encompassing love.

"I think we should declare the honeymoon over," Sam said to Drew later, as they were having lunch, knee to knee in the cramped kitchen.

"What? And I thought we were just getting good at it."

"Not that part of the honeymoon. That can last forever. It's the stuff in between."

"Meaning?"

"Meaning, we've got to look for work," Sam said. "Obviously, neither one of us can go back to DMC, but I'm a good mechanic. I should be able to find a job in a garage."

Drew scowled. "No, I don't want you to do that."

Sam looked at him. She'd been afraid of this. It was one thing for a man of Drew's background to give up his fortune for the woman he loved; it was quite another to face the fact that his wife was a grease monkey.

"It's not a very classy job, but it's what I do, Drew. And I do it well enough to make some money. And right now your main credential is that you're the disinherited son of Forrest Symington, so I might be more employable than you are."

"I don't doubt that for a minute."

"Then why don't you want me to get a job? Do you have something up your sleeve that I don't know about?"

"Yes."

"What is it?"

"A small trust fund that my grandfather left to me. It's mine free and clear. No one else can touch it. Even my father couldn't cut it off. Believe me, he tried."

Sam's heart was sinking. For some reason she had assumed that when Drew gave up his privileged life, he would embrace her working-class ethic. She tried to tell herself not to be disappointed, that he didn't have to be like her to love her, and vice versa.

"Listen, sweetheart," she began carefully. "It's your money, and if you want to live on it, that's fine. But I can't. I have to work for a living. I've been doing it since I was a little girl, and I can't change it now."

"What do you mean?"

"I mean I'm not going to let you support me on your trust fund."

"Oh, good. Because I'm afraid it's not really enough money for both of us."

"I see," said Sam, a little taken aback. She didn't really see at all. She had understood that Drew might have problems adjusting to poverty, but this attitude was way beyond her expectations.

"Okay," she went on, trying to sound nonchalant while she recovered some equilibrium. "I guess we could divide our resources. Once I get a job, I'll have an idea of what I can afford, and then if you match it, we'll know where we stand, financially speaking."

"What are you talking about?" Drew looked genuinely bewildered, which confused Sam even more.

"Well, what are *you* talking about?"

"I'm talking about liquidating my trust fund and using the cash as seed money to set up our own company. Half and half. My money, your invention. If we can manufacture the Mylometer and sell it to the auto industry, I think we could do pretty well. D'Uberville Motor Company won't buy it, considering my father stole your patent and was forced to give it back, but we can offer it to GM and Chrysler and all the others."

Sam was silent. Her eyes were brimming with tears.

"What's wrong?" asked Drew, concerned. "Don't you want to be my business partner?"

"Oh, God, of course I do."

"Then why are you crying?"

"Because I'm so happy. And I'm so stupid. I keep thinking I'm wrong about you, but you keep proving I'm not. You are utterly perfect."

"No, I'm not."

"You're not?"

"No. Sometimes I'm too demanding."

"In what way?"

"Come back to bed, I'll show you."

Sam had to smile then. "Maybe it's a little too soon for the honeymoon to be over."

"I think you're right."

"Tomorrow."

"Tomorrow."

"I wonder if it will feel different making love with a business partner."

"Only one way to find out," and with that, he lifted her from her chair, knocking over his own, slung her over his shoulder to her laughing protests, and carried her back to the bedroom.

Bethany Havenhurst wasn't quite sure why she'd called the Symingtons and had herself invited to Belvedere for dinner. She hadn't seen them since the night her engagement to their son had been irretrievably and irrevocably broken.

Knowing how protective Drew had been of his mother, she knew that he would never have revealed the complete circumstances of their breakup. Mathilde would never know that Bethany had tried to keep Drew by threatening to expose a family scandal: that Mathilde, an unadmitted but thoroughly advanced alcoholic, had been driving on the Grande Corniche in the south of France, and had hit and killed a young bride on her wedding day. Mathilde had fled the scene, leaving Drew to take the blame and pay the price. Bethany's plan had backfired, however, after Drew had learned a little too much about Bethany's insatiable appetites, but he'd agreed to keep her secrets if she kept his.

But the other Symingtons didn't know anything about that. All they knew was that Drew had given up Bethany—a girl they'd known all her life, a girl who was one of *them*—for a low-class, gold-digging, factory worker, and they, as well as she, considered it a rotten deal.

She'd dressed carefully for the occasion, selecting a floor-length navy Chanel shirtwaist with white cuffs and collar and gold buttons, dark enough to enhance her quality of bereaved beauty without being unduly somber. Mathilde, as usual, looked regal and unreachable, in a column of pleated burgundy silk by Mary McFadden that set off her ebony hair with its streak of silver. Sarah, Drew's sister, was there too, dressed just as fashionably, but somehow, as everyone including her husband James was aware, Sarah never quite attained the standard of attractiveness set by the rest of them.

Drew's name was never mentioned, but his presence rested so heavily among them that he might as well have been seated at the head of the table.

"C'est bon that you are here, my dear." Mathilde patted Bethany's hand as the butler poured more wine. "We do not wish to lose you."

Even though we've lost our son, Bethany silently finished for her. She said aloud, "I wanted to call sooner, but . . ."

Bethany understood the conventions of the unstated. She rather enjoyed playing the role of the scorned woman, and she wondered how much mileage she could get out of it.

"Well, it's good you did," added Forrest, a little gruffly. *The hell with that boy. Who needs him!*

"Sarah and I have been talking about ringing you up," James said, sounding more pompous and affected than usual. "But things have been so hectic at DMC lately that I haven't had a chance to breathe." *Since I've been scrambling to establish myself in my erstwhile brother-in-law's position now that there's a vacancy for heir to the throne.*

"I hope you're not expecting it to let up," said Forrest. *You're the only option I've got left, so you'd better not disappoint me.*

"On the contrary." *I want it all.*

"It makes you wonder about the possibility of life without cars," Sarah interjected, only half joking. *Maybe Drew did the right thing. At least he's got someone to love.*

By dessert, the dynamics of the situation were clear to Bethany. On the outside, the Symington family appeared seamless, as though a minor growth had been excised and the skin had healed without a scar. But Bethany could see the far-reaching effects of Drew's banishment and, like a vulture drawn to the possibility of carrion even before the death itself, she could sense herself circling the family unit.

"If you'll all excuse me," James said, when they had finished coffee, "I'm going to go outside for some air."

"You are still smoking?" Mathilde's tone was disapproving.

"Not much, and not in front of you, *chère maman.*"

"So unhealthy," said Mathilde, sipping her second brandy, the irony of the situation escaping her completely.

"I think I'll join you, if you don't mind. It's been such a long time since I was here, and I've always loved the gardens at night," Bethany said, injecting a hint of sadness into her voice to ensure that the unspoken misery of her abandonment was clear to them all.

"I don't mind at all," said James, with the correct measure of solicitousness, as he touched his wife's shoulder to dispel any hint of impropriety and then helped Bethany from her chair.

The late night air was cool and fresh, and the gardens, lit by spotlights hidden in the flower beds and tapers along the walks, were indeed lovely. But as they strolled, Bethany was far more aware of the scent of the man beside her than of the night-blooming jasmine that bordered the carved stone path. James was certainly clean; he smelled of soap and Armani for Men, and a little smoke from his cigarette. But he also emitted another odor, musky and almost rank, like that of an animal on the prowl—pheromones, exuded to attract a mate in heat. It was the smell of desire, and Bethany, recognizing it, smiled and knew she had found her access. The Symingtons owed her, though exactly *what* they owed her she wasn't sure. She only knew that James would somehow help her get it.

"It's a lovely night," Bethany said softly, pressing James's arm a little tighter.

She felt him respond immediately and knew her assumptions about him had not been wrong.

"I didn't notice the weather earlier," he answered, "but it's damn beautiful right now." He had stopped and turned to look at her. His tone was unmistakable.

"Your wife must be waiting for you," she said, her meaning clear.

"She's waited for me before," he answered, just as cogent. Bethany looked at him from under her dark lashes. She shivered a little, faking a chill and a vulnerability she did not feel. Instantly his arms were around her.

"You're cold."

"Not anymore." Her voice conveyed gratitude. The veil of night hid the disdain in her eyes.

He kissed her then, not gently, but with naked desire, pushing his tongue between her teeth, exploring her mouth. She felt him harden against her. He was already panting. This was not a man with a slow hand; she could tell that right away.

"James, please." She extricated herself, as if with difficulty. "This is wrong."

"I can't help myself. You're so beautiful. I've wanted to kiss you ever since you first came home with Drew. The guy's an idiot. He never knew what he had. But I did."

Under cover of darkness, Bethany smiled. Somehow he didn't sound so affected anymore. It was difficult for a man to be pompous with a hard-on. "It's not that I don't want to . . ."

"Then why stop?"

"Your wife. Your in-laws. This is their home."

"You're right. Meet me someplace. Your place. Any place."

"But the Symingtons—"

"Fuck the Symingtons," James burst out. "Don't you feel that way? They think just because they are who they are, everybody's supposed to kowtow, act like them, think like them, be like them. But we're not like them, are we? They're ice, we're fire. Isn't that right?"

He pushed himself on her again. She opened her mouth for him. His hands moved to her breasts, crushing them. She did not protest. She didn't really mind. Maybe there was more to James than his association with the simple Sarah had led her to believe. This might be fun as well as work.

"Oh, I'm so confused!" Bethany tried to sound demure, but she noticed her nipples were visibly erect through the thin chiffon of her gown. He noticed too.

"James?" Sarah was calling him.

He looked at Bethany, desperate not to close the door on opportunity knocking. "Let's at least talk about it. Tomorrow. At your place. I'll be there at four."

"But what about Forrest? Don't you work with him?"

"I'll say I have to go out to a meeting. I'll be there, don't worry."

"James?" Sarah was calling again.

"I'm coming, sweetheart."

Bethany folded her arms over her bosom and started moving back to the house. James hurried after her.

"Okay, Bethany? Okay? Four o'clock?"

She smiled, feeling his urgent need. She was in control again, and she liked it. "Okay. But just to talk."

"Right." James grinned, already planning. He could be there by four; they'd be in bed by four-thirty. He could be home by six. Two hours for a meeting. That was acceptable.

Once inside, Bethany took her leave, declining James's chivalrous offer to see her home. She needed to be alone, to think, to plan, to figure out exactly what she wanted and how she could use James to get it.

"Want a refill?" asked Pete, holding the bottle of cheap white wine over Melinda's glass.

"No, thanks," said Melinda, eyeing the poster in front of her that warned she could be endangering the health of her unborn child. She'd talked to her doctor about drinking alcohol, and he'd said a glass of wine once in a while wouldn't do the baby any harm, especially if it calmed Melinda down. And these days she needed as much calming down as she could get.

"Come on," Pete offered again. "On the house."

She shook her head. Pete still didn't know that she was pregnant, and she wasn't making any announcements.

Anyway, she didn't really need the wine. What she needed was to get out of her parents' house. Forrest Symington had agreed to give her a cash settlement to keep his paternity a secret, but the lawyers were still dickering over the details, and she had yet to see a penny. Which meant she couldn't afford to get her own place.

Melinda sighed, and took a tiny sip of the wine in

her glass, just to give herself something to do. Who was she kidding? The truth was, even if she'd had the money, she wouldn't have been so quick to move out. The baby was due in four months, and she was scared to face childbirth alone. The future as a single mother was daunting, and she was relying on her mother's support to help her through it. But in the meantime her status as a single woman with nothing to do was sheer boredom and her mother's constant hovering wasn't helping one bit.

She'd taken to going out for a drive after dinner every night, if her father wasn't on the night shift at the plant and didn't need the car. Harvey Myles had lost some seniority on the line at DMC since the scandals his daughters had caused with the Symington regime, but at least he'd kept his job, the union had seen to that. But none of the rest of them would ever work for the D'Uberville Motor Company again, that was for sure.

Not that Melinda wanted to. Still, she had to admit that she missed being Forrest Symington's personal assistant, both the personal and the assistant parts. She'd enjoyed the luxury and the limos, the private moments and the public meetings. It had given her a taste of a way of life she was increasingly afraid she might never get again, and she was equally convinced she could not live without it.

"So what's going on with you?" Pete was in front of her again. It was a weeknight, and the bar at Bamboo Bernie's wasn't very busy.

"Nothing much," she said, knowing Pete couldn't begin to understand her problems.

"So . . . uh . . . what do you hear from Sam?" He was trying to sound as if he didn't much care, but Melinda knew he was still smarting from what might possibly have been his first and last rejection.

He'd been engaged to Samantha once, before Sam met Drew Symington. Pete was good-looking and a big star on the dirt-track circuit. At the time, Melinda had been convinced that Sam had gotten herself a damn good catch. But now, having ventured beyond lunch-bucket territory herself, she could understand why Sam had always insisted there must be something more to life than what Oakdale, a job on the line, and a working-stiff husband had to offer.

"We haven't seen her since the wedding," Melinda said, not wanting to elaborate.

But Pete wanted elaboration. "Honeymoon, huh?"

"Yeah."

"Where'd they go?"

"Nowhere."

"Really?"

"Uh-huh. They figured they couldn't spare the money."

Pete snorted. "Shit. She dumps me for a zillionaire and ends up with nothing. I would have at least taken her to Daytona Beach."

"Got a race there, huh?"

"Yup. I'm sponsored," he said proudly. "They're even putting me up at the Holiday Inn. Double room, all expenses paid. Old Sammy could have done worse than me. Hell, she did! Without the D'Uberville money, Drew Symington's a loser. A honeymoon in Oakdale—what a fucking joke!" Chortling, he moved off to serve his other customers, filling shot glasses to overflowing. Nothing like a sense of superiority, no matter how mistaken, to make one feel magnanimous.

Melinda knew that for Sam, it wasn't the economics that mattered; it was the attitude. Even though Drew was cut off from his family and without a prospect in the world, Sam believed he was her soul mate. But, Melinda thought, that's not going to do it for me. Sensitivity and understanding aren't enough. Sensitivity and understanding and a hefty bank account to back them up, now, that's something to aim for.

She went to take another small sip, and suddenly felt a hand on her arm, stopping her glass in midair.

"I don't think you should be doing that."

Melinda turned to find Jack Bader in her face.

"Excuse me," she said, shaking his hand off her arm, "You must have mistaken me for someone who cares what you think. Pete," she called. "I'll take that refill now, if you're still pouring."

"Sure thing, babe." She knew she wasn't going to drink it, but she needed to show that nosy son of a bitch that he might be able to influence her sister but he had no hold on her.

"Can you read?" He pointed to the sign she'd been guiltily studying all night.

"Can you?" she countered, grabbing a napkin

and a pencil and expressing herself succinctly by printing two words in big block letters and shoving it under his nose.

" 'Fuck off,' " he read aloud, making it sound like he'd expected the Declaration of Independence. "Oh, of course. I remember. You're the pretty sister. Sam's the smart one."

"Fuck off," she spoke the words this time, flushing angrily.

"You might want to improve your vocabulary before your baby's born. Although if you keep on drinking that swill, it might not matter. If your baby's brain is damaged, it won't understand anything you say anyway."

"My baby is none of your damn business!" She had raised her voice louder than she intended. The rest of the people at the bar were looking at her. Two steps, and Pete was in front of her.

"Hey, Melinda, are you having a baby?"

Melinda shook her head, exasperated. "Yeah, Pete, what about it?"

"Well, you shouldn't be drinking. Didn't you see that sign? Hey, I don't want to be responsible for any tragedies." And before she could say anything, he'd whisked away her glass and poured the wine into the sink. The other people at the bar applauded. Jack didn't even look at her, but she knew he was gloating.

She threw five dollars on the bar, got off her stool, and stalked out. She was furious. He hadn't been in there five minutes and he'd managed to enrage and humiliate her. She wanted to go back in and smack him and tell him that the stress he had caused her was far worse for her baby than the two sips of wine she'd had. Instead, she took five deep breaths and promised herself that someday, somehow, she'd get out of Oakdale and away from stupid, meddling, ignorant busybodies like Jack Bader.

3

Every day, whether he admitted it to himself or not, Forrest Symington felt the loss of his son more deeply. Those who were close to him saw his pain, and the few who had the nerve tried to suggest some form of reconciliation, reminding him in subtle ways that Mathilde had married him when he was below her station, and her family hadn't disowned them. Quite the contrary. The D'Ubervilles had seen to it that Forrest was given every privilege and opportunity so that, before long, people had quite forgotten that Mathilde had married beneath her. Or at the very least, the fact was never mentioned. But Forrest knew, and could not say, that the horrifying coincidence of Drew marrying Melinda's sister, and then taking her side against him, made any sort of magnanimity impossible. Instead, he toed a hard line, insisting that

43

Sarah was his only child now and that her husband, James, would serve just as well as the next in line at DMC.

Although Forrest said that James was capable of being the heir to the D'Uberville Motor Company, he knew it wasn't true, and so did everyone else. As eager as James appeared to be, Forrest knew that James didn't have the talent to be successful in the motor industry because his heart didn't feel it and his brain didn't get it. And topping the list of truths that Forrest insisted on denying was the fact that if James had not been married to Sarah, he wouldn't even have him working at DMC, let alone be grooming him to take over.

James had no idea he had just been assessed and found wanting when he entered Forrest's office to tell his father-in-law he was leaving early for a meeting and might not be back. Forrest was suddenly flooded with memories of his own early departures. The one thing he did admit to himself was that he missed Melinda. Her warmth, her youth, her sex, her humor—they'd made each day alive and exciting. He knew he'd have no trouble finding a substitute, if he wanted one. But he'd come so close to losing it all with her—his family, his wealth, and his reputation—that he wasn't sure anymore that another woman would be worth the risk. And although there had been so many others before Melinda, and there could be more after her, at the moment he was still all too aware that she had been special. In his way, he had loved her, and if she hadn't become pregnant, he might have gone on leaving his office early for years to come.

"My leaving early isn't a problem, is it, sir?" James asked, noticing his scowl.

Forrest studied his son-in-law. If this jerk was cheating on his daughter, as he'd done . . .

". . . Because if it is, I can make it a point to get back. I just thought it would be a good idea for me to spend some casual time with some of the union big shots before contract negotiations come up again, so I've arranged to have cocktails with them. I wanted to stick around and schmooz with them for a while, have a few drinks, tell some jokes. Show them the boss can be a regular guy. You know what I mean, sir . . . Dad?"

Forrest cringed inwardly. He hated it when James called him Dad. He was just sucking up, as though the word alone could bring them closer. He also hadn't failed to notice that James was referring to himself as the boss. He would have liked to reprimand him, but he felt a little guilty for projecting his own sexual proclivities onto his daughter's husband.

"Fine idea, take all the time you want," he said, with a lot more warmth than he felt.

Bethany had debated just how naive to play the scene with James. She had started out by wearing a fairly demure dress with buttons all the way down the front that popped open at the least provocation. They could discuss the situation, she could play little girl lost, and then things could "just happen."

In the end, she'd decided against it. James already had a little girl lost in his wife, and he'd made it clear in the garden that he wasn't enamored of long courtships. Besides, she didn't want to waste time. She had a feeling that James could lose interest as quickly as he found it. He had a wandering eye, and she didn't want it to wander somewhere else before she'd had a chance to get what she wanted.

Bethany still wasn't exactly sure what that was. She had wanted to marry into the Symington family, but even if she could get James to divorce Sarah for her, it would be defeating her purpose. Then neither one of them would be connected to the seat of power, and there'd be no point in marrying James. Unless, of course, James somehow managed to take over the number one position from Forrest. She knew that was far-fetched, but she owned stock in DMC, and she knew most of the board members. A hostile takeover was always a possibility. She laughed to think of herself and James, ensconced as the reigning couple in Woodland Cliffs while the Symingtons groveled at their feet. That wasn't necessarily a realistic picture, but it was delicious, and it excited her.

The doorbell rang. She quickly slipped off her dress and put on a silk robe, discarding her underwear along the way. She wanted James to be as vulnerable to temptation as possible.

"Did you have any trouble getting away?" Bethany queried as she opened the door. She could see she had made the right choice of clothing. James was almost salivating as he entered the apartment.

"No, I said I had a meeting with union big

shots." James laughed, his hands already inside her robe, between her legs.

She was ready for him. James had a feeling she was one of those women who were always ready. For a moment he wondered if it was his presence that excited her, if she was that way all the time, or if she had done something to herself in preparation before he arrived. Either way, it meant less work for him. He liked not feeling responsible, knowing that whatever Bethany wanted or needed, she'd get it, with or without him. In seconds he was inside her, pumping his way to his own release.

Later, sprawled out on Bethany's bed, waiting for her, he luxuriated in his good fortune. She was different from the other women whom he used but didn't know. Different from his wife, who was as dry as parchment and whom he knew but couldn't use. Bethany and James knew each other, understood that they could use each other. There was comfort in that, and even more, there was possibility.

James eyed Bethany as she returned from the kitchen, wearing nothing but a smile, carrying a silver tray with a bottle of champagne, a tin of caviar, and two spoons. He felt a twinge in his groin as he thought about spreading the caviar over her body and licking it off. He knew she wouldn't object. Motioning her closer, he picked up the phone.

"Hi, sweetheart. Listen, I'm sorry, but I'm going to be late again tonight. . . . Union meeting—nothing I can do about it. . . . Well, you know, with

Drew gone, your dad is relying on me a lot more, . . . Okay. Don't wait up."

He hung up the phone. Bethany had placed the tray at the side of the bed. She was holding out the tin of caviar and a spoon.

"Lie down," he said.

"What? Don't you want your treat?"

"Oh, but I do. I want all my treats. I'm a very greedy boy."

He took the caviar and pushed her onto the bed. She laughed and obligingly lay back. Slowly he began spooning the caviar onto her breasts, circling the nipples. There were so many little black eggs. This was going to take a long, long time.

At home, Sarah told the cook to forget about dinner.

"What about you, madam? Even if your husband isn't coming home, you have to eat."

"Thanks, but I'm not really hungry. If I want something, I can just open a tin of pâté or something. You might as well go home early," she added, knowing that would forestall any argument. The last thing she wanted was servants waiting on her alone, making assumptions about her misery and pitying her solitude.

The truth was, she felt pitiable and extremely sorry for herself. She looked in the mirror and saw herself as she imagined others must see her: a drab, washed-out woman, dressed expensively but carelessly, looking dowdy and unattractive and older than her years. She was only twenty-eight, but six

years of marriage to James had rushed her head-
long into middle age. No wonder he didn't want to
come home at night.

"No!" she said aloud to herself in the mirror,
interrupting her own thoughts. "He didn't come
home at night even before I looked like this. That's
why I look like this!"

It was true. In the early days, Sarah's blond hair,
wide blue eyes, and fair skin, had given her the
classic beauty of a fragile porcelain doll. On the
Continent, she'd been a standout among the many
dark-haired, lusty offspring of down-at-the-heels
nobility from countries that had long since ceased
to exist. Visiting friends in Ibiza, James had noticed her immediately and, to his credit, divined
that she didn't really belong in the Euro-trash
crowd with which she was running. Once he found
out who she was, he had pursued her relentlessly,
not immune to her allure, but certainly aware of
her family heritage.

At twenty-two, she hadn't been a virgin when she
was married. She had lost her virginity at eighteen
to the son of the gardener at her Swiss finishing
school. She had had sex only that once, and only
because she'd been so anxious to get rid of her
virginity and participate in the knowing talk with
the other girls in the dormitory. After that, there
had been the occasional frantic groping in the back
of a limo with one European playboy or another,
after having too much to drink at a party. But she
was never quite sure if she should consider those
encounters as actual sexual experiences, since she

could never quite remember exactly what she had done. When James came into the picture, his insistent devotion had convinced her that he would be her first real lover. To her astonishment, he had refused, asserting that he loved her too much to use her that way. He wanted to take her home, introduce himself to her parents, and ask for her hand in marriage. She had been so disarmed by his old-fashioned appeal, so different from that of the alcohol-sodden, lust-filled entreaties she usually heard, that she had fallen instantly and madly in love. To her parents' delight, she and James had been married on the grounds of Belvedere a few short months later.

Taking no chances, James had resisted the urge to sleep with her before the wedding, in spite of Sarah's many enticements. But once she was his wife, he took her often and without ceremony. At the beginning, Sarah had been disconcerted to find her new husband on her, in her, and done with her in a matter of minutes. She'd acquiesced at first, saying nothing, assuming that the anticipation of waiting had made him too eager and her too needy.

After a while, she'd tried to stall the act itself, guiding his hand to where she wanted it, to raise her level of excitement. But he'd seemed so impatient that the effect had been just the opposite, making her body shut down and dry up, even though her heart was willing. Not giving up, she'd experimented with other techniques, delighting him by taking him in her mouth and concentrating all her attention on pleasing him. But when she looked for a little reciprocal action, it was not forthcoming, and Sarah had had to admit to herself that while James appeared to be a devoted husband, he was a selfish lover.

For James, the novelty of Sarah, like that of the other women he had known, had worn off quickly. In the bedroom he was willing to do his duty, but he would not put a lot of effort into it. For himself, he found it easier and a lot more pleasant to continue his frequent dalliances with women who asked nothing of him except perhaps a meal and a little cash. All his energy he reserved for making himself an indispensable part of the Symington family, catering to Sarah's mother, kowtowing to her father, and waiting for the day, which seemed to have arrived, when he could make his move.

For Sarah, the change, though gradual, had been decidedly dramatic. Seeing that her husband no longer found her attractive, Sarah ceased to be attractive. Believing he no longer cared for her, she stopped caring for herself.

Dinners at Belvedere, which happened at least twice a week, did nothing to fortify her. Once he'd married his daughter off acceptably, Forrest ceased to actually notice Sarah. She didn't doubt that her father loved her, but since every observable emotion in his life was directly tied to his company and the auto industry, she didn't expect much from him. While Drew was with them, Forrest had focused his parental pride on his son. With Drew gone, he'd had to transfer some semblance of it to James, who ostensibly was taking Drew's place. But

Sarah had nothing to do with cars, so beyond a formally affectionate exchange of small talk, her father hardly noticed her.

Sarah would have liked to confide in her mother, but Mathilde's alcoholic torpor discouraged approach. The two women had once been close. Sarah still had fond memories of summers on the Riviera, with French cousins racing around the villa grounds and of a warm, sweet-smelling mother who bathed her and tucked her into bed at night. But something had happened to Mathilde—something that Sarah was not allowed to question—and she had retreated behind an impenetrable veil, leaving Sarah to get through the rest of her life alone.

Only Drew was aware of how different his sister had become. But even though they had been close when they were younger, as adults their paths had diverged. The choices they'd made in their lives had tended to pull them apart rather than bring them together. Sarah had always felt that Bethany was too shallow for Drew, but until Drew realized it himself and married Samantha, whom Sarah had never met, he wouldn't discuss his engagement with her. Drew had always seen through James's continual fawning, and suspected that James was not the loving husband he made himself out to be. But Sarah, convinced that in some way she had brought James's indifference upon herself, refused to confirm Drew's misgivings. Accepting her punishment, she had played out her role of dutiful wife.

Since Drew had been banished from the family, there had been fewer dinners at Belvedere, and

Sarah was relieved not to have to keep up the pretense. But it was a mixed blessing. At least in front of her family, James continued to shower her with attention, and contrived though it was, it was better than the nothing she was getting now. She was lonelier than ever, and she sorely missed her brother. She tried to imagine what life must be like for Drew's wife, who was from an ordinary family where people married whomever they wanted and sisters-in-law went shopping together and everybody got along and met for barbecues. She bet that was what Drew's life would be like with his new family, and for a moment she envied him. Mostly, she just wanted to see him and know that he was happy and tell him that marrying the "right sort of person" wasn't all it was cracked up to be.

"Why don't I visit Drew?" she said, surprising herself with the sound of her own voice. "I don't even know where they are," she answered.

She'd taken to talking to herself lately, dispelling the feeling of isolation with the sound of simulated conversation.

"You know where her family lives," she told herself. "You could go ask them. They'll know where Drew is."

She dug around her desk, looking for the invitation to the wedding that had come over a month ago, and to which she'd never even responded. She had wanted to go, but James and her parents had been adamant, and she'd lost her nerve. She'd kept the invitation, though, thinking she could at least send a gift later, when things had cooled down.

"Mom and Dad will kill me if they find out.

"Why should they find out?" she argued with herself. "I'm not going to tell them.

"What about James? He's so happy with his new job, I know he doesn't want things patched up with Drew.

"The hell with James," she said, very loud, and felt instantly free. "I'm going to see my brother."

She freed the invitation from under a pile of fashion magazines and studied it: "Diane and Harvey Myles request the honor of your presence at the marriage of their daughter Samantha to Andrew Forrest Symington, at their home, Twenty-two Thayer Street, Oakdale . . ."

She was having second thoughts. She wanted to see Drew, not these Myles people. She tried calling Information, but the only listing for Andrew Symington was his old phone number at Belvedere. She asked for a number for Samantha Myles, but was informed the number was unlisted. She wondered why a factory worker would need an unlisted number, and then remembered that her brother's wife had been instrumental in thwarting DMC's plans to build a new plant, and thought it was wise. She could just call the bride's parents and ask for Drew's number, but she was afraid they might not give it to her. She needed to go there, convince them that she was sincere and that she meant the newlyweds no harm.

"Stop being an idiot. Just go," she scolded herself. And before she could change her mind, she was out the door.

She had a little trouble finding Thayer Street. She

realized she knew Paris better than she knew this part of town. She had been raised to think that nice girls from good families in Woodland Cliffs had no business in Oakdale, and now, driving around the slightly run-down but quiet, clean streets, she had the grace to be embarrassed. Finally she pulled up in front of a simple clapboard house with a small, scruffy front yard, separated from its neighbors by a sparse line of juniper bushes. It was hard for her to imagine her brother Drew getting married in a place like this. The caretaker's cottage at Belvedere had more style. For a moment she wondered how he could possibly give up the life they enjoyed for this bare-bones existence. Then she heard a laugh from inside, thought about her own empty mansion, and began to understand.

"What am I doing here?" she said aloud, getting out of the car. "They're probably going to spit at me." But she didn't really believe they would. She had a feeling that Drew's wife's parents would be more polite to her than her parents had been to them.

Halfway up the walk she hesitated. "What can they do to me except tell me to get lost? James does that to me every day. Not in so many words, of course." She gave a sardonic laugh, and then stopped herself. Something, someone, was moving in the bushes.

"Who's there?" she called out nervously, flustered to be caught talking to herself. There was no response. She stood still, holding her breath. Another rustle. She thought she saw a glint at eye level. Definitely a person, not a thing.

"Who is it?" she asked again, waiting for an answer, ready to bolt if she got one.

She peered into the bushes. Someone she didn't know was in there. She looked at the house. Strangers were in there too. She lost her nerve and ran to the safety of her car. She'd find another way to get to Drew. But not tonight. Right now she just wanted to get back to the safety of Woodland Cliffs. And to her lonely but familiar home.

By the time Drew got home to their little apartment, it was after midnight and Sam was already asleep. She'd obviously been waiting for him, propped up on the pillows with a book open on her lap. She was wearing a nightgown of white muslin that had slipped off one shoulder, and he could see the faint outline of a rosy nipple through the thin fabric. She was an intoxicating mixture of innocence and sensuality, and Drew couldn't decide if he should tuck her in or ravish her. Watching her breast rise and fall, he was leaning toward attack when she opened her eyes and smiled at him.

"You just saved yourself from being sexually assaulted in your sleep."

"Oh, darn," she kidded. "I could pretend," she added hopefully.

"Nope. Wouldn't work."

"Then you'll just have to do it with me awake."

He didn't need a second invitation. Even though they'd been together over a month, their lovemaking hadn't diminished in intensity. They were continually surprised by their constant desire for each other. Enough just never seemed to be enough.

As much as they felt the need to begin to build a new life for themselves, it took all their willpower to resist the ever-beckoning bed and attend to business. Still, the last thing they did before going out on their individual errands, and the first thing they did upon returning to their lair, was to make love. And only afterward could they discuss the day's events.

"So, what's your news?" Drew asked sleepily, after he'd been temporarily sated and sedated.

"You go first," Sam said, snuggling into his arms. "Yours is more important."

Drew hesitated, not wanting to spoil the feeling of well-being that suffused them both.

"Your news is not good, is it?" asked Sam, sensing his reluctance.

"Aren't you tired? Wouldn't you rather go to sleep and talk about it in the morning?"

"No," said Sam, sitting up. "I'd rather stay up and worry with you than let you stay up and worry alone."

"Okay, since you asked. The bank said no."

"I figured. Did you offer the equipment as collateral?"

"I offered the equipment. I offered the space. I offered our unborn children. No go."

"Did the banker say why he turned us down?"

"Yes. He didn't want to explain, I have to grant him that. He was pretty embarrassed about it. But he told me the D'Uberville Motor Company had substantial deposits in his bank, and that my father had made it perfectly clear that if they helped me in any way, DMC would pull out. The bank just couldn't afford to let that happen. He felt bad. He picked up the tab for dinner."

"Big deal. So I guess that's it. We've already been turned down by everyone else. You said this bank was our last resort."

"I was wrong."

"Really? Do you think there's a bank in the entire state that your father doesn't have some control over?"

"I doubt it."

"Then what are we going to do?"

"Go out of state."

Sam looked at her husband and tried to keep her disappointment and panic at bay. They'd had such hopes, such plans. They had figured with the half-million dollars from Drew's trust and a matching loan, they could build their own plant and begin production of the Mylometer within a year. Once auto engineers were introduced to her invention, Sam had no doubt that it would be just a matter of time before she and Drew would be supplying the entire industry—with the exception, of course, of DMC—and they'd be well on their way to a hugely lucrative business. It had been exciting for Sam to think that what had been taken away from Drew because of who she was might be regained because of what she did.

But it seemed they had figured wrong. Forrest Symington's vindictiveness went far beyond what she'd expect a man to do to his only son, no matter how embittered their relationship. Effectively, Forrest had not only banished Drew from his home and family but had seen to it that he was exiled as well from any semblance of his former lifestyle.

She started to cry. "It's no use. Your father probably has half the U.S. Senate in his pocket. He's one of the biggest political contributors in the country. Do you think the situation will be any different in Ohio or Iowa?"

"No." He was wiping away her tears with the hem of his T-shirt. "That's why I have to go very far out of state. Like Europe."

She stopped crying, baffled. "What are you talking about?"

"Honey, the Symingtons are powerful people, but they don't rule the world. When I was in Europe, I made some contacts. And believe it or not, some of them have more money than my father—or my mother, for that matter."

"You don't mind going to them?"

"Why should I? I'm offering them a solid investment, not begging for a handout. High-performance, environmentally sound cars are a necessity for the future. Your invention can make them a reality for the present. Who wouldn't be interested!"

"You make it sound great."

"It *is* great. Don't underestimate yourself and what you've done. Believe me, if your invention wasn't worth developing, my father would never have tried to steal it from you."

"Do you really think you could get money in Europe?"

"There's only one way to find out."

They were quiet for a moment, both thinking. Sam wanted to believe what Drew said, that all things were possible, but his plan seemed so remote, so difficult. Her eyes filled with tears again.

"Drew, I'm sorry."

"For what?"

"For making your life so difficult."

Her vulnerability and concern touched him. As he kissed away her tears, he became aroused again. Everything about her seemed to arouse him. He lifted the blanket for her to see.

"Do I look like a man who's unhappy?"

Only later did he get around to asking her what had happened during her day.

"I got a job," she said. "Healy's Garage. It's only fourteen dollars an hour, but it's off the books."

"O ye of little faith."

"It's not that. I believe you can make this all happen. It's just that while we're waiting for your trust to be liquidated, and for you to raise the other half a million, we're going to need a way to pay the rent."

"You've got a point."

He hadn't been enthusiastic about her finding a job in a garage when she'd first suggested it. She didn't blame him. Life with her had to be quite a change for someone who was used to dressing for dinner and then socializing with women who spent their days preparing for their evenings. She knew he loved her, but she wagered he hadn't bargained on coming home to a mate who was covered with grease and smelled like gasoline. She was sure

Bethany Havenhurst would have a good laugh about that.

"Do you find it embarrassing to be married to a mechanic?" she asked, hating herself for being so insecure.

"Do you find it embarrassing to be married to a man who has to live off his wife?"

"That's just temporary."

"So's you're being a mechanic."

"I love you," she said, amazed that, despite having been raised the way he was, he was still not a snob.

"And I love you," he said, wondering how she could be so beautiful and brilliant and still not be conceited.

4

"Maybe you should come to London with me, Sam. You've still got time to pack."

"Oh, Drew. We've been through this a hundred times. It just doesn't make sense."

Drew knew that Sam was right. They'd been going back and forth on it all week. Practically, there was no reason for Sam to go with him. He intended to reach out to his contacts with a strictly personal appeal based on his family background and reputation. Certainly he'd talk about the industry-wide ramifications of Sam's invention. But, much as they both hated to admit it, he would probably find it easier to interest serious investors if they didn't actually meet her. Not too many Old World financial barons were equipped to deal with a gorgeous female automotive genius. They'd think Drew was just trying to give his new little woman something to do—instead of the other way around.

Emotionally, Drew couldn't bear the thought of being without Sam even for a day, let alone a week. "It wouldn't be that expensive, Sam. I mean, we could share a room," he teased.

"Yeah, and if we did, we'd probably never leave it."

"You've got a point there."

She hated to have him leave her as much as he hated to go. But he'd told her himself how expensive London was. Even staying in a single room in a cheap hotel, they'd both still have to eat. And then there was the plane fare. They had gone to buy Drew's ticket together, and he had been positively relieved when the travel agent quoted him the price for a coach ticket. Compared to first class, which was what he was used to flying, it seemed a veritable bargain. Sam, on the other hand, never having spent more on a trip than excursion fare to Orlando, was shocked. The ticket cost more than a month's rent, and if things didn't go as well as Drew hoped, they'd need that money for the apartment.

"You'll only be gone for a week," she whispered, her arms around his neck, sounding braver than she felt.

"That'll seem like an eternity." He kissed her. She looked at her watch. "Am I boring you?" he asked, trying to keep the mood jocular. "Or are you expecting someone to arrive the minute I leave?"

"None of the above." She laughed. "I was just thinking . . . Since the plane doesn't leave for an hour, and I'm not going to pack, that leaves us about fifteen minutes. Too short?"

He didn't need to answer. He was already unbuttoning her shirt.

"This puts a new twist on the notion of having one for the road," he said as he gently pushed her down on the bed. Then, for the next fifteen minutes, neither one of them uttered a word. Their hearts and their bodies said all that needed to be said.

They were already closing the door to the plane when Drew came racing to the gate. At first the ground attendant refused to let him pass, but Drew, still languorous in the aftermath of an incredible climax with his wife, had only to look at her from under his dark lashes, and she relented.

A little out of breath, Drew entered the plane and automatically turned to his left. He felt a moment of confusion, as he saw all the seats were filled. The flight attendant checked his boarding pass.

"You're in coach, sir. That's to your right toward the rear." She was smiling benignly, but he felt like a fool.

"Of course," he muttered and began to push his way down the narrow aisle, mumbling apologies as the Hermès carry-on bag slung over his shoulder knocked against the seats on either side.

This is not possible, he thought to himself as he saw the tight little space that waited for him between a rather large man and a woman holding an infant on her lap. He turned to the flight attendant, who was now standing behind him, urging him into his spot.

"I don't think I can fit in there," he said, giving her his most charming smile. It had worked on the ground crew, but it had no effect here.

"I'm afraid you're going to have to," she said, and he thought he detected a slight hint of belligerence. "It's the last seat in the house. Now, if you'll kindly take your seat, we can prepare for takeoff." He heard a definite note of reprimand and saw that people in the area were eyeing him with impatience. He looked helplessly at the bag over his shoulder. He was used to smiling and deferential flight attendants taking his bags from him the moment he entered the cabin.

"You'll have to put that in the overhead bin, sir."

He opened the latch above him and was rewarded with a heavy man's coat falling onto his head. He stuffed it back in and tried another bin and another.

"They all seem to be full."

"Then you'll have to place it under the seat in front of you," the attendant said with a trace of annoyance.

He looked in the direction she pointed. There was precious little room for his legs as it was. "Couldn't you put it in—"

"No," she said curtly, cutting him off. "This flight is completely booked. The bag goes below the seat or into the baggage area, which would mean opening the doors and . . ."

He didn't need to hear more. Another attendant had joined the first, obviously wondering about the delay. "Fine. I'll put it under the seat."

The woman with the baby got up so he could

squeeze his way into his designated spot. The baby woke up and began to cry. The attendants began their safety demonstrations. The baby cried louder. Feeling as though he'd been folded into a cage, Drew felt a pang of longing for the first-class amenities, which he'd always taken for granted. He suddenly missed the cheap champagne and orange juice, which he never drank. He yearned for the fawning attention, which used to annoy him: a stewardess who introduced herself, called him by his first name, and offered him selections from a menu, which he never ate.

People fly this way all the time and survive very nicely, he told himself over and over again, as if repeating a mantra. But he had never done it before, and by the time the flight was over, seven hours later, he looked forward to never having to fly coach again.

He was exhausted when he emerged into Heathrow at a little after six in the morning, having slept perhaps a total of thirty minutes through the endless night. He looked around, half expecting to see a liveried chauffeur bearing a sign with his name on it, waiting to take his bag and usher him into a waiting limousine. Not this time, he reminded himself, a little disgusted with his involuntary elitist reactions but too tired to control them.

He resisted the urge to just jump into a taxi and instead made his way to the underground. Never having been in the London tube before, he was pleased to find it reasonably comfortable and inestimably quieter than his seat over the airplane wing had been. Resting his head on the bag on his lap, lulled by the whoosh of the electric wheels, he fell into a heavy sleep.

He woke to find a mass of humanity crushing in on him. The car had been empty when he got in at Heathrow, but this was the morning rush hour, and while he slept, he had been joined by a crowd of Londoners on their way to work. He had no idea where he was and couldn't see the signs for the people, as the train pulled into the next station.

"Excuse me, what stop is this?" he asked, addressing no one in particular.

"Piccadilly," came the response.

He jumped up from his seat and, with apologies, elbowed his way through the crowd, ignoring the mumbled curses, until, pushed along more by momentum than by design, he found himself deposited on the platform seconds before the doors closed behind him.

Emerging into the gray morning at Piccadilly Circus, he suddenly felt revived. This was the London he knew. Chill and damp, to be sure, but interesting and alive just the same. He had chosen a budget hotel on Broadwick Street, walking distance from Piccadilly and the Ritz, where he usually stayed. He knew he could have gotten more for his money farther from Mayfair, but this was an area he knew well, and where he felt at home.

He was also aware that if he was seeking investments, he couldn't appear to be down on his luck. He hoped that the personal tribulations of an American automotive dynasty hadn't commanded much attention across the ocean, but he knew there was a good chance that people would have heard about his circumstances. It was important for him to act as if being disinherited had hardly affected his fortunes, and as if this new enterprise was an adventure rather than a survival tactic.

Still smarting from his new role as Everyman, Drew was relieved to see that the lobby of the Royal Broadwick, though not at all regal, was clean and pleasant enough.

Living on the cheap might not be so bad after all, he thought, as he approached the desk and, smiling optimistically, greeted the clerk. "Good morning. I have a reservation in the name of Symington?"

The clerk, tinkering with a screwdriver at something under the desk, looked up for a moment, then went back to his work.

"Excuse me . . ." Drew began, with an emphasis that revealed the full extent of his annoyance.

"I see ya, guv," said the clerk. "No need to get your knickers in a twist."

Drew forced himself to retain his composure, again conscious of the notable difference between the treatment given to the rich and that accorded to everyone else. He was very tired. Shouting at the clerk would not get him a room any faster.

"Could I get a room, please?" he said with deliberate calm.

"D'ya have a reservation?"

"I just said I did."

"Name?"

"Symington. S-y-m—"

"I can spell, guv. Here it is. Symington, Andrew. Single room with bath for one week." Drew signed the registration form, paid thirty pounds in advance for the first night, and was handed a key. "Room three-fourteen. Third floor on the left. You'll have to take the stairs. Lift is broken."

Drew shook his head but said nothing. What was the point? He usually spent thirty pounds on tips alone during his first day at the Ritz. Wearily he started up the stairs.

"W.C. is at the end of the hall," the clerk called after him.

"I beg your pardon?"

"W.C. Toilet. At the end of the hall."

Now there was a point in protesting. Coming back down the steps, he confronted the clerk. "I reserved a room with private bath."

"That's what you've got. Private bath."

"But you said—"

"Toilet, guv. There's a bath in the room, and the toilet's down the hall. We don't have toilets in the rooms. That would be nasty."

Drew mentally kicked himself. He had assumed a private bath would include a toilet. It did at the Ritz. He was flooded with a fatigue so profound he felt he was drowning. Slowly he trudged back up the stairs. He'd stay here for now, call home, get a few hours' sleep, set up some appointments, then find another hotel tomorrow.

Barely allowing the state of the room to enter his consciousness, Drew dropped his bag and looked around for the phone. There wasn't one.

"God damn it. What the hell am I doing here?" he said aloud, frustrated at the situation and angry at himself for not being able to cope with it better. But a sigh of relief escaped his body as he lay down and found the bed to be smooth and soft. He'd just lie here for a few minutes, pull himself together, then go and find a phone. In seconds he was asleep, dreaming of his wife.

"At least you have a husband," Melinda said to her sister. She knew she was whining, but she didn't care. She'd come for tea and sympathy, and since Sam had run out of tea, she was damn sure going to get all the sympathy she could.

"Yeah. I wish he'd call," Sam replied, distracted.

Melinda gave up. She could see she wasn't going to get much encouragement here. At least not until Drew had called Sam.

"He'll call. He probably got in late or something."

"I guess," said Sam, not satisfied. "This is the first time we've been apart since we've been married."

"You've only been married a month."

"I still miss him," Sam said forlornly.

"Do you think you could miss him and talk to me at the same time?"

"I'm sorry. What were you saying?"

"I was saying that I feel awful and I look worse. I hate living at home, but I don't know where else to go. Mom is on my case all the time about going to the singles group at the church, before I really start to show. As if I can hook someone in to marrying me by the day after tomorrow and make him think the baby is his, just five months premature. Dad wants me to call Forrest's lawyer and try to get child-support money before the baby is born."

Sam forced herself to stop staring at the phone. Maybe it was like a watched pot, and it wouldn't ring as long as she looked at it. She tried to focus on Melinda. "Are you okay at home?"

Melinda gave up. "You didn't hear a word I said, did you?"

"I'm sorry," said Sam again, meaning it. "Tell me again."

"Never mind, it's not important," said Melinda, feeling more depressed than when she came.

The doorbell rang. Sam's face lit up. "I bet he sent a telegram or flowers or something. That would be just like Drew. Who is it?" she called out hopefully.

"Me, Jack."

Melinda groaned. Now she was really depressed. Sam opened the door, greeting him flatly, barely responding to his hearty hug.

Jack looked from Sam's open disappointment to Melinda's open disgust. "I've come at a bad time, have I?"

"Not really," Sam said apologetically. "I'm just waiting for Drew to call. He landed in London hours ago, and I still haven't heard from him. I'm a little worried."

"I'm just leaving," added Melinda, by way of her own explanation.

"No, don't go," implored Sam, her instinct for hospitality suddenly kicking in. "I'll make you both tea."

"You don't have any," Melinda reminded her.

"Okay, coffee. A glass of wine. Whatever."

"She can't have wine," Jack interjected.

"Oh, please, let's not start that again." This visit was not turning out the way she had hoped. "Bye, Sam. I'm sure he'll call. Excuse me," she said to Jack, inching past him at the door. "I have to go jump in the river and drown myself."

"What did she say?" Sam asked Jack moments after Melinda had left.

"She said she had to go drown herself."

"Oh, God. She was really depressed. I should have listened to her, but I couldn't concentrate."

"Don't worry. I think she was just kidding."

"Of course she was. You do think so, don't you? She couldn't have really meant it."

"I'm sure she didn't mean it."

"What if she did?" Sam knew she was losing it, but she couldn't think straight anymore. In her heart she knew she had nothing to worry about. But somehow she couldn't stop herself from worrying about everything. "Go after her, Jack. Just make sure."

"Sam, she didn't mean it, I assure you. It was just a joke."

"What if it wasn't?"

"Sam, your sister doesn't like me. It won't make her feel better if I grill her about her intentions."

"You don't even have to talk to her. Just follow her home, make sure she gets there all right."

"This is stupid."

"I know. But hurry, so you don't miss her. I'd go myself, but I have to wait for Drew to call."

Jack sighed. "I knew I came at a bad time." But he raced down the stairs and got into his car, just as Melinda was pulling out in hers.

He followed her for a while, cursing softly under his breath, tempted to just turn around and head home. But he'd promised Sam he'd make sure she got home, and the Myles place was only five minutes away. It occurred to him that they'd been driving ten minutes already. They should have been there by now. He started paying attention to the street signs instead of just following Melinda's taillights. He knew why it was taking so long. They weren't heading toward her house; they were going to the river.

"Don't do this," he said, watching as she parked her car in the deserted lot by the bridge. The roadway had been closed for repairs ever since the new tunnel had been built. There was no traffic and no cover. He wasn't sure what to do. If he pulled in after her, she'd see him. He turned off his lights and let the car coast a little closer before bringing it to a silent stop. He suddenly remembered everything he'd ever heard about suicidal people: listen to their warnings; believe them when they say they are going to kill themselves. He felt like a fool for resisting Sam's superior instincts. His eyes strained in the dark to make out Melinda's shape as she got out of her car and headed toward the bridge.

Careful not to slam the car door, he quietly made his way behind her. He realized how ill equipped he was to handle this sort of crisis. But there was no time to go get help. He had always disdained car phones as an affectation, but now he cursed himself for his proletarian posturing. He started to rehearse soothing phrases in his mind:

"You don't want to die. . . . No, that was too harsh: you don't really want to do this. . . . That was better. Things can't be that bad. . . . Too negative. He needed to stress the positive: you have so much to live for. . . ."

Then he heard the splash, loud and hard. He stopped thinking and started running. He saw her standing on the pedestrian walkway, leaning over the railing. In an instant he was at her side, grabbing her, pulling her back and away from the rail, away from the water. She was screaming, struggling against him. He was afraid to let her go, afraid she'd try to jump again. Suddenly a thought occurred to him: if she was in his arms, she couldn't have made that splash. Abruptly he let her go.

She pulled away, ready to run, looking over her shoulder for an instant to see if her assailant had a weapon. She stopped short.

"Jack?" she gasped, incredulous, then furious. "What the hell do you think you're doing?"

He was confused, and getting angry as well. "What the hell were *you* doing?"

"Throwing rocks in the water. Is there a law against that?"

"Not if you don't jump in after them."

"Jump? Are you crazy?"

"No. Are you?"

They were screaming at each other. Jack looked at her, the absurdity of the situation starting to take hold somewhere in his gut.

"You weren't going to jump?" he asked, quieting.

"Of course not."

He paused for a moment. "Oh. Never mind," he said and started to laugh.

"What's so funny? You almost scared me to death," Melinda said, but she was already laughing too.

"I'm sorry," he said, choking out the words while he wiped tears from his eyes. "Sam thought you were going to drown yourself . . ." He was laughing too hard to continue.

When she could talk, she asked, "Why did Sam think I was going to drown myself?"

"Because you said you were."

"I did? When?"

"Before you left her place."

"Well, if I did, I didn't mean it."

"That's what I said, but Sam wasn't sure, so she asked me to follow you. Then you came to the river, and I thought, Oh, shit, Sam was right. And then I heard the splash."

"It was just a rock."

"Now you tell me. Why were you throwing rocks in the water?"

"To keep myself from jumping," she said, and they were laughing again.

Later, after they had driven in tandem to the Oakdale Diner and Melinda finally had the cup of tea she'd been trying to get all evening, she was surprised to find that she was getting the sympathy as well.

"So you weren't going to jump. But are you really okay?"

"Yeah, sure. I mean, I'm depressed, but not any more than normal for a pregnant woman without a husband, a home, or a job."

"Fair enough. So what's the downside?"

She laughed, as he had hoped she would. "Let's face it," she said. "My past is disgusting, my present is dreary, and my future looks dismal."

"Do I detect a note of self-pity?" he asked in a mocking Church Lady tone, but she could hear his kindness.

"Absolutely," she responded defiantly. "I can't seem to get any pity from anyone else."

"You're right. You're too pretty to pity."

She looked at him and saw he was being serious.

"I'm getting a little Rubenesque for average American tastes, and what do looks have to do with anything?"

"Nothing. Everything. I'm not talking about how attractive you are, which, incidentally, you are. Some people actually find what nature does quite beautiful. But that's beside the point. What I'm talking about is your inner light. It's shining."

"This isn't just another way of telling me I'm a dim bulb, is it?"

He laughed. "No, although I wouldn't blame you if that's what you expected of me." He liked the way she deflected compliments, even though he saw she was pleased. "And I don't mean this to sound like psychobabble, either. Whatever your circumstances are, something about you says you're not unhappy about being pregnant."

She smiled at his insight. "You're right. I'm not. I want this baby, even if no one else does. I feel dejected once in a while because I'm embarrassed, and I'm definitely scared, and I know the baby's going to cramp my style. But way down deep I don't care. I think having this baby is going to be good."

"I think so, too. Because you want your life to be good and you're the kind of person who gets what she wants."

"I didn't get Forrest Symington," she said quietly, before she could stop herself.

"Are you sure you wanted him?" Jack asked, then got up to pay the check before she could answer.

"Why did you cancel dinner at your parents' tonight?" James asked Sarah.

"I don't know. Because it gets so boring. Don't you think so?"

"Well, they *are* your parents." The truth was, James found the evenings more boring when he was at home with Sarah. At least, when he was at his in-laws', he could work on Mathilde and show the Symingtons how indispensable he was becoming.

"Ever since Drew's been gone—" Sarah began.

"Let's not start that again. Your father knew what he was doing. Drew put your parents in a very awkward position, and he had no right to do that."

"Oh, for God's sake, he fell in love, that's all.

And from everything I can see, there's nothing wrong with his wife. She's smart, she's pretty, she loves him. And he's still their son . . . and my brother."

"I don't see him making any overtures toward reconciliation."

"He knows my father too well. Maybe if I spoke to him, I could serve as a liaison."

"Honey, you know how I feel about that. I don't want you caught in the middle of an ugly family battle. Drew's problem has nothing to do with us, we should just keep out of it."

Drew's estrangement had everything to do with James, but he was not about to admit that to his wife. The last thing in the world he wanted was for Drew to make peace with Forrest and come back into the fold. James was putting in long, hard, and boring hours, trying to make the Symingtons think of him as the only son—and heir—they had left. With Drew back in the picture his plans would be ruined.

"I think you're wrong. My father is just being stubborn because Drew didn't marry a girl from the right circles, like Bethany."

James quickly crossed his legs to keep his wife from seeing his reaction to the mention of Bethany. What had started as just a minor excursion into abandoned territory was turning into a rousing adventure and a possible gold mine of opportunity. He and Bethany were not yet certain how they were going to parlay their dalliance into power, but they were both aware that there was a purpose to their play. In the meantime, James was reaping the benefits. With Bethany, satisfaction was always guaranteed.

He looked at his watch. It wasn't that late. He knew Bethany was home tonight; he'd called her before he left the office. And the probable alternative was watching a nature documentary on educational television with Sarah, followed by a chaste kiss and a good night's sleep. He could still get the good night's sleep.

"Oh, my God!" he exclaimed, trying to sound like a man in trouble.

"What's wrong?" Sarah asked solicitously.

"I just realized I forgot to bring home a report that I was supposed to work on after dinner. I have to go back to the office and get it."

"All right. We're just having soup and salad. I'll wait for you."

"You know what, honey? Don't bother. I was only going to work on the report at home because I thought we were going to your parents'. But the truth is, it'll be easier for me to work at the office. I've got all the materials I need there, so this is really kind of a blessing."

Sarah was disappointed. Not that she expected they'd do much besides watch television, but James was company. She regretted having canceled dinner at Belvedere, but it was too late to change her mind now. James was already out the door, telling her not to wait up. She channel-surfed for a few minutes, but the thought of learning about the plight of the coyotes was not appealing. After turning off the television, she wandered around the silent house. She thought of calling her mother, but she knew that by now Mathilde would have had too many cocktails to be really coherent, especially since there were no guests to monitor her behavior.

Sarah knew what she really wanted to do. She had chickened out last time, imagining someone watching her from the bushes near the Myles house. But she had been silly. She'd knock on their door tonight and find out where the newlyweds were living. She didn't care what the Myles family thought of her. Drew was her brother, and she wanted to see him.

She had no trouble finding the place this time. The lights were on, and she could see some movement in the house. She tried not to think about what she'd say or how she'd feel if they were hostile.

"You are such a wimp!" She laughed at herself, giving the car door an aggressive slam to emphasize her determination. She walked purposefully up the drive, then stopped and shuddered. She felt it again. Someone was watching her from the bushes. Forcing herself not to run, she peered into the darkness. She saw his eyes first and then the rest of him, crouching.

"I'm calling the police," she shouted and ran back toward her car.

He was on her in a minute, holding his hand over her mouth. His grip felt firm but somehow gentle. He was pleading. "Please don't do that. I'm not harming anyone. Please."

Suddenly she wasn't frightened anymore. She indicated she wanted to speak.

"You won't scream?" he asked.

She shook her head no. He let her go without hesitation. She turned and looked at him. He looked to be about her age, dressed decently but not expensively. His hair was dark and so were his eyes. She felt something warm and familiar when she looked into them.

I must be crazy, she thought, but she tried to sound stern. "Why are you following me?"

"I'm not," he said, sounding genuinely surprised.

"Don't give me that. I saw you the last time I came here, too. Are you spying for my father? Is this his way of finding out if I've gone against his orders and contacted Drew?"

"I don't know what you're talking about."

She could see that he didn't. "But you were here before when I was here."

"I'm always here," he said quietly.

"Why?"

"I . . . I can't tell you." He seemed pained. "But I swear to you, I'm just watching them. I . . . I need to see who they are. I'm not going to hurt them or anything. Please don't tell."

She thought about it. She probably should go straight to the door, warn the Myles family about the prowler in their front yard, and ask them to call the police. He was looking at her with round eyes filled with fear and anguish. His distress was palpable, and she felt it imperceptibly linking to her own.

She had no idea who he was or what he was doing there, but for some reason she felt she understood him.

"I am definitely crazy," she said aloud.

"You won't call the police?"

"No. But stay away from here, okay? You can't hang out in people's bushes and watch them, for whatever reason."

"Fine. I'm going. Thank you."

She watched him hurry off. There was a grace in his movements that surprised her. She went back to her car. She'd used up all her assertiveness with this stranger. She didn't have the strength to confront Mr. Myles.

"Jeez, I'm going to feel awful if I find out in the papers tomorrow that he broke in and killed them," she said to herself. She considered driving to the nearest precinct and at least informing the police that she had seen a prowler. Then she remembered his eyes. They had been pleading, but under the fear there had been gentleness. He wasn't going to harm anyone; she was sure of that. She scolded herself for being a romantic fool. How could she possibly know what a prowler was capable of doing? But still, she could not make herself drive to the police station. She reminded herself that she didn't want anyone to know she'd been making forays into Oakdale. If she went to the police, they'd insist on knowing who she was and what she was doing there. Best to just let it go, she told herself, aware she was rationalizing a totally irrational need to protect someone she didn't know and would never meet again.

Slowly Sarah drove home, still thinking about the stranger. Somehow it was comforting to think that there was someone more alone and frightened than she was. For once she didn't care whether James came home tonight or not.

❧ 5 ❧

Drew opened his eyes. A dim gray light, filtered through dirty windows, cast desultory shadows around the ugliest room he had ever seen. He closed his eyes again, hoping he was dreaming and would wake to find himself in Sam's bed, her warm body next to his. He moved his arm, tentatively reaching out to the space beside him and was disappointed to encounter only cold, dank, empty air. He let out a sigh of profound dejection. He knew where he was. He wished he didn't.

He studied his watch. It said eight o'clock. But he was hard pressed to tell if it was day or night. He went to the window and looked down on a brood of black umbrellas, scurrying through the ever-present London drizzle—to work, or from work, he had no idea. He felt an urge to empty his bladder, and became even more depressed as he

lumbered down the hall to the toilet, only to find it
locked. Frustrated, he rattled the handle, then
heard sounds he had no interest hearing from
within: a whisper, a moan, a giggle, a rustle of
clothing. He felt groggy and disoriented, but he
knew for a certainty that he had to get out of this
place. He turned to go back to his room, and the
door marked W.C. opened. A man and a woman
emerged, the man zipping up his fly, while the
woman counted a handful of pound notes and
slipped them down the front of her dress.

"G'morning," she said, giving him a black-
toothed grin as they headed down the stairs.

At least he knew what time of day it was.

He'd slept for thirteen hours straight. He calculated that it would be about two in the morning in
Oakdale. He wanted desperately to hear Sam's
voice, but he knew she'd certainly be asleep. He
looked at himself in the cracked mirror above the
washstand in his room. His hair was matted, his
face unshaven, and his clothes looked as if he'd
slept in them, because he had. He decided to use
the one amenity provided in this dreary hotel, his
private shower. He would get cleaned up and
change, then check out and find another hotel. By
then, it would be morning in America, and he could
call his wife.

Clean and wearing fresh clothes, Drew looked
and felt like a new person. He stood in front of the
desk, his bag at his feet, waiting to check out. The
clerk, his back to the desk, his feet propped against

the wall, was in the midst of a clearly personal phone call. Drew coughed politely. Without turning around, the clerk covered the receiver with his hand and called out, "Hold your horses, guv. I'm busy here."

Drew seethed. There was a bell on the desk. He slammed his hand down on it hard, and it let out a piercing clang.

"What the—" the clerk began, whipping around in his seat. But the minute he saw Drew, his demeanor changed. "I'll have to call you back," he said hurriedly as he hung up the phone and rushed over to the desk, an obsequious grin on his face. "I'm so sorry to keep you waiting, sir. How can I help?"

He knew it was a shallow thought, but Drew couldn't help being pleased at the sudden change in attitude precipitated by his change in apparel. "I'm checking out."

"Checking out?" asked the clerk, confused. "You were staying here?"

"Symington."

The clerk did a double take. Could this be the same bleary-eyed man who had arrived the day before looking like a shaggy cur? His gaze intensified. Indeed it was.

"Symington, of course. Let's see. Oh, I see you were registered to stay a week, sir."

"That's right. But I'm checking out."

"Is something not to your satisfaction?"

"Yes, everything."

"Perhaps we could—"

"You could give me a receipt, take back your key

and let me get out of here," he said bluntly, losing patience.

"I see," the clerk stiffened, but the grin remained. "I'm afraid we'll have to charge you for the week."

"What?"

The clerk eyed him from head to foot. There was no mistaking the expensive cut of the clothes. "That's right," he went on, confident of his mark. "We've had to turn down other bookings for that room. Yours was a guaranteed stay."

"There are only three guarantees," Drew answered, his voice ominously quiet. "One, that I am leaving now. Two, that I will pay for one night and one night only. And three, if you think you're going to get me to pay for a whole week, I will have the American ambassador barking up your ass so quickly that you won't have time to take a leak before they charge you with creating an international incident."

"I understand, sir. No problem, sir. One night it is, then," said the clerk, as Drew had known he would. He also knew his tactics weren't admirable, and they certainly weren't fair, but that was the way of the world. If you looked as if you had money, people always believed you had power. As a customer, you were always right not because it was your prerogative but because you paid for the privilege. And the more you could pay, the more privileged you were. None of this was new information, but Drew had never been forced to think about it before. He walked out of the hotel smiling. It was good to be aware.

Outside, the air was sticky and damp. He slipped on his trench coat, feeling too warm, but without it, he would get too wet. He needed all his willpower not to walk the two short blocks to the Ritz and just check in. The staff knew him well there. Even without a reservation, he would be given a suite, or at least one of their better rooms. He could have a lovely English breakfast sent to his room, and he was certain that even without his asking, they'd remember to bring him American coffee instead of tea. Then he remembered that breakfast alone would cost more than the room he had just abandoned. And the room itself would eat up an entire month's budget for him and Sam in Oakdale.

For a moment depression descended on him like the mist over Piccadilly. But just as suddenly it turned into elation. Where was his spirit of adventure? He'd been in London countless times, but never on such a tight budget. He always stayed at the Ritz, ate at Walton's or Carrier's, went to Langan's for a nightcap. This trip to London was different. Life was starting again for him, and for Sam, and bringing with it all the fear and excitement of the unknown. He had a challenge to face and a reason to succeed. The rest of his life depended on his success.

Hoisting his bag, he hopped a red double-decker bus marked Victoria Station and settled into a seat on the upper deck. As he watched the sights go by, he realized that the last time he had been on a bus was when his parents had brought him to England as a little boy, and his nanny had taken him for a bus ride after countless hours of begging. He remembered how he had accosted his mother at tea, regaling her with his great adventure. Mathilde had been kind but distant and had quietly instructed the nanny not to subject her son to possible exposure to pedestrian germs again. During the rest of his trip he had been shunted by limousine to museums and palaces. But the high point, without a doubt, had been the bus ride, a thrill that even the changing of the guard, viewed as it was from a privileged perch on the chauffeur's shoulders, could not supplant. Riding a London bus was still fun, he decided, and promised himself that when he returned one day, with Sam and their children, and a healthy bank account, he would escort them all on a tour of the city, viewed from the top of a red double-decker bus.

By the time the bus let him off at Victoria Station, Drew was in fine spirits. He made his way to the Tourist Information Center and was pleased to find he was the only customer. A young blond woman with apple cheeks, looking like an advertisement for the English countryside, turned to him with a smile.

"Good morning," she greeted him cheerily. "Can I help you?"

"Yes, as a matter of fact, you can," he said, putting his bag down at his feet. "I need accommodations here in London, preferably somewhere around this area, and I wondered if you could recommend a hotel and make a reservation for me."

"That's what we do," she said, pulling out her printed list of hotels, separated into regions and categorized by price range. She gave him a friendly once-over, not failing to notice the striking contrast between his blue eyes and his black hair as well as the expensive cut of his suit. He was American, but he was definitely not one of the usual backpacking students or traveling dropouts who formed the bulk of her clientele.

She leaned over the counter so that he could read the list with her, glad that she'd bothered to put on perfume this morning. She wanted to ask what a man like him—well bred and wealthy, from the look of him—was doing at her post in Victoria Station. Why hadn't his secretary or his travel agent—she noticed his wedding band—or his wife booked him a room before he got to England? But even though he was smiling and his eyes were kind, his bearing was somehow aristocratic, and she didn't want to seem forward.

"Here we are," she said, indicating the top hotels, demarcated by five stars and the heading "superdeluxe." "A lot of the best choices are nearby. There's the Connaught, the Ritz, Brown's . . ."

He stopped her. She wore a name tag, and he read it. "Thank you, Anne, but I know those places. Actually I am looking for something a little more modest."

"I understand," she said, not understanding at all. She liked that he had bothered to register her name and use it. "If you want something a little more low-key, there's the Stafford in Saint James's. It's a lovely Edwardian—"

Again he interrupted. He knew the Stafford; it

could be even more expensive than the Ritz. He explained gently, "What I meant was that I need something more along the lines of a decent budget hotel."

She was as surprised as if he had told her he was looking for the gay baths. Her instincts had always been good, and she was as certain that this man was rich as that he was straight. He didn't even seem particularly eccentric. She reminded herself to mind her own business, and hastily flipped the pages of her booklet to the budget category, studying several entries at length, looking up at him from under her eyelashes occasionally, then shaking her head and moving on to the next.

Drew watched her watching him, amused. He knew he'd astonished her. He had never been so conscious of the impression wealth made on other people until he'd lost his. He had a feeling he was going to learn important lessons he would not soon forget. That made him think about Sam, how she was turning his life around and how her influence was all for the better. He missed her and wanted her desperately. He looked at his watch, calculating quickly. Ten a.m. in London meant four a.m. in Oakdale, still too early to call.

"Here's one," said Anne, interrupting his thoughts. "It's right off Sloane Square. That's a lovely area, very central. You can get a single with private bath for about twenty pounds. Will that do?"

"Does private bath mean a toilet as well?"

"I assume so, but I can check."

"Please do. And ask about a telephone in the room as well."

He waited while she called, watching the morning commuter crowd thinning out. He was always amazed at how many London men actually wore bowler hats and carried black umbrellas.

As Anne talked on the phone, she gave him a thumb's-up sign and a questioning smile. He nodded, relieved. But then worried a little as he saw her frown. "Oh, I see," she said into the phone. "Let me just ask the gentleman."

He leaned forward, "Is there a problem?"

"It seems they're fully booked at the moment. They will have a room for tonight, but their checkout time isn't until noon, so you wouldn't be able to get in until after that. Is that all right?"

"Fine." He could check his bag into a locker, have some breakfast, take a walk, then go to the hotel in time to call Sam just as she was getting up.

"They need a credit card to hold it."

He got out his wallet from his coat pocket and handed her a card. She looked at it—a platinum American Express card with the name Andrew Symington. She had not been wrong about him: this man was no tourist on a budget. She was intensely curious, but she reminded herself that he was married, she was working, and she'd better keep her mouth shut and stay out of trouble. She completed the business of booking the room and handed him back his card.

"Thanks very much, Anne. You've been a real lifesaver."

"You're quite welcome, Mr. Symington. Glad to have helped."

She watched him walk away and stop by the row of lockers to put away his bag. She saw him look outside, smile at the appearance of a wavering sun, take off his trench coat, and throw it in the locker. He had a lovely smile, and she began to fantasize about the possibility of meeting another handsome, rich American, preferably not married next time. After all, her job did put her in constant contact with the public; that was part of its attraction.

Her reverie was interrupted by an overweight German proffering a map to her and struggling to make himself understood while his wife shouted "Za Tover uf Lon-don" over and over again. Sighing, she took up her red pencil, put on a smile, and started to mark the map. It was business as usual. By the time she looked up, Andrew Symington was gone.

Instinct more than inclination took Drew to Harrods. Going in through the Brompton Road entrance he quickly passed by the men's accessories, not even tempted by the cashmere scarves he used to buy by the dozen. His thoughts were on Sam. He wanted to get her something beautiful in exchange for the beauty she had brought to his life.

He wandered through the small leather goods, past the Filofax products and hand-stitched travel bags. He picked up a pair of elbow-length kid gloves lined with cashmere, soft as a baby's bottom. How lovely they would be with his wife's hands inside, nestled in his palms. He turned them over to look at the price tag: ninety-eight pounds—over two hundred dollars. They were exquisite, but he had decided he wouldn't spend over fifty pounds. Even that was more than they could afford, but it was much less than Sam deserved.

He knew better than to stop at the jewelry counter, and headed straight for women's fashions, not quite sure what he was hoping to find. As he wandered through stacks of sweaters and racks of clothing, his eye would occasionally be caught by something special that he was sure would please Sam, but invariably the price was way beyond his allotted figure. He looked around him in frustration. He had been to Harrods countless times, but he'd never noticed how unmanageably large it was before. Shopping here had always been so easy: walk in, spot something you like, buy it, and leave; the task never took very long. And indeed he'd already spotted a dozen things he liked. Unfortunately none of them were in his price range.

A saleswoman approached him, smiling. "You look a little lost, sir. Can I help?"

"Actually, yes. I'm looking for a gift for my wife."

Her smile broadened. A wealthy American, exactly the kind of customer she liked. "Well, tell me a little bit about her. What's she like?"

"She's spectacular."

The saleswoman laughed. "You'll have to be a bit more specific. Is she sporty? Elegant?"

"I guess you'd say she's sporty. She likes cars," he

said, understating the reality, knowing it would be impossible to explain Sam.

"What about a driving suit?"

"Sounds intriguing. What is it?"

She led him toward the designer section. "This is new in the Katherine Hammett line. It's really just leggings and a blazer. But very sharp." She pulled an outfit off the rack and held it in front of her to display its clean lines. He liked it immediately and knew the rust color would look sensational with Sam's hair.

"I'll take it," he said, falling reflexively into his former ways, beaming at the saleswoman, who beamed right back. Then suddenly he remembered that he was not the same kind of shopper he had once been. "Uh . . . how much is it?" he asked, knowing before he heard the answer that the price would be too high.

She checked the tag and gave him a quick look, certain the cost would be no problem. "Two hundred sixty pounds for the jacket and one hundred twenty for the pants."

He coughed. "Actually, I'm afraid that's a little more than I wanted to spend."

She was surprised. He didn't look to be the type who cared. "How much did you have in mind?"

"Around fifty pounds," he said, without emotion.

The saleswoman's face fell. She never would understand Americans. Why would this man, who dressed in an Armani suit and thought his wife was spectacular, want to spend only fifty pounds on her? She didn't feel like wasting any more of her time. "Perhaps another department," she said dismissively. "Or Selfridge's on Oxford Street."

"Thank you," Drew said, ignoring her rudeness as he turned away. That kind of attitude didn't surprise him anymore. What shocked him was how he had managed to insulate himself for so long from the treatment that normal people received in their everyday lives.

"Welcome to the real world," he said to himself with deep irony, "where every day's a new adventure."

He looked around, feeling like a child out of his element, and then suddenly he knew exactly what he wanted to get for Sam. He headed straight for the toy department, and there he saw it. A row of stuffed Paddington bears, in an array of sizes, all wearing the signature blue coat and yellow hat, with a pinned-on sign saying, "Please take care of this bear." And he knew Sam would. Just as she would take care of him.

A saleswoman approached. He had learned his lesson. "How much are the bears?" he asked before even indicating his interest.

"The smallest is twelve, the biggest is thirty-eight, and I'll have to check on the middle size."

"Don't bother. I'll take the big one."

"Very good. Is it a gift?" she asked, a little coyly.

"It most certainly is." He followed her to the cash register as he reached for his wallet.

"What's wrong, sir?" She had seen his face as she prepared to wrap the bear.

"My wallet. It's gone."

"Are you certain?" She was as alarmed as he was.

He checked his inside jacket pocket once more, and then he remembered. "Damn. I left it in my trench coat. It was raining this morning when I first went out, and my wallet was in my coat. Then, when the rain stopped, I put away my coat, but I forgot to take my wallet."

She was understanding, offering to hold the bear for him, but he'd had enough shopping for one day. The morning had been a fiasco.

He looked at his watch: eleven-thirty. He could pick up his bag, check into his hotel, and call Sam. Anxious to get out of Harrods, he made his apologies and headed for the Basil Street exit, intending to take a brisk walk to Victoria Station.

There was no warning. One moment he was impatiently waiting with a crowd of shoppers for his turn out the door; the next, he was lifted off the ground and propelled into the cold, damp air. The blast was deafening, ringing in his ears, blocking out all sound, all sensation. He knew he was lying on the sidewalk. It felt hard and chill beneath him. For a moment he was grateful for a halo of warmth around his head, a wet cushion of heat that seemed to be spreading down the side of his face. Then he realized it was blood, his own, emanating from a cut somewhere near his eye. He couldn't tell exactly where he was injured, because he couldn't feel, but he could hear again—screams, running feet, shouts, commands, sirens. The sounds of danger. He felt strangely dissociated. He knew he had to leave this place, but he couldn't remember how to stand. Feet were pounding all around him, near his head, his legs. He began to fear that someone might step on him and crush him. With fear came will. He forced himself to stand up. Something hurt, but he didn't know what. He tried to move away from the chaos and stumbled off Basil Street toward Hans Place. He collapsed and was aware that something, someone, broke his fall. Then he lost consciousness.

"Why don't you just leave the answering machine on?" Melinda spoke groggily into the phone. She'd stayed up much later than usual talking with Jack the night before, and she would have still been asleep if not for the call from her sister.

"Because he's calling from London, and I don't want him to just talk to a machine."

"Leave a message with your number at work."

"Please, Melinda," pleaded Sam. "It's not as if you've got a heavy schedule."

"How kind of you to remind me."

"Come on, I didn't mean anything. I'm just worried. What if something's wrong and he can only make one phone call, and there's no one here? I would have just stayed home myself, but I can't miss work. I just started."

"Okay, okay. I'll come and baby-sit your phone."

"Thanks. You're an angel."

"It's all right. I mean, it's not as if I've got a heavy schedule."

"I said I was sorry."

"I know. I know. Don't worry. I'll be there. Give me half an hour."

She was there in twenty minutes, and Sam hugged her hard, knowing the Myles Militia was still intact. Sam had tried not to overstate her concern, but Melinda had sensed enough worry to come without too much coaxing, and to come fast.

"You know, an idea occurred to me after I said I'd come, so I'm here," Melinda began before she was even in the door. "Why don't you just call him?"

Sam gave her a give-me-a-break look. "I did. The hotel where he was supposed to be staying said he'd checked out."

"Didn't he say where he was going?"

"I asked. The clerk said he didn't know. Actually he was kind of rude."

"Maybe that's why Drew checked out."

"Maybe. But why didn't he call and tell me?"

"What's the difference in time?"

"Six hours."

"So if he left the hotel any time after six, it would have been the middle of the night for you. He probably just didn't want to wake you up. I bet he calls the minute you walk out the door."

"That's what I bet, too. That's why I want you here."

"So I'm here. Go. Then he'll call and I can go home."

"You'll call me as soon as he calls?"

"What do you think?"

"Okay. Thanks." Sam started out, then stopped. "Melinda?"

"What honey?" Melinda could hear the tension

99

in her sister's voice. She felt for her, and at the same time she was a little jealous. How wonderful to be so in love that if you didn't hear from your beloved for twenty-four hours you thought the world had come to an end.

"You don't think anything could be wrong, do you?"

"Of course not. Drew got to his hotel. He didn't like it. He found someplace else, but by the time he got there it was too late to call you. He's only been gone a day, for God's sake."

Sam laughed at herself. "I know. It feels like forever. Am I being an idiot?"

"Yes, you are. What's with you and this imminent doom thing? First you send Jack after me because you think I'm going to kill myself . . ."

Sam felt like an even bigger fool. "I didn't really," she tried to explain her worry away. "You were just so down, I wanted to make sure you didn't do anything stupid."

"Like kill myself."

"No. Like . . . I don't know. I'm sorry. Drew's not here, and I'm reacting to everything in the extreme."

"It's all right. Just go to work. You need this job."

"You're right," Sam said, giving her sister another hug. "I'll talk to you soon."

Melinda felt relieved when Sam had gone, taking her tension with her, and she looked forward to settling down with a cup of tea and the stack of magazines she'd brought along.

The doorbell rang, and Melinda sighed as she got up to answer.

"What did you forget?" she asked, flinging the door open.

"Nothing that I know of," said Jack, looking as surprised to see her as she was to see him.

"Are you following me again?" she asked, only half joking.

"I think it's more like you're preceding me, in this case. I came to see how Sam was doing. I presume you're doing the same."

"Not voluntarily. She's gone to work. I got enlisted to guard the phone."

"Drew didn't call."

"Good guess. But I'm sure he will. And I'll be right here, wasting my day, because my sister didn't want her husband to have to talk to a machine."

"You don't seem too upset."

"Hey, we sisters look out for each other, no matter how stupid that may seem. And I owe her. After all, she did send you out after me last night."

"I can't tell if you're being sarcastic or serious."

"Neither can I," she said, but she was smiling.

Jack glanced at his watch. It was getting late, and he was expected at the office. He'd been working in the union legal department ever since the Save the Millpond project. That had gotten the D'Uberville Motor Company to abandon its plans to build a new automotive plant that would have destroyed the environment and polluted Oakdale's water supply. Jack had originally come to Oakdale to work on the line and get away from practicing law. But once it became known that he actually was an attorney, no factory would take him, and the union had pressed him into service. They gave him a small salary, and in exchange, he argued the pro bono cases of workers with grievances against management.

He had enjoyed his stint as a laborer, getting his hands dirty and actually being able to see what he had built at the end of the day. But at least the kind of law he was practicing now was a lot more satisfying than the cold-blooded corporate career he had abandoned several years before. For one thing, even though he got kidded about his manhood, nobody questioned his right to wear his thick blond hair in a ponytail. For another, as long as he got his work done and showed up for meetings, no one kept track of the hours he put in. There were no senior partners to impress, no competition to outdo. Which meant that if he wanted to come in an hour late today, no one really minded.

"Is that a cup of tea on the table?" he asked Melinda innocently.

"Yes, it is," she responded, playing along. "But it's mine. You'll have to get your own."

"Fair enough." He'd spent a lot of time at Sam's place over the summer, and unceremoniously dumped his coat on the coach and headed into the kitchen.

"Oh, my God," gasped Melinda, stopping him short.

"What? You told me to make my own tea."

"It's not that. It moved."

"What? The kitchen?"

"No, stupid. My baby."

She was holding her hand on her belly and grinning. He started to grin too and, without thinking, came over to her, hand outstretched. He stopped himself, realizing that just because Melinda was pregnant, her belly was not public property. He was about to ask, but she had already taken his hand in hers and was guiding it. He loved the fact that she was so excited.

"Feel it?" she asked. "There."

He pressed his hand onto her and held it there, "I don't feel anything."

"I know. He stopped. Wait."

They stood there together, both holding their breath. Melinda passed her hand gently over her stomach.

"Oh, my God," said Jack. Melinda beamed and said, "There. Did you feel it?"

"I felt it," he said. "Kind of like a rolling motion."

"That was it. The kid's moving around. It feels so weird."

"It's alive!" Jack said in an eerie voice, and they both laughed.

They stood still for a few more moments, but there was no repeat performance.

"I think he's done," said Melinda, moving away, suddenly embarrassed to be standing so intimately with a man she didn't know all that well.

Jack felt exhilarated. "I've never felt a baby move before. That was exciting."

"I thought so too," she said, pleased that he seemed to share her joy.

"Will you let me do that again sometime?"

"Sure," she said. "But I have a feeling the novelty will wear off pretty quickly."

"I don't see how it could," said Jack. "The miracle of birth."

"If you're going to start sounding like a Hallmark card, you'll have to leave," she scolded, but she was happy. There were going to be a lot of milestones in the next few months, even years, that she would have to face alone. She was glad that this had not been one of them.

❦6❦

"What the fuck are we supposed to do with him?" Colim Kilpatrick was driving through the London traffic and looking back over his shoulder onto the floor of the backseat at the same time. A car honked loudly, signaling that he wasn't managing to do either with particular success.

"You just keep your eyes on the road. I'll take care of him," answered Moira O'Brian from the floor, where she cradled the stranger's head in her lap.

"Let's just open the door and dump him," offered Seamus Ferguson, ready to act on his words.

"No," shouted Moira. "That's all we need. Someone spotting us dumping a body in the middle of the road, taking down our license, and calling the police. Use your brains."

"Me, use my brains? How the hell did that

bleeding fucker end up in our car in the first place? Care to explain that?"

Moira couldn't explain it. He had fallen on top of her, just as she was about to get into the car, and she had pulled him in with her. It was beyond explanation, beyond reason. He had looked at her with deep blue wounded eyes, just before he'd passed out, and she had responded in an instant of insanity. Without articulating her fears, she had been certain that if she left him, he would be trampled to death or, worse, run over by the back wheels of Colim's car as they made their hasty getaway. She felt responsible for the stranger. With perfect equanimity, she had helped to detonate a bomb at the back door of Harrods, causing a great deal of damage, perhaps even death, and yet she felt responsible for this one man. If she could save him, maybe somehow it would not matter what happened to the others.

"I acted on instinct" was all she said.

Seamus wasn't satisfied, as she knew he would not be. Justifiably. "An instinct to get us caught?" he snorted. "An instinct to make sure someone could identify us, in case our plan worked and we got away?"

"He can't identify us. He's unconscious," she said quietly, although she had felt the strong beat of his pulse and knew he would recover.

"That's not exactly the point, is it, Moira?" asked Colim. They were heading north on Camden High Street, out of the main flow of traffic, and he was already feeling calmer. Soon they'd be on the A1, and there'd be no stops until they hit the cabin on the outskirts of Barrow in Cumbria, where the army had set up a safe house for them. Although it was questionable whether the place would still be safe with Moira and their wounded passenger along.

"Look," said Moira, improvising, aware that she had some serious explaining to do. "This guy's a toff. His suit must have cost a bloody fortune."

"Who gives a shit what he's wearing? He's fucking bleeding to death in our backseat."

Moira saw she wasn't going to get around Seamus very easily. "He's not going to die."

"How the fuck do you know?"

"Because we're not going to let him die, you asshole. We can use him." She was getting angry now too. She tried to calm herself. It wouldn't do for all of them to be screaming at each other. They were meant to spend the next month lying low in a small cabin together, and it wouldn't help to be at each other's throats.

Seamus was already puffing out his cheeks with another curse, but Colim cut him off. "Shut up, Seamus. Go on, Moira. I'm really interested. How are *we* going to use him? I mean, Seamus and I don't go for men, so if that's what you had in mind . . ."

"Is that why you brought him? So you could fuck him?" asked Seamus. "Christ, Moira, I'll fuck you if that's your problem."

"You're a pig, Seamus, you know that? We'd have to be stuck in that cabin for decades before I'd let you lay a hand on me."

Colim was starting to feel exhilarated. The radio

was on, and the news bulletins about the bomb at Harrods were coming nonstop. The authorities had been called, so the IRA was getting proper credit, but it was clear that the police hadn't a clue as to how the bomb had been placed or who, exactly, had placed it. The figures for the wounded were changing by the moment, but it looked to be fifty or sixty people. No deaths reported yet, but that was just as well. As far as Colim was concerned, injuries were just as effective at getting the point across.

He'd been upset when he got to the car and found Moira on the floor with the man. They'd agreed to separate after the bomb had been planted and to approach the car from different directions. He hadn't considered it necessary to tell her not to pick up any strangers. Moira had always been a good soldier. That was why she'd been picked for this mission. He was still waiting to hear her reasons.

"So, Moira me darlin', are you going to tell us what made you do such a stupid thing?" Colim asked.

He sounded genial enough, but Moira knew her time was up. Colim wasn't like Seamus. She couldn't brush him off with a curse and an insult. "I don't think it was so stupid, Colim. Really. We're always talking about the advantages of taking hostages. This one fell right into our laps." She was making up excuses as she went along, but Colim was looking at her in the rearview mirror, and Seamus was looking at Colim, so she knew she wasn't doing too badly.

"None of us knew if we'd been spotted or whether the Brits were on to us," she went on. "I don't know who this guy is, but I know he's not some poor slob nobody cares about. This bloke's got money, and if he's got money, he's got influence. If anything goes wrong, we've got something to bargain with. If not, we can get rid of him. I figured we could keep him until we know we're in the clear."

Colim smiled. He knew she was a good soldier. "Check his pockets and find out who he is."

Seamus said nothing, but his hands were already groping in the stranger's pockets, following orders. Moira gave a silent grateful prayer. She was in the clear, for now.

"What have we got here?" said Seamus, pulling out a handful of bills. "Twenty pounds, just loose in his pocket."

Moira gave him a triumphant look, "Which means he must have more in his wallet."

"I'm less interested in the money than in his name. Let me see his wallet." Colim kept one hand on the wheel and reached over the seat into the back with the other, his fingers curling with impatience.

"There's no wallet," said Seamus, starting his search again.

"What?"

"No wallet."

"No license? Credit cards? Business card?"

"Nothing. Just that loose twenty pounds."

"That doesn't make sense," said Moira, starting to get nervous again.

Colim started to laugh. The others didn't get the

joke. "People are no damn good," he said by way of explanation. "Don't you see? Some bugger saw him staggering, figured he was an easy mark, and lifted his wallet from him."

"That's disgusting," said Seamus, outraged. Moira looked at him in disbelief. She saw no point in reminding him that he'd just pocketed twenty pounds he'd found on an unconscious man. It would just start another argument, and she'd noticed the man was starting to stir. She knew it was as irrational as anything else she'd done that day, but she didn't want him to wake to hear them fighting.

"It doesn't matter," she said quietly. "He'll tell us who he is when he comes to."

They drove the rest of the way in silence, with Colim occasionally flicking on the radio for an update on the news reports. He was pleased. They had done enough damage to garner major coverage, and the point of the mission, of all their missions, was to attract attention to their cause. Most regular programming had been suspended in favor of on-the-scene accounts, and one station was airing a history of unrest in Northern Ireland, and a catalog of IRA activity for the last twenty years.

Seamus whooped with delight at the body count. "You'd think the bastards would get the point, wouldn't you? No complaints, though. Keeps us in business," he laughed, slapping his thigh.

"What will you do if this conflict is resolved, Seamus? Become an ax murderer?" Colim asked. He was smiling, but Moira could see that even though he was usually pretty tolerant of the personal opinions of his cohorts as long as they performed as commanded, he was offended at Seamus's disregard for human life.

It was the thing she liked about Colim and most of the other people in the army. Even though they firmly believed that the end justified the means, they were not callous about the damage they inflicted. They were in a battle for their very existence, and the guerrilla tactics they were forced to employ were their only hope for victory. Like soldiers anywhere, they saw themselves not as purveyors of death but rather as fighters for freedom. Still, their ranks were occasionally tarnished by people like Seamus, street thugs who had found their way into the cause, more as a channel for their hostility than as an expression of their ideology.

Moira wished they could screen out the mercenary and the mad. But the ranks of true believers were dwindling, and these days they took help where they could get it.

When, after several hours, they turned onto the dirt road that led through the woods and to their cabin, Moira was grateful. She had remained on the floor, with the stranger's head in her lap, for the entire journey, and her back was killing her. He had moved a little and moaned once or twice, but he had not regained consciousness. She touched his forehead and was alarmed at the dry heat beneath her fingers. It wouldn't help him to wake up on the floor of a car, covered with blood, Seamus's gun pointing in his face.

The cabin was smaller than she had expected, but it was adequate. It had a large main room, a kitchen, and a small bedroom. Best of all, it was well stocked and clean. She had spent many a month eating nothing but Spam out of a tin in safe houses that were encrusted with filth and overrun with vermin. A quick look inside the kitchen cabinets had revealed a store of rice, pasta, dried soups, juices, and cereals. She found bread and chicken in the freezer, and even some fresh fruits and vegetables in the refrigerator.

Moira checked out the bedroom and was delighted to find someone had even gone to the trouble of putting clean sheets on the bed. "Bring him in here, but be careful," she instructed.

"Why are we giving the stiff the only bed?" complained Seamus. "He's supposed to be the hostage, not the guest of honor."

"Geneva Convention rules," said Moira, hoping to shut him up.

"Fuck the Geneva Convention and its rules."

She should have known better. "Look, we don't have to tell him he's a hostage right off. Let him think we're friends and get him to cooperate."

"I don't need to be someone's bleeding friend to get cooperation," said Seamus, pounding a fist into his hand for emphasis.

"He's going to figure it out the first time he tries to walk outside," said Colim, looking at her.

She avoided his eyes. She knew he was suspicious of her motives, and he was right. "I know that. But why encounter resistance before you have to? He's not going to be able to move around much for a while. We can get all the information we need and maybe even make a deal for him before he's even out of bed."

"And I suppose you're going to nurse him?"

"Well, I could." She tried to sound nonchalant.

Seamus guffawed, but Colim waved him to silence. "Do you know what you're doing? If he sees you, he can identify you."

"You said yourself that we might need some leverage. We won't have any if we've got to shoot him to keep him from escaping." Moira knew she sounded too defensive, but she couldn't help it. For some reason it was important to her that this man think of her as his friend before he knew she was his jailer.

Colim walked around the cabin, assessing the situation. "All right. If you're willing to nurse him, why should I give a fuck? Keep him in the bedroom and away from us. I don't want him to see me."

"Same here," chimed in Seamus. "If I see his eyes, I kill him."

Moira ignored him. She felt jubilant. "No problem. There's a lock on the bedroom door. He won't come out of that room if you're anywhere in sight, I promise."

They laid the hostage on the bed and left her in there with him, locking the door from the outside. Colim told her to knock two short, one long, if she wanted to get out. If he didn't hear the specific knock signal, he wouldn't open the door. She was glad they had refused to help her undress him and clean him up. It made the task more arduous but more enjoyable as well. His cut had long since clotted, but there was dried blood everywhere. Gingerly she removed his soiled clothing item by item, leaving only his shorts. Even unconscious, she wanted him to retain his dignity, so she resisted the temptation to peek inside. After soaking a cloth in tepid water, she gently washed away the soot and blood, remnants of a trauma she had caused, and was gratified to find his temperature subsiding under her cool caress.

Colim came in and watched her for a moment. "Pretty, isn't, he?" was his only comment.

"Yes," she answered, with more fervor than she had intended, "Very."

Sarah Fielding was shopping with her mother, Mathilde D'Uberville Symington, at the Woodland Cliffs Galleria. As far as Sarah was concerned, the primary purpose of the outing had been to speak to her mother about Drew outside the confines of Belvedere and beyond the sphere of influence of her father. Since Sarah had twice lost her nerve following up on Drew herself, she had decided to attempt an official change in family policy. Still, they had managed to find a couple of nice things at Saks, so even if she couldn't get her mother to agree on a new course of action concerning her brother, the trip would not be a total waste.

"Drew is your son, Maman," Sarah was saying, as if the older woman were not aware of that biological fact. "Don't you miss him?"

"Of course, I do, *chérie. Mais qu'est-ce que je peux faire?* It is your father who has decided."

"You can make him change his mind."

"Pouf," she made an airy motion of dismissal. "And how do I do that?"

"I don't know," said Sarah, dejected. "Threaten to do something with your stock."

"Don't be foolish. I couldn't make Drew change his mind, and I couldn't make Forrest change his. The whole thing is *quelque chose stupide.* Drew should have married Bethany, and there would be no problem.

"I never liked Bethany." Sarah looked at her mother. For just a moment Mathilde looked horribly sad and vulnerable. But then the older woman shook herself.

"Well, *you* were not the one who was supposed to marry her." Mathilde checked her watch. *"Mon Dieu,* the afternoon is over," she said, as if surprised. "Let's go home and have a drink."

Sarah sighed. If it was cocktail hour, she knew she'd lost momentum for the day. Mathilde was already motioning to Robert, who walked a discreet distance behind them, carrying their packages, to bring around the car.

"You go ahead, Maman. I want to look around some more. I'll come over later, okay?"

"What are you looking for?"

Sarah hesitated. She couldn't tell her mother she wanted to look for a man she had spotted once in some bushes, but that was the truth. She had thought she'd caught a glimpse of him going into the Cozy Corner Café, and she was desperate to follow. But her mother's Bruno Magli heels were already rapidly clicking toward the approaching limousine, and she realized that Mathilde wanted a drink too badly to care about anything else.

"Just some stuff."

"Bien, chérie, à toute à l'heure."

Sarah watched the car pull away, and then backtracked to the coffee shop, dodging dawdling shoppers who stepped into her path. She paused outside the door, angry at herself for always pausing, always hesitating, never just doing exactly what she felt like doing when she felt like doing it. But still, she might have turned away had someone not come up behind her, wanting to enter, forcing her to move inside to clear the way.

She had never been inside the Cozy Corner before. Usually, if she got hungry while at the Galleria, she made her way to Petrov's for tea and a little caviar on toast points. The coffee shop, while clearly not chic, did strike her as cozy, with its red-checkered tablecloths and wooden booths cushioned in dark red leatherlike vinyl. He was sitting in a booth, hunkered over a newspaper and a cup of coffee, wire-rimmed glasses perched on his nose, his dark hair tousled, his sweater unraveling at the sleeve. There was something vulnerable and endearing about him, and she couldn't believe that she had been frightened or suspicious of him.

She slid into the booth across from him, intending to watch him, as he had been watching her. She was certain he wouldn't notice her, and even if he did, she doubted that he would recognize or re-

member her. She was wrong. He lifted his eyes
from the paper and saw her, and smiled.

"Well, if it isn't the lady in the dark."

She wasn't sure what to say.

"If you're alone, why don't you join me?" he
went on.

She felt embarrassed, as if *she* had been the one
hiding in the bushes. Then, to try to deny to herself
that she could possibly be such a wimp, she slipped
into the booth beside him.

"I didn't think you'd remember me," she said,
silently castigating herself for telling the simple
truth, and at the same time amazed that she felt
comfortable doing it.

"Of course I remembered you. You could have
gotten me into a lot of trouble, and you didn't. You
were very kind."

"And probably too trusting."

"Well, I don't think so."

"I have to admit, I checked the papers the next
day to see if you'd done anything to make head-
lines."

He laughed, and she laughed with him, certain
now that her instincts had been correct. This man
would never intentionally hurt a fly.

The waitress came over. "Found a friend, hon?"
she asked pleasantly.

Sarah wasn't sure what to say, but he was already
answering for her: "She certainly has."

"That's nice," said the waitress with a motherly
smile. "What'll it be?"

For some reason Sarah was reminded of a nanny
her mother had hired when she was about six years

old. The woman had been gray-haired and a little overweight, and Sarah had immediately pretended she was her grandmother and not the hired help. She had taken Sarah to the kitchen and made her a grilled cheese sandwich. Then Mathilde had found them happily munching away, to the cook's chagrin. The woman had disappeared the next day, and in her place had appeared "Mademoiselle," a cold French disciplinarian whom Sarah and Drew had immediately dubbed "the Fish." There were no more grilled cheese sandwiches in the kitchen after that, just foie gras on silver platters in the den, which, to a couple of kids, was nothing more than disgusting liver they were forced to eat and pretend to enjoy. To this day Sarah detested foie gras in any form.

"I'll have a grilled cheese sandwich," she said, beaming. She liked this place, she liked the waitress, she liked the man across from her. They all seemed kind and, well, cozy.

"Does this mean I'm going to get an explanation?" she asked, emboldened.

"Would you settle for an introduction?" he asked.

"It's a start."

"Ian Taylor." He stuck out his hand.

She took it. It was firm and warm. "Sarah Symington," she said, and then realized what she'd done, "I mean, Fielding."

He looked at her questioningly. Most people didn't have to take two stabs at their name. They got it in one try.

118

She blushed. "Fielding. My name is Sarah Field ing. Symington is my maiden name."

"How long have you been married?"

"Six years."

He laughed. "I see. It's taken you quite a while to get used to it."

"Not really," she was laughing too. She didn't know how he did it, but he'd managed to turn her embarrassment into amusement. "I don't know why I said Symington. It just slipped out. Wishful thinking, maybe."

"I'm not touching that one," he said gracefully.

"You're right. Thank you. I owe you one."

"No, I owe you one. Let me pay for your lunch and we can call it even."

"It's a deal," she said, biting into her dripping, greasy sandwich.

He watched her eat and it made him smile. She looked like a little girl, relishing every morsel. "You really love grilled cheese, don't you?"

"Actually, I think I've only had it once before in my life. When I was six years old."

"No kidding. Where did you grow up? Antarctica?"

"Right here. But sometimes it seemed just as remote, and just as cold. I was the embodiment of that old cliché, the poor little rich girl. Where did you grow up?" She knew he wasn't from around there; he hadn't reacted to the name Symington.

"I guess you could say I was your exact opposite, the happy little orphan boy."

"Seriously?"

"Uh-huh. I was given up for adoption at birth. But was raised by some wonderful people who gave me more love and attention than I probably deserved."

"I doubt that."

"What? That I was adopted?"

"No, of course not. That you didn't deserve all the love you got. All children deserve love. They don't need much of anything else." The instant the words were out of her mouth, she regretted them. It was the kind of remark that would have caused James to instantly heap scorn on what he called her maudlin attitude toward children.

"Spoken like a true poor little rich girl," said Ian quietly. But there was kindness in his voice and she knew he was not making fun of her.

"What do you do besides hide in people's bushes?" she asked, to direct the conversation away from herself.

"I have coffee with beautiful strangers."

She blushed, and suddenly felt beautiful. "I assume that neither one of those activities helps you pay the rent. Unless you really are a private detective." The thought had just occurred to her—a trickle of suspicion, opening into a flood of doubts. She waited, fervently praying for his denial.

"I'm a teacher," he said simply, and she was awash with joy, all misgivings gone. She looked at his wire-rimmed glasses and rumpled hair and knew it was the perfect occupation for him.

"What do you teach?"

"Math to high school kids."

"Do you like it?"

"Yes. They're inner city kids. Math is really only a part of it. For them, life is an obstacle course, and I'm trying to teach them how to navigate. I feel good when one of them gets through."

There was no pride in what he said; it was just a statement of fact. She felt proud for him. "Why aren't you teaching now?"

"It's summer. I spend my vacations hiding in people's bushes." They laughed together. She liked that he didn't hesitate to make fun of himself.

"Are you going to tell me why?"

"Not this time. I'm not going to lurk in the bushes anymore, but I can't talk about it yet."

There was nothing jovial in his voice, and she realized that whatever the mystery was, it was a cause of pain to him. She was familiar with secret anguish; she would not ask him again. At the same time she felt exhilarated, not only because she recognized a fellow traveler in the area of private sorrow but because he had said, "not this time," suggesting there would be a next time.

"Okay," she said, and the way she said it made it a caress.

"Do you come here often?" he asked.

"To the Galleria?"

"Well, specifically, to this café."

"All the time," she said, then told him the truth. "Actually, I've never been here before in my life. But I could easily start coming here all the time."

"Good," he laughed. "Then come tomorrow."

"All right. Same time, same station?"

"Why not?"

She could think of a hundred reasons why not, but she didn't offer any.

"At least I know he's not dead," Sam said to Melinda and Jack, whose services she'd enlisted for the evening, to keep her from going insane alone.

"Good," said Jack. "So you're not crazy enough to imagine the worst."

"Yes, she is," said Melinda. "She knows Drew's not dead, because she already called the American embassy and made them check all the morgues and hospitals in and around London."

"There's nothing wrong with being efficient," Jack said, putting the best light on it. "Did the people at the embassy have anything else to say?"

"They certainly did," Sam said indignantly. "They wanted to know if he drank, if he saw other women, if he showed signs of depression, and if we fought a lot at home. When I told them he'd checked out of his hotel and hadn't called me, they wanted to know if he was in financial trouble or running from the law, or if he might have a more personal reason for wanting to disappear. I felt like a contestant on *Divorce Court.*"

"What about that explosion at Harrods?"

"All injuries and fatalities have been accounted for. No Americans involved."

"Are they going to put out an APB or something?"

"They said they can't. With adults they have to wait seventy-two hours. They said there's no evidence of foul play, and there's no law that says that a man has to call his wife."

"That's it?"

"No. They suggested that a lot of men find getting married traumatic, and he might just need one last wild weekend. And that I should just calm down and maybe go out myself and have a good time."

Sam saw Melinda and Jack looking at each other. "Oh, no, don't you two start that bullshit too."

"We're not saying Drew is out screwing around," said Melinda, trying to calm her sister. "It's just that it might be premature to panic. There could be a lot of reasons why he changed his hotel and didn't call. He could just be caught up in his business, that's all."

Sam stared at her sister. "Do you really think he would just not bother to call me? Or forget? Or not know I was worried?"

Melinda didn't say anything. She didn't think so, but it wouldn't make Sam feel any better to hear that.

Jack looked at his watch. "It's the middle of the night in London, so we're not going to find any help now. Why don't you have something to eat, get a good night's sleep, and I'll come over and make some calls with you in the morning? Maybe if I speak legalese I can get some response."

"I'm not hungry and I can't sleep," said Sam, her eyes filling with tears. Melinda felt like crying with her. It had always been like that. When one sister cried, so did the other.

"Okay, honey. Why don't we do this? You come out to dinner with Jack and me. Then we'll come back and wait with you until it gets late enough for things to open up over there, and Jack can call." She was offering Jack's services at three A.M. without consulting him, but she knew he wouldn't mind.

Sam sniffled and nodded.

"You've got to eat," said Jack, "and I'm not calling unless you finish everything on your plate." This was rewarded with a weak laugh, as the sisters preceded him out the door arm in arm.

"Thank you, both of you," said Sam. "I'm sure everyone is right and Drew's okay, but I've got to know what's happened."

"Don't worry about it," said Melinda. "Another few months and you'll be staying up nights with me."

"I'm looking forward to it," said Sam, hugging her. "But Drew will be with me. Because I swear to you, after this, I'm never letting that creep out of my sight again."

Dinner was difficult. Melinda and Jack took turns trying to entertain, or at least distract Sam, but she couldn't stop brooding about the dire possibilities. She pushed her food around on her plate, and only made a halfhearted attempt to actually eat some. She knew they were only trying to help, but every word of encouragement, every bid for laughter, just increased her anxiety. She looked at her watch—still hours to go. She felt the desperation take hold, and before the tears could come, she excused herself and went to the ladies' room to weep for a few moments in peace.

"We're not doing too great here, are we?" Melinda said to Jack, as she watched her sister go.

"Hey, don't you start getting disheartened on me," Jack commanded. "I've got all I can do keeping up the spirits of one sister. I can't take both of you on."

"Actually, that's kind of what you've done, isn't it? Taken both of us on."

"Well, you seem to have come in a matched set," he responded, making light of it.

She leaned over and kissed his cheek. "For someone I thought I hated, you turned out to be a pretty nice guy."

"For someone I thought was a spoiled brat, you're not so bad yourself." He patted her belly in a friendly, proprietary way, and Melinda was glad he was there. Somehow, when Jack was around, she could believe that everything would turn out okay.

Unfortunately, believing didn't always make it so, and when Jack managed to get through to the deputy consul at the embassy in London, identifying himself as the attorney for Mrs. Andrew Symington, the response he got was not much more encouraging than what Sam had learned herself.

"It's not everything you wanted, but it's something," he said to Sam as he hung up. "They've agreed to talk to the Metropolitan Police of London, otherwise known as Scotland Yard. They're still not convinced that Drew didn't just disappear of his own accord, but they're willing to look into it."

"What do they need to convince them," Sam said angrily. "A body?"

Jack tried to keep things in perspective for her. "Come on, Sam, don't get worked up. The whole point is that there is no body. Which is good, right?"

"Let's just take it one step at a time," said Melinda. "Let's see what the police come up with, and we'll take it from there. I mean, Scotland Yard is legendary for figuring out these kinds of things, right?"

Sam looked at her sister and her best friend. They were so earnest, trying so hard to calm her. She noticed that all the while they were talking, Jack had his arm around Melinda's shoulder, and both of them seemed to take it for granted. For the first time that evening, she smiled.

"What?" asked Melinda, pleased to see that something was cheering her up, even if she had no idea what it was.

"Nothing," said Sam, not wanting to make them self-conscious. "Jack, take my sister home. She's six months pregnant and she shouldn't be up so late."

"Are you going to be okay?" asked Melinda, as concerned for her sister as Sam was for her.

"I'll be fine. I'll do just what you said. I'll go to bed and get some sleep and take it one day at a time and wait and see what happens."

But after Jack and Melinda had gone, Sam didn't go to bed right away. She sat up at the kitchen table, looking at her wedding photographs. It didn't matter that they weren't professional, just snapshots of the bride and groom, and friends and relatives. They were precious moments captured, cherished faces remembered. Finally she fell asleep, head cradled in her arms on the table, clutching a picture of the man she loved.

✑ 7 ✑

Someone was pounding a drum with a rhythmic, unvarying beat, never stopping, never changing. There was no music, no melody, just boom, boom, boom, boom, faint in volume, but close at hand. Drew tried to place the sound, near or far, inside or out, tom-toms or timpani. It was several moments before he understood that the sound was within him. He was hearing his own pulse, the beat of his own blood, throbbing through a pain in his head.

He opened his eyes, expecting clarification. He understood that he was lying in a bed, that he must have been asleep, but nothing else was clear. It was dark. He felt hot, thirsty, frightened.

A sound came from his throat that he had not intended to make. He did not recognize his voice.

Instantly she was at his side. She had been asleep in a wing chair beside the bed, and he had not noticed her. Her voice was soothing, her tone pleased.

"You've come around. Thank God. Not that I ever had a doubt."

He tried to say something, but it came out, "Ah . . . ah . . . ah . . ."

"Shh," she said, putting a cool hand on his forehead, instantly comforting him. "No need to wake the others." She held out a glass, positioning a straw in his mouth. "Drink," she commanded, and he obeyed, wondering how she had deciphered his monosyllables into a correct interpretation of his desires.

He drank until his thirst was gone. She stroked his forehead, and he felt the heat subside. With her at his side, he felt no fear. Now there was only fatigue.

"Sleep," she said, again reading his thoughts.

She moved away. Moving for the first time, he grabbed her hand. "Don't go," he whispered, amazing himself with real speech.

"Don't worry," she said gently. "I've been by your side all week, and I'm surely not going to leave you now."

A week, he thought. He had been in this place for a week. But what was this place? Who was this woman? He knew he should know something, but he couldn't figure out what it was. Shadows moved on the wall as trees, backlit by the moon, projected a silhouette of branches through a small window. The window was open. He could feel a warm breeze that smelled of flowers. He could feel her hand caress his brow. He felt safe. He slept.

When he opened his eyes again, it was light. He had no way of knowing if he'd slept for hours or days. But she was there, smiling at him. The pounding in his head was gone. He smiled back at her.

"Hello," she said, brightly. "It's lovely to see you awake."

She had a lilt to her voice and a lovely accent, probably Irish, he guessed.

"Hello," he answered, sitting up gingerly. She rushed to put a pillow behind his head. Moving wasn't easy. He still didn't know what had happened to him, but he knew it wasn't all good. "Excuse me if I'm being rude, but where am I and who are you?"

"You're in a cabin in northern England, and my name is Moira."

He had hoped for something a little less vague, but it was a start. His guess had been right: she was Irish. She put out her hand. "It's nice to finally meet you, Mr. . . . ?"

She was waiting for him to fill in the blank. He felt confused. Something was wrong. He didn't know what to say.

"And your name is?" Moira was prodding.

"Don't you know me?" he asked, avoiding her question by asking one of his own.

She was still smiling. "You've been unconscious, so we haven't been properly introduced."

"How did I get here?"

"I brought you here."

"Why, if you don't know me?" She could see he

was getting agitated. He'd been unconscious for over a week. It wasn't surprising that he'd be disoriented. She tried to sound reassuring.

"You were in an accident. I found you and brought you here to look after you."

"Why? Why didn't I go to a hospital?"

She hadn't expected these questions to come up so quickly. She'd somehow imagined that he would see her, introduce himself, and thank her for saving his life, or some such fantasy. It was too soon for him to challenge her. She forced herself to appear calm.

"It's all right now. You're fine. You don't need to be in a hospital. Is there someone you'd like me to contact for you? Your wife, perhaps?" He had been wearing a wedding band when she found him. She had taken it off, afraid his hands might swell with the fever. She had meant to put it back on him as he recovered, but somehow she hadn't gotten around to it.

She saw him glancing at his hand for the ring that wasn't there. She didn't tell him about it. Let him tell her.

"My wife?" he repeated, as if learning a foreign language. "I don't know."

She didn't understand. For a moment, hope rose and fell with her breath. Perhaps he was divorced or at least not getting along. "Well, if not your wife, what about some other family member? Surely they'll be missing you by now."

"I don't know," he answered again, more emphatically.

Something cold gripped her chest. She was afraid to ask the next question, afraid she had already heard the answer. She wished she could tell him that his life might depend on what he said next, but she could only ask, "Who are you? What's your name?"

And he answered, as she had feared he would, "I don't know."

"Holy Mary, Mother of God!" she exclaimed, sounding more vehement than she had intended. "Do you remember anything at all?"

She looked at him, saw how frightened he was, and forgot her own fear. She sat on the edge of the bed and took his hand. "Ah, look. It's nothing to worry about. You've had a nasty bump on the head—a concussion, no doubt. You've been dead to the world for a week. It's not surprising you might have a small memory gap. It'll come back to you."

The panic began somewhere down in his gut and moved rapidly upward. He felt he was going to vomit, and broke out in a cold sweat. Instantly she was proffering a bucket, holding his head, then bathing his brow.

"I may not know who I am," he said, feeling spent and weary, "but I know you are an angel of mercy."

"I wouldn't say that," she said truthfully, but she was glad he thought so, even for a moment.

He wanted to get up, get dressed, and go find out who he was, although he had no idea where to go or how to find out anything. But the minute he tried to raise his head, he knew it was an impossible dream.

Moira saw it too; his face looked drawn, and his eyelids were heavy.

"If you think I'm letting you up in your condition, Yank, you'd better think again," she chided gently.

"Yank." He smiled.

"It's one thing we do know. You're definitely an American." She saw his eyes closing. "That's right. Get some sleep. When you wake up, the cobwebs will probably be all cleared up."

He opened his eyes briefly and reached for her hand. "Thank you, Moira," he said, so sweetly that she wanted to cry.

"You're welcome, Yank," she whispered, and didn't remove her hand until he was fast asleep.

By the time Moira emerged from the bedroom, Colim and Seamus were waiting. She had wanted to avoid a confrontation, but she saw it was inevitable.

"Well?" was all Colim said, but his tone demanded answers she knew she didn't have.

"Well what?" She decided to play dumb, even though she knew it wouldn't win her much.

"What did he say?"

"Nothing."

"Don't give us that crap," Seamus interrupted, his fuse as short as ever. "We heard you talking to him."

"Then why are you asking?" She was baiting him, but she couldn't help it. He invited it.

Colim saw what was coming and intervened. It was bad enough being stuck in this cage together without being at each other's throats day and night.

"Moira, will you please just tell us who he is?"

"I don't know, Colim."

"What the fuck? Didn't you ask him his name?" Seamus spit out before Colim could shut him up.

"Of course I did, you fool."

"Then who is he?" asked Colim, speaking slowly, as though to a child.

"I don't know," she repeated.

Seamus started to say something, but Colim motioned him to keep his mouth shut. "Why not?" asked Colim and there was something ominous in his attitude that made Moira shiver.

"Because he doesn't know," she said quietly.

"What is this shit?" Seamus was shouting again.

Colim just waited for her to explain herself. She saw she had no choice. "He doesn't remember. He suffered a bad blow to the head; he's been unconscious for a week. It's not surprising."

"Then what the fuck good is he to us? Let's dump him."

"No!" She knew it wouldn't help to panic, but she couldn't help being afraid for the American. If Colim wasn't on her side, there wouldn't be much she could do to save him. She looked at Colim.

"Does he remember anything?" Colim asked.

"Not much at the moment. He doesn't know who he is, what happened to him, or how he got here. He thinks I'm some kind of angel of mercy."

"Oh, and I bet you just love that, don't you?" said Seamus.

She shot him a look with daggers, but said nothing. It was true, she did.

"He just needs time," said Moira. "I'm sure his memory will come back to him when he's a little stronger. We've got nothing to lose at this point, and maybe a great deal to gain."

"A week," said Colim. "Then we'll see. But I'm warning you now, Moira. If he gives us any trouble—"

"I know," said Moira, cutting him off. She didn't need to hear the possible consequences.

Suddenly there was a crash, and Moira turned to find Seamus attacking their only radio with a hammer.

"What the hell are you doing?" she asked, afraid he was using it as a substitute for their hostage's head.

"I've smashed the radio."

"We can see that," said Colim. "What for?"

"He doesn't know we're IRA. Best he not find out. He might hear something about the explosion and get his memory back."

"That's what we want, you idiot," Colim was furious.

"No." Moira shocked them all by agreeing with Seamus. "Seamus is right. We want him to remember about himself, not about us. We should keep away the papers as well."

Grudgingly Colim agreed, "But if we can't use him, we can't keep him. Just remember that."

Moira nodded, pleased. She had won some time for her and her Yank. Eventually she'd have to tell him who they were and what they did. But in her own time, in her own way, when she could put the best possible light on it, and when she felt that no matter what she told him, he'd still choose to stay with her forever.

Moira went back into the room and sat in the chair by his bed again, the chair where she had spent most of her hours during the past week, watching him sleep. He was restless, frowning and making small noises in his throat, like a frightened puppy. She put her hand on his head and caressed his brow.

"Shhh. It's all right. I'm here. Moira's with you."

He became still then, his face relaxed. She sighed. One week was not a lot of time. She had no desire to jeopardize the cause. It was all she had lived for, fought for, for the past ten years. She'd left the home she loved in South Armagh, across the Irish Sea and inland from where they were now. She'd forsaken her widowed mother and eleven sisters and brothers. She'd abandoned her own future and all possibility of having a normal life. She'd given up everything to free Ireland. She still wanted to free Ireland, but she didn't want to give up this man to do it. She had just one week. One week to make him one of them, or lose him.

Driving her beat-up car through the gates of Belvedere, Samantha Myles suddenly understood the distance that Andrew Symington had had to come to marry her. Of course, she had known from long before she had even met him, that the Symingtons were of a different economic and social class than her family. But reading about them in the society columns or driving past the high-walled estate, with its rolling hills and turreted compound barely visible, could not convey the visceral experience of what it must have meant to drive up this graveled path, past acres of perfectly manicured lawns and landscaped gardens, to approach the colonnaded facade of the ultimate in mansions, and call it home.

She was met at the head of the drive by a liveried servant, clearly alerted to her arrival, who relieved her of her keys and ushered her up the steps to the grand portal. But before she could raise her hand to the silver and brass knocker shaped like the head of a lion, the door opened.

"Please follow me," Robert said, without questioning her identity. She smiled to herself as she walked behind him, realizing that if she had hoped to disarm her hostile in-laws with the element of surprise, that hope had long since dissipated.

"Mr. Symington will be with you in a moment," Robert intoned, as he deposited her in the library and backed out of the room, closing the heavy mahogany doors behind him. She had caught only a glimpse beyond the foyer to the formal dining room and the salon leading onto the terrace and into the garden. That brief glance was enough to let her know that, as extravagant as she had imagined her husband's upbringing to have been, she had underestimated the opulence by far.

Nervously she waited for Forrest Symington to arrive. She had not specified whom she wanted to see, simply announced her name when asked to identify herself at the gate. She wondered who had decided that he would see her alone, and why. She didn't know if that was good or bad.

His entrance surprised her, coming as it did not from the double doors in front of her, but from behind her. She jumped a little as she heard a door shut and turned to see him approaching. She couldn't be sure, but she thought he looked gratified by her discomfiture. She had been nervous, even frightened. But the pettiness of his pleasure put things back in perspective. He had intended to catch her off guard, and he had succeeded. But he could not sway her from her course.

"Mr. Symington," she began, forgoing polite formalities, which she knew he would not appreciate, "I think Drew might be in trouble and I need your help."

"I'm sorry, young lady," he replied without hesitation, as though she were a stranger. "You've come to the wrong place."

"You don't understand," she said, not allowing her resolve to weaken, in spite of his unresponsiveness. "Your son went to London over a week ago, and I haven't heard from him. I think something might have happened to him."

She watched his face, looking for a flicker of concern or understanding. There was none.

"No," he said, "*you* don't understand. I do not have a son. By his choice and yours, not mine. I have no interest in helping either you or him. You're wasting my time and yours."

She couldn't believe what she was hearing. Perhaps she had been too brusque, hadn't communicated the gravity of the situation. "Please, Mr. Symington, just listen to me. Drew has disappeared. Even Scotland Yard hasn't been able to find him. He . . ." She hesitated. She hadn't even said the words to herself. "He could be dead."

"He is already dead to me. He died the day he married you. Anything that has happened to him since that day is irrelevant, as far as I'm concerned."

She stared at him, profoundly shocked. She hadn't expected to win Forrest Symington's help without a struggle, but she hadn't even guessed at the depth of his bitterness.

"He is your son," she said quietly, but with outrage encasing each word.

"No," said Forrest, just as emphatically. "He is your husband."

She wanted to cry, but she would not. Not in front of this hateful man, who had somehow sired her wonderful Drew, all the more miraculous for his callous roots. Frustration and fear had made her weak, and she had come seeking solace as much as assistance. But now her anger would make her strong. Tears were pointless, and she suddenly knew with a dreadful certainty, that if she was ever going to find Drew, she would have to do it herself.

"You're right," she said, her voice as cold as his had been. "Talking to you is a waste of time."

She thought she heard the door behind her again, and whirled around, refusing to allow another emotional ambush. But there was no one there.

"I can see myself out," she said, marching toward the double doors without looking back.

On the way home she stopped at her parents' house.

"I've got to go to England," she told them. "It's the only way I can hope to find out what's going on. I talk to Scotland Yard every day, but they're giving me the runaround and there's nothing I can do about it."

"What do you think you can do if you're there?" asked Harvey.

"Park myself on the doorstep if I have to until I get some answers. I don't know. But I can't just sit here and wait. I'll go crazy."

Diane hesitated for a minute, then said, "You know, we're just getting by on Dad's salary, so we haven't been saving much. But I've still got about three hundred and twenty dollars in the Christmas fund. It's yours."

Sam looked at her father. He nodded. "We'd just end up spending it on you and your sister anyway. Take it."

"I love you two," Sam said, hugging them both. The Symingtons' affluence notwithstanding, she saw how deprived Drew's childhood must have been. She was the one who had the family fortune.

By the time she got home, Melinda and Jack were waiting at her front door.

"Mom called me, and I called Jack," Melinda said by way of explanation.

"What took you so long?" asked Jack, meaning it as a joke.

But Sam was too serious to see the humor. "I stopped at the travel agency," she said, letting them all into her apartment. "But a trip to London is going to cost over a thousand dollars. I don't have it."

"You do now," said Melinda.

"What?"

Jack looked at Melinda, and in unison, they said, "Ta-da!" each holding out a hand with a flourish.

"What's this?" asked Sam, eyeing their two fists full of bills.

"Money," said Melinda, as if she were instructing an alien.

"I know that. Whose?"

"Yours," said Jack. "Take it."

"I can't."

"Of course you can. You just said you didn't have enough for the ticket."

"Melinda, you're going to have a baby. You're going to need it yourself."

"I'm not having it yet. And when I do, the father, whose name I will not mention, is supposed to start making regular child-support payments."

"What if he doesn't?"

"Well, then, I've got a lawyer who'll work on contingency. He'll take the bastard to court and sue the hell out of him. Right, Jack?"

"Right, babe. Take the money, Sam. You need it and you know it."

"Call us when you've got a reservation. We'll drive you to the airport. Come on, Jack. Sam's got to pack."

Sam noticed there was a lot of *us*-ing and *we*-ing going on, but she said nothing. She hugged them both and let them go, then sat down to figure out exactly what she had and what she'd need.

Her financial situation was definitely borderline. Even with all the contributions, once she'd paid for the ticket, she would have only a couple of hundred dollars left. She felt, in her very soul, that if she went to England, she would find Drew. But she couldn't guarantee it would happen in a matter of days. What would she do if she ran out of money? There was no more where this came from. She didn't know anyone in England; she would have no one to turn to. She began to feel overwhelmed. How could she help if she ended up on the streets of London, as lost as Drew?

She counted the money again, as if somehow the result might be different the second time around. The doorbell rang, startling her, making her scatter the bills on the table and at her feet.

"Who is it?" she asked reflexively, assuming it was one of her family members checking up on her, as usual.

She recognized the voice before she actually heard the name.

"It is Mathilde."

Quickly she gathered up the strewn bills and stuffed them away, preparing herself for a fight. It took her a moment to realize that her mother-in-law had identified herself by her first name alone: this was not to be a power play. She opened the door, wide enough for Mathilde to step in without being asked.

"I am sorry it is so late," she said.

"That's all right," said Sam. She waited. She had not forgotten that the last time she had met this woman, she had assumed the best, only to be confronted with the worst. She would not make the same mistake twice.

"May I sit?"

"Of course."

Mathilde lowered herself onto the sofa, taking in the small apartment in one sweeping glance. She could not imagine her son living in this mouse hole, but at the same time she was aware that she would have been profoundly grateful to see him there at that very moment. She looked at her daughter-in-law. Sam was undeniably beautiful. Mathilde thought she must also be remarkable in other ways for Drew to be content with the life he was forced to live with her. She hoped Drew was not mistaken in his judgment. His life might depend on it.

"I heard you talking to my husband this afternoon."

Sam nodded. She *had* heard the door close behind her; Mathilde must have been eavesdropping.

"Is it true? Has something happened to Andrew?"

"I don't know. All I know is that he's missing. He went to London about a week ago and I haven't heard from him since."

"Did you telephone the Ritz?"

"He wasn't staying at the Ritz. We can't afford it," she added pointedly. She saw Mathilde wince, and was sorry. "But, yes, I did call the hotel where he was supposed to be. All they told me was that he had checked out and left no forwarding address."

"Why would he do that?"

"I don't know. But I'm going to find out."

"And the police?"

"They've been informed. But they haven't found out anything. I don't think they will unless I go there."

"You are going to London?"

"Yes."

"Do you know people there? Do you have some connections?"

"No."

"I do."

She took a Mont Blanc pen from her purse and tore a page out of a Fendi notebook. Sam watched her write, still not entirely sure what was happening.

Mathilde handed her the paper. "His name is Michael Litton. He is attaché to the American ambassador."

"I've already spoken to the deputy consul," Sam said. "He's the one who got in touch with Scotland Yard."

"It doesn't matter. Michael is well connected. His mother, Delphine, has been my friend since we were children in France together. Her grandfather was Georges Pompidou. Her husband is a Kennedy cousin. Michael knows everyone. He will help you."

"Thank you," Sam said simply, taking the paper and studying it.

"You'll need this, too." Sam looked up. Mathilde was holding out an envelope. She took the envelope and opened it. It was filled with hundred-dollar bills, too many to count. Her mouth fell open.

Mathilde was closing her purse and getting up to go. "You don't know how long you must be there. You might need to hire private detectives. They can be *très cher*. You have to be prepared."

"I don't know what to say."

"Say you will not come home until you have found my son."

"I can promise you that," Sam said fervently.

Mathilde knew, without a doubt, that she meant it, and was profoundly grateful.

"I love him too," Mathilde said.

"I know."

"I would go with you, but Forrest . . ."

"I understand."

There was a pause, as she went to the door. "If you need more," Mathilde said, indicating the envelope in Sam's hand, "Just call me. Forrest is never home during the day. Never."

"This should be enough." From the look and heft of it, she thought there must be several thousand dollars there.

"May I ask, *s'il vous plaît,* for you to call me anyway? With news, if you have."

"I'll call you," Sam said quietly, and then added, "Don't worry. I'm sure Drew is all right."

Mathilde smiled at her. *"Il n'est pas mort.* If he were dead, I would know, in here," she said, indicating her heart. "Do you think that's stupid?"

Sam looked at her. Mathilde seemed, suddenly, less formidable and more foreign. She looked out of place and fragile, and Sam imagined she must feel that way in her life.

"No," said Sam, "I believe exactly the same thing. And I'm going to find him and bring him home."

"Merci, ma chérie," said Mathilde, and then surprised them both by leaning forward and kissing Sam on the cheek.

After she'd gone, Sam counted the money: ten thousand dollars in hundred-dollar bills. She called the airline and made a reservation. By this time tomorrow she would be in London.

"Maybe we should take a trip together," Bethany said to James as they lay in her bed.

"Very funny," said James.

"No, I mean it."

"What do you propose I tell my wife."

"That you're going away on business."

"Are you forgetting that I work for my father-in-law? Sarah doesn't ask a lot of questions, but it wouldn't take much for her to divine the truth. And then I wouldn't work for my father-in-law anymore."

"Aren't you bored?"

"Where? Here? At work? At home?"

"Everywhere!"

Bethany was bored. She'd become involved with James because, at the time, she'd thought that being with her ex-fiancée's brother-in-law would give her continued access to the family. The Symingtons exuded a power that she'd felt through Drew, and she wasn't ready to give that up, even though she had been forced to give up on Drew. But though James was expected to take Drew's place in the family hierarchy, his strength seemed diluted, as though it came to him only by default and only in a watered-down state.

Even his lovemaking had proved to be uninteresting. Unlike Bethany's previous lovers, who had shared her taste for the bizarre, and unlike even Drew, who had responded to her imaginative sex play with amusement but had still rewarded her originality with his well-practiced ardor, James was a rapacious lover who had neither the skill nor the patience to reciprocate her erotic love play.

"I'm getting bored right now," James said, interrupting her reverie, "But I could get a lot less bored if you'd give me a blow job."

Bethany sat up and poured herself a glass of wine. She'd already had him in her mouth once tonight and had gotten nothing in return, and she'd be damned if she'd do it again. She was starting to feel that little throb between her legs that told her if she didn't come soon, she was going to hurt. She looked at James. His cock was standing straight up, but she knew it would do her no good. She turned on the music, low and slow.

"I'll dance; you watch," she said, taking his hand, and putting it on his own member. He didn't need further instructions.

Closing her eyes, she swayed to the music, letting

her hands move up her body, squeezing her breasts together, reaching out her tongue to flick each nipple. She heard James moan, "Oh, baby, do it," heard the sticky slap of skin on skin.

She blocked him out of her mind, concentrating on herself, pressing her fingers, first one, then two, then three, into her private spaces, moving them in and out, around and around, building to the moment of stillness, when conscious movement was no longer necessary, and her body took over, opening and closing on itself, as she counted the spasms to her final release.

Afterward, James complimented her on her performance, and she saw she would need to change the sheets before she slept tonight. She sighed. Why was she bothering? James would be worth this much work if he were president of the D'Uberville Motor Company. And then she had her answer.

"James," she said, twining her body around his, "do you love your wife?"

"Give me a break."

"Do you like working for your father-in-law?"

"Are you kidding?"

"Have you ever thought of getting rid of them both?"

"Often. But I'm not prepared to exchange the mansion my father-in-law bought for my wife for a ten-foot cell."

"There are legal ways."

"Do you think that if I divorced my wife, I'd get to keep my job, let alone anything else?"

"If you were the boss you would."

"And how do you propose I become the boss?"

"A hostile takeover."

"Very funny," he said, but he looked at her and knew she wasn't joking.

"My family owns a lot of stock in DMC. My mother is on the board, and since my father died, she votes the way I tell her to. I've known a lot of the other board members for years. In fact, quite a number of them have watched me grow up—with great interest, I might add. And you know I can be very influential when I want to be." She smoothed her hand over his body in case he didn't get her meaning. But James understood her perfectly.

"You're living in a dream," he said. "You think sex is going to convince these guys that Forrest Symington should be overthrown? They're businessmen. They're not going to jeopardize their profits for a piece of ass."

Bethany was getting angry. He was so small-minded, so stupid. She needed someone with vision, but James was all she had to work with. "You're the one who's not in the real world. Have you read a newspaper in the past twenty years? Does the name Profumo mean anything to you, or Packwood, or the Duke of Windsor, for that matter? Give the right men the right piece of ass, as you so delicately put it, and they'll jeopardize their mothers, their children, and the Constitution all at the same time."

James started to laugh. She was probably right. "Why, Bethany? Why do you want to do this?"

"Because I want to be the second Mrs. Fielding,

wife of the CEO of the largest, most successful corporation in the state."

He was still laughing, "Why don't you just go for the top job yourself?"

"Because that's not what I do," she said.

Bethany knew her strengths, and running a company wasn't one of them. Running the man behind it, however, was something else again. She considered herself a facilitator, although others, less kindly, might have called her a manipulator. And her life had been a master class, training her for the ultimate in control.

"Mommy's coming," her father used to say. "Let's not tell her about the games we've been playing. It will be our secret."

At first, confused as she was, she had simply agreed, assuming that all little girls played secret games with their fathers. But once she understood she was different, the abuse had made her angry, and with the anger came the understanding that everything, even endurance, had a price.

The next time her father reminded her to keep their secret, she said, "Of course, Daddy." Then, as though speaking of a totally unrelated subject, she had added, "Daddy? Can I have a pony?"

She'd gotten the pony and everything else she'd asked for, including boarding school in Switzerland, which had brought an end to the games and the generosity that came with them. But by that time she had learned her lesson well. With love came abuse, but with sex came control.

"What's the matter, James?" she asked, stroking

him for emphasis. "Don't you want to get rid of your mousy little wife and run your own big company?"

He pushed away her hand. She'd already made her point, and now he needed to keep his mind clear. "Do you really think you could deliver enough votes over to me for a hostile takeover?"

"Do you think you can handle it if I do?"

"Of course I can. I'm in the number two spot now," James reminded her. "No one else is primed to move into Forrest's position. The Symingtons have been running the company for too long. I think it's time for a new regime to take over."

"I agree, darling. And when that happens, I will be right by your side. Or, as I'm sure you're aware, it won't happen at all."

James looked at Bethany, lying there. She looked soft and pliant, but she was as tough as steel. He realized she was using him, but he was smart enough to know he wasn't smart enough to take over the company without her. Bethany's fire was a lot more interesting than the Symingtons' frying pan, and if the strategy worked, they'd both have what they wanted.

"Do a little preliminary research, why don't you?" James said as he was getting dressed. "Put together a list of people we can count on. Then we can see if this maneuver is worth the risk."

"I'll do that," she agreed, as she kissed him good-bye. But she didn't have to do research to know that a takeover would be worth it. She couldn't hurt Drew, but she could hurt his family, and he would know that the disaster was a direct result of what he had done to her. It wasn't living well, or success, or any other cute little epigram that was the best revenge. You just can't beat the real thing, she thought. *Revenge* is the best revenge.

⨖ 8 ⨖

When Moira came in with his breakfast tray on the fifth day after he'd regained consciousness, he wasn't in his bed.

"Yank? Where are you?" she called out, panicking for a moment, until she saw that the window was still locked. They'd all been in the living room; he could not have gotten out any other way.

"In here," he shouted back from the bathroom. "I'll be right out."

It was his first foray out of bed, and it pleased and frightened her. Before, he had been a patient; now he would have to become a prisoner. She couldn't bear the thought of the glimmer of affection that she had seen flickering in his eyes being extinguished by a cloud of betrayal. But the moment he tried to venture out of the safe haven of his

153

recovery room, he would know the truth, and in this case it would not set him free.

The door to the bathroom opened, and he stood before her, wearing nothing but a towel around his waist and a smile on his face. He was freshly shaven, and his hair, still wet from the shower, gleamed like ebony. His blue eyes were clear and laughing, and she couldn't suppress the little gasp of joy that escaped at the very sight of him.

"My goodness, Yank, aren't you the pretty picture?"

"I thought it was about time you saw the real me. Whoever he is," he added with a laugh.

Being able to get up and take a shower made him feel like a real person. Lying between the white sheets, unable to remember anything about himself, he had felt like an amoeba, floating in an extrinsic element. For the first time since the accident, he had seen himself in the mirror, and the image had felt familiar somehow. And though he still could not remember his name, he answered to "Yank" and was comfortable with it.

"I like what I see. But don't you think you'd best get back into bed and not overdo it?"

"I do not. I think you should find me some clothes and take me for a walk, and get me to a policeman so I can start trying to figure out who I am."

Moira was desperate for time. She wanted another day for him to look at her as a woman and not a warden. Colim and Seamus had gone to a meeting with another IRA contingent and wouldn't be back until nightfall. She had given the past six years to

God and country; surely she could take one damn day for herself.

"How about we start with the clothes and the walk and see how you do with it? I'm not going to have you pushing yourself and having a relapse."

"I wouldn't do that. You saved my life once already. It would be asking too much to make you do it again."

She brought him a clean shirt and jeans, borrowed from Colim, who was close to his size, and left him while he dressed, although she'd seen plenty of him while she'd been caring for him. But seeing him standing made it different, and she suddenly felt shy.

When he was dressed, he joined her in the living room.

"Where are the guys?" he asked. He'd never seen them, but he'd heard their voices. She had told him they were her cousins who shared her house.

"They've gone for supplies," she said. "So we've got the place to ourselves. We can do whatever we like."

"I'll tell you the truth, Moira. The only thing I really want to do now is contact some authority and start the process of finding out who I am."

She tried to sound playful and nonchalant. "What's the hurry, Yank? One more day won't make any difference, and it'll give you a chance to build up some more strength."

"It makes a difference to me. There could be people looking for me, things I should be doing. I don't know. But I can't go on in limbo this way."

"The boys took the car. It's too far to walk to the village."

"I'll hitchhike."

"Oh, you're not likely to get a ride. No one comes out this way."

"I'll take my chances. I'll start walking. Just point me in the right direction."

She saw it was no use. Even if she could put him off for today, he would be too anxious for her to even pretend they were just two normal people having a normal afternoon. And she'd still have to tell him tomorrow.

She swallowed hard. "I can't let you go."

He smiled at her benignly, certain she was just being overly cautious out of concern for his health. "I'm fine now. Really I am. You ought to know. You're the one who nursed me."

He headed for the door. She stepped in front of it. She didn't want to have to pull the gun. "Please, Yank. Sit down. You can't go."

He saw she was being serious, but he didn't understand. "Why not?"

"Sit down and I'll tell you."

Her eyes were filling with tears, and she was shaking. She had appeared so strong to him when he was lying helpless in the bed. Now he saw she wasn't much more than a girl. He wanted to comfort her, as she had done for him so many times when he had awakened in the cold sweat of his fear of the unknown.

"What is it?" He put his arms around her.

"I'm sorry," she sobbed, clinging to him, as he held her closer.

"What do you have to be sorry for? You've been wonderful."

"No, I haven't."

"Yes, you have." He laughed, entirely unaware of the gravity of the situation. "You've got me head over heels in love with you."

She could tell he wasn't being completely serious, but it thrilled her to hear him say it anyway.

"You won't even like me when you hear what I have to say."

"I doubt that. But why don't you spit it out and we'll find out for sure."

She sat down beside him and looked at the floor, took a deep breath, and said, "You are being held as a hostage by the Irish Republican Army."

He started to laugh, and she looked at him sharply. Only at that moment did it occur to him that her statement might be true.

"Do you want to explain that?"

"Your accident wasn't exactly an accident. You were caught in a bomb explosion at Harrods."

"Did you and your cousins detonate the bomb?"

"They're not really my cousins."

He said nothing for a moment, letting the reality sink in. This was inconceivable. It was the sort of thing you read about in the newspapers, but never believed could happen to you.

"Why did you bring me here?"

"You were hurt. I was afraid you'd be trampled. You looked kind of rich, and I persuaded the others not to dump you by saying we could hold you for ransom once we found out who you were. But your wallet must have been stolen, and then you came to and didn't remember who you were. So that shot that plan."

He had the urge to laugh again, but he saw by her face that she spoke in deadly earnest. He decided he'd heard enough.

"I'm walking out of here, Moira."

"Don't try," she pleaded. "I can't let you leave."

"I'm going," he said and he walked to the door.

"Yank," she called, and he knew he'd better turn around. She was pointing a revolver right at him and it was clear she knew how to use it.

"Are you going to kill me, Moira? After all the work you did to save my life?"

She tried to make her face hard, but her lips were quivering, and she knew it wasn't working. She put the gun down.

"You're right, Yank. I couldn't hurt you. But if they come back and find you gone, they'll kill me."

He looked at her, forlorn and frightened. "Come with me, then. We can both escape."

She laughed bitterly. "To where? You don't even know who you are, let alone where you're going. And me? The IRA will find me. They're not forgiving. They don't take well to traitors."

"I don't buy that. There's got to be some way of finding out who I am and getting you protection. The authorities—"

"Who do you think the damn authorities are?" she interrupted, frustration turning her fear to anger. "We're in Britain, for God's sake. What protection do you suppose they're going to offer an Irish Republican? Prison? I don't consider that a secure future."

"Maybe you could make a deal."

"Oh, Yank," she said sadly, "as if I would. You don't know the Irish." She looked at him, and he saw in her eyes such tenderness that it made his heart melt. "Go," she said. "You'll need a head start."

He came back and dropped onto the sofa beside her. How could he leave her to a certain death when she had saved him from his own? "I don't believe this," he said. "You're really in the IRA?"

She nodded, rueful, not expecting him to understand. But he needed to understand. She had been his angel. Her presence had soothed his spirit after countless nightmares and nameless terrors. He felt he owed it to her to at least try to comprehend what was clearly the essence of her life.

"Why did you join?" he asked her.

"I guess it was because of the hunger strikers."

"I beg your pardon?"

"No, of course, you wouldn't remember. Even if you didn't have amnesia, you probably wouldn't remember. I don't think anyone outside of Ireland does. But in South Armagh, where I come from, you can't help remembering. Raymond McCreesh, one of the ones who died, he was one of our boys."

"What happened?"

"It was 1981. They were in the Maze–Long Kesh prison outside of Belfast, put there by the British, and they were fighting to be recognized as political prisoners rather than criminals. They went on a hunger strike, and then one by one, they started to die. As each one died, another would stop eating to take his place. And the British did nothing. The church did nothing. Dublin did nothing. They just let the boys die. Bobby Sands was the first to go. Raymond died a couple of weeks later. He hadn't eaten for sixty-one days. He was twenty-four years old."

"Did you know him?"

"In South Armagh, you know everybody. I was just eleven, but Raymond and I had been neighbors all my life. He was in my brother's class in school. You know, he was just one of us. But after he died, he became a hero to us."

"Where's your brother now?" he asked, afraid he already knew the answer.

"Dead. Killed in Loughgall six years later, shot down by the British."

"I'm sorry," he said, meaning it. She spoke matter-of-factly, but the sadness in her voice was unmistakable. "Do you have other brothers?"

"Loads." She laughed, the sorrow sinking back to its normal place, somewhere in the back of her heart and mind. "And sisters too."

"Are they all in the IRA?"

"No, not all. But some. We almost can't help it. It's like a duty. To carry on the fight for the ones who died. Otherwise, what was the point of their dying? We couldn't live with that. It's easier to live with the knowledge that it could happen to you as well."

"Aren't you afraid?"

"All the time. But I'd be afraid even if I wasn't in the IRA. You're from America. You don't understand what it's like to live in a place where you feel you're not free, where another country's soldiers patrol your streets and control your lives."

"You know, Moira," he said cautiously, "I don't remember anything about my life, but I do still have a vague recollection of current events. There's another side to this story as well, isn't there?"

"Of course there is. There's always another side in any conflict. But that's not my side. I can't help what I believe. I got my convictions with my Mum's milk."

He was quiet for a long time. She was afraid to look at him, certain she'd see revulsion in his eyes, where before she'd seen affection.

"Do you hate me?" she finally asked.

"No, I feel sorry for you."

"Why?"

"Because you're twenty-four, and your life has been a legacy of hate and death. It's a harsh existence."

"Twenty-five."

"What?"

"I'm twenty-five. Today."

"Today's your birthday?"

She nodded.

"This is awful," he said. "You should be out celebrating with friends, drinking champagne, dancing, having a party, instead of hiding in some cabin in the middle of nowhere."

She shrugged. "It could be worse," she said, meaning it. "At least I've got company."

He moved closer to her and put his hands on her shoulders, feeling her deprivation as deeply as if it were his own.

"Haven't you ever wanted anything besides freedom for Ireland and vengeance for the death of your loved ones? Don't you want something for yourself?"

"Yes." She wouldn't look at him.

"What?" he asked, turning her face up to his.

"You," she said, looking into his eyes, challenging him to act on his empathy.

"How can you? You don't even know who I am."

"I knew from the minute I saw you. I'm not so much the good soldier as I pretend to be with Colim and Seamus. I took you with us for myself, not for the Republican cause. It was a truly selfish act, and I wouldn't blame you if you could never forgive me."

Her eyes were filled with tears, which could not blur her need or mask her desire. He let her go, but still she did not turn her face away. She looked at him, vulnerable and unguarded, letting him see the private pain, the depth of yearning. He understood the toll the years of dedication to a cause had taken on her soul. She was asking him to save her as surely as she had saved him. He could not refuse. He owed her his life; how could he deny her his love?

He put his arms around her and gently pressed his lips against hers. She stood stiff for a moment in the unfamiliarity of his embrace, and then the hunger took over as she moved against him, devouring each kiss greedily. He felt something stirring inside him, and with it a yearning that seemed not to be focused on the woman in his arms but on something far away, just out of reach. He saw a flash of something remembered his hand entwined in silken flame. He opened his eyes with a start, expecting to see the reality of what he had just imagined. But it was Moira in his arms, her hair as straight and black as his own, her skin fair, her cheeks flushed. She looked at him with violet eyes filled with love, and though he longed to make that connection to his past, he knew he could not deny her this moment.

She was already leading him to the bed, shyly but insistently. He let her unbutton his shirt, then placed his hands under her sweater, feeling her breasts, warm and firm. He pulled the sweater off over her head, then removed the rest of their clothing, first hers, then his own.

She reached out to him, and he hesitated a moment, something inside him making him hold back.

"Yank?" she called to him softly, and he looked at her. She wasn't a soldier of the IRA now. She was a fragile Irish beauty, and her need and vulnerability made him ache for her.

"I'm here, Moira," he whispered, lowering himself on top of her.

She lay still for a moment, eyes closed, as if in silent prayer. He kissed her gently and she responded, opening her legs around him. He put himself inside her slowly, feeling the desire, but the strangeness as well. He felt resistance, and stopped for a moment, confused, then understood.

"Oh, my God, Moira. You're—"

"Please, Yank. Don't stop. It's what I want. It's all I want."

He had started what he could not stop. He could only make it worth the doing. She had lost so much in her young life, he would not let her lose the wonder of this moment.

He eased himself into her a little more, felt her stiffen.

"Am I hurting you?"

"Only a little."

He kept his body still, but moved his lips over her face, pressed his tongue into her mouth. She received him, groaning with pleasure, and with the gentlest of thrusts he pushed himself past the barrier and eased into the warm, welcoming space of a woman.

"How does it feel now?" he asked, slowly rocking them both with the tender rhythm of desire.

"Wonderful," she said simply, moving with him at first. Then her passion took over and quickened the pace for both of them.

He followed her lead, giving her what she wanted, letting her body tell him when it was time to move slowly and when to be more insistent.

Her breath was coming faster now, and she was moaning softly, lifting her mouth to his to stifle her cries. Her body arched, and he held her against him, letting her feel his loss of control, so that she could let go of her own.

She gasped, and he felt her quiver, her body closing in on his, tensing and releasing in quick succession. Gently he lowered her to the bed, and started to ease out of her. But she quickly pulled him back, holding him with her legs.

"Don't go," she pleaded. "I can't be sure, but I don't think I'm done yet."

Without allowing their bodies to separate, he turned them around so that they were both sitting up, and she was on him instead of under him. She laughed, delighted at the maneuver, but caught her breath when he lifted her from his lap, balancing her on the tip of his still erect member, then let her slide down its length. Over and over again he repeated the action until she was panting, her body moving up and down of its own accord, her nails digging into his back. She screamed and fell upon him, clinging to him, coming over and over again in a paroxysm of passion that left them both breathless.

"Happy birthday, dear Moira," he sang in a whisper, as they collapsed onto the bed, still joined together. "Happy birthday to you."

Having seen the inside of Belvedere, Sam could understand why her husband had checked out of the Royal Broadwick Hotel. She found room 314, where Drew had spent his last known day, to be a sad little room. The furniture was drab, the drapes shabby, the carpet worn. For someone raised in elegance and luxury, used to staying abroad in hotels called the Ritz, an ugly room with a toilet down the hall must have represented the nadir of his new life. He'd been such a good sport about giving up all the luxuries, telling her they meant nothing to him. All that counted, he'd said, was being with her. Now he didn't even have that.

She forced herself to stop thinking about what might have happened to him, stop speculating. Worrying about him would only make her start crying again, and she had no more time for tears. She had called Michael Litton at the American embassy, and he would be arriving any minute. She couldn't let him think she was hysterical. She needed to present herself as a strong woman, as someone whose demands could not be dismissed.

There was a knock on the door. She took a deep breath, blinked away the last of the tears, straightened her shoulders, and opened the door. She was taken aback.

"You're not Mr. Litton?"

"I'm afraid I am. Is there a problem?"

"No, of course not," she said, embarrassed, afraid she'd started off on the wrong foot. "It's just that, since you're a friend of Mrs. Symington, I expected someone older, and . . . I don't know . . . shorter."

He laughed, as she'd hoped he would. "I have to admit you're not what I had envisioned either." He had expected a horsey-faced society deb, not this earthy, flame-haired beauty.

"I'm sorry I can't offer you anything, Mr. Litton. As you can see, this room is not exactly inviting. But I thought you might want to see the place where Drew was last seen."

"That's fine, Mrs. Symington. But since I'm not that older, shorter guy, I'd appreciate it if you would call me Michael."

"All right. If you call me Sam." He gave her a look. "It's short for Samantha."

He smiled. The name suited her. "I've got to ask you a few questions, Sam, and I hope you won't think I'm being rude."

"What was a Symington doing in a place like this?"

"You guessed it."

"I didn't go into detail on the phone, Mr. Li . . . Michael. But my husband was disinherited for marrying me. He was here because this was the only hotel we could afford."

Michael shook his head. "I don't know the Symingtons all that well, even though my mother and Mathilde are best friends, but I never took them for fools."

"Thank you," she said simply, knowing he just meant to show he was on her side, and for that she was grateful.

"Have you talked to the personnel here?" he asked.

"Yes. Apparently when Drew realized there were no telephones in the rooms and the toilet was down the hall, he decided to check out. He stayed here one night, that's all."

"He didn't call to tell you where he was going?"

"No. I think maybe he didn't have a chance. This room has no phone, and something happened to him before he got to one."

"You don't suppose he could be in another hotel, and simply neglected to call?"

"I've been asked that question a lot. Do you believe that's what happened?"

He looked at her. She was an outstanding beauty; she seemed intelligent and sensitive, considering she'd been given quite the runaround. It was highly unlikely that any man in his right mind would forget to call her.

"How long has your husband been missing?"

"Thirteen days."

He thought back and put a date on it. "So he disappeared around the time of the Harrods bombing."

"Yes. I checked into that. But there were no unclaimed or unidentified victims."

"I see. We might need to put out some kind of bulletin, maybe publish a request for information in the papers."

Sam knew she couldn't afford to alienate her only ally, but she was boiling over. "Damn it, that's what I asked for over a week ago. Why wouldn't anyone at your goddamn embassy listen to me?"

"I'll be honest with you, Sam. I checked into it. There's a record of your call, and the police even discussed the matter with the embassy. But the truth is, they thought you were a crackpot. Forrest Symington is a known commodity. Everyone figured if his son was missing, we'd have heard from him."

"Do you want to see my marriage license?"

"No, I believe you." He paused, then added sheepishly, "Anyway, Mathilde called me and told me you'd be coming."

She gave a sardonic laugh. "And I always thought money just bought material things. I'm just beginning to realize that in some circles there's a price on trust, respect, and affection, too. Well, thanks to Mathilde I've got money now. And I'm willing to spend whatever it takes to find my husband." She went to her purse and grabbed a fistful of bills from an envelope, proffering them to him.

He could see she was angry, and it was critical to him that he be able to calm her. "Put your money away, Sam. I'm going to help you."

"I'm sorry," she said, embarrassed by her outburst. "I didn't mean that you . . ."

He was glad she could see he was different. He wanted to help her. But he also wanted her to like him.

"Meanwhile, since we're not going to learn anything of importance here, why don't we get you out of this dump?"

"No. The money isn't mine; it's Mathilde's. I'd rather use it for expenses in the search than spend it on myself. I don't want to have to ask her for more. Besides, this place doesn't bother me. I'm used to sharing a bathroom."

"Aside from the amenities, we need you near a phone. But if you don't want to spend money, I've got an alternative."

She looked at him quizzically, and he hesitated. No ulterior motive lay behind what he was about to offer, but he was afraid she'd misunderstand.

"Yes?" she prodded him.

"I've got a small house in Hampstead. It's twenty minutes from London center, but it borders on a field of heather, and you could have some peace.

"That's very kind of you, but your wife . . . ?"

"Actually my wife left me several months ago. So it's just me. But there's a guest room; in fact, it's a guest floor. So you'd have plenty of privacy."

Now it was her turn to hesitate.

"The important thing is," Michael went on, "it's got several telephone lines and a fax machine. If you were there, we could set it up as a twenty-four-hour headquarters without having to go through hotel switchboards or worry that our messages weren't getting through. If you're concerned about propriety—"

"No," Sam interrupted. "I'm only concerned about finding my husband. And you're right. Staying here isn't going to make the search any easier. Let's go."

On the drive to Hampstead, Michael suggested several possible approaches to the search. She was grateful to him for realizing that small talk would have been intolerable to her at this point, and for treating her like a thinking, intelligent being instead of like a fragile woman who had to be coddled and placated.

"My first instinct," he said, "is to go public. It's not the sort of thing the embassy likes to do, but a lot of time has been lost already."

"You mean put up notices, place ads in the paper, that sort of thing?"

"That, too. But I think we should make Drew's disappearance a news event—hold a press conference, make a personal appeal for information, get you on the telly, as they say here."

"Sounds good to me."

"Well, it could get us results. But I have to warn you. This will be a big story, and Fleet Street will be after you with all they've got."

"That's what we want, isn't it?"

"Yes and no. We want attention, and you'll definitely get that. But let's face it. Poor girl marries rich heir who gets disinherited, then disappears. That story's an irresistible target for exploitation."

He glanced over at her. She'd swept her amber hair into a ponytail at the nape of her neck to keep it off her face. She was wearing no makeup, and looked as if she hadn't had a good night's sleep in weeks. She was still gorgeous. "And the way you look is going to keep the paparazzi on your heels day and night."

"If it helps to find Drew, I'll handle it."

"I'm glad we decided to move you out to Hampstead. If we're careful, we might be able to keep them from finding out where you're staying, and at least you won't trip over them every time you walk out the door."

The house in Hampstead was everything Michael had said, but nothing like Sam expected. For some reason, when he mentioned a small house, she'd envisioned a little two-story house, like the ones in her parents' neighborhood. Instead, she found a narrow four-story row house, attached to other houses of similar design, all painstakingly restored with original detail. Michael's house was painted a dusty delft blue, with white decorative arches around the oak door and framing the casement windows. Yellow marigolds spilled from window boxes, and two gaslights flanked the doorway, offering an antiquated welcome.

The small but inviting foyer led into a sitting room with deep green walls, brightened by an overstuffed sofa and chairs in a rose chintz pattern.

A piano stood in a corner of the room, topped with photographs in silver frames. On the walls were paintings of gardens and dogs. Sam had seen a room like this only once before—in an architectural magazine in a doctor's office.

"And your wife was British?" she asked without thinking.

Michael laughed. "Still is. How could you tell? I did the restoration. She did the decorating."

"It's very charming. Very English."

"What can I say? She had good taste, good breeding, but bad judgment."

"Where is she now?"

"Last I heard, on a yacht in Portofino with a Greek shipping magnate who's twice as old as I am and twenty times richer."

Sam shook her head. "The money thing again. Probably because I never had any, it never occurred to me that it was often used to buy souls."

"Actually I think she really loves the guy. She started up with him when she was seventeen. She only married me because he's got a wife stashed away somewhere and refused to get a divorce. Of course, I didn't know any of this at the time. She left when I found out."

"I'm sorry. I didn't mean to pry."

"That's all right. There's going to be a lot of delving into your private life over the next few days. This won't even the score, but when things get rough, you can just remember that at least you don't have anything as bad as that to cover up."

She laughed. She already felt calmer, as though

things were starting to happen. She was flooded with gratitude. "Michael, I don't know how to thank you."

He could think of several ways, none of which he'd dare to propose. He scolded himself into remembering what she was doing there. "Let's wait until we find your husband. Then we'll figure something out."

Michael arranged to have the press conference that afternoon at the embassy. Before the journalists arrived, she met with a Captain Bruce Hastings from Scotland Yard, and though it wasn't the first time someone from the Yard had heard her tale, it was the first time she felt that Drew's disappearance was being treated as a serious problem. When she went to meet the press, Hastings was at her side, looking solemn and in control. The irony did not escape her, but it didn't matter. Nothing matters if it brings Drew back, she said to herself.

She had expected a few reporters and maybe a television camera. Nothing had prepared her for the mob that confronted her when she stepped up to the lectern. She hadn't borne the Symington name long enough to know what kind of curiosity it generated. She felt a moment of panic and a yearning to flee. But Michael, who had his hand on her arm, guiding her, gave it a little squeeze, and she understood that he would be there to help her. He introduced her and informed the press that she'd be making a brief statement, after which they would answer some questions.

The lights were dizzying, and the microphones

thrust in her face made her feel as though she was under attack. In her head, she repeated what was quickly becoming her mantra: nothing matters if it will bring Drew back.

She began slowly. "Thirteen days ago my husband, Andrew Symington, disappeared. The last known person to have seen him was a clerk at the Royal Broadwick Hotel. He could tell me only that my husband checked out; he had no idea where he was going. We have searched all public facilities, including hospitals and morgues, to no avail. No one has contacted me with information or with a request for ransom. I am desperate with worry, and I beseech anyone who might have information as to my husband's whereabouts, to contact Captain Hastings or me directly. I will protect all sources of information. I am not interested in pursuing a criminal prosecution. I only want my husband back. Thank you."

She stepped away from the microphone to a barrage of "Mrs. Symington! Mrs. Symington!" as reporters clamored to get her attention. She looked to Michael.

"You don't have to answer questions if you don't want to. They'll probably get very personal," he said under his breath.

"Will it help?"

"How can we know?"

"Nothing matters if it will bring Drew back," she said as much to herself as to him.

"I'm sorry?" He hadn't heard her, but she was already stepping back to the microphone, pointing at a reporter who was screaming her name over and over again.

"Mrs. Symington, is it true that your husband was disinherited when he married you?"

Michael raised his hand in disgust and started to approach the microphone, but Sam waved him back. Nothing matters . . .

"Yes," she answered evenly. "It's true. But I can't see how that would be relevant to his disappearance."

She tried to turn to someone else, but the same reporter continued insistently. "The Symingtons are a very powerful family. Couldn't they have arranged to get their son away from you?"

"My husband's family may not approve of our marriage, but they are not criminals."

"Mrs. Symington," someone was yelling over the crowd, "what business brought your husband to London?"

"He was looking into the possibility of European financing for an automotive venture of our own."

"If you don't think Forrest Symington would take drastic measures for personal reasons, do you think he might do so for professional reasons?"

"Please. I'm not trying to turn this into an attack on the Symingtons. I just want to find my husband."

"How have Forrest Symington and Mathilde D'Uberville Symington reacted to their son's disappearance?"

Sam thought about Forrest's hardened face and Mathilde's secret plea and knew that to speak of either of them would amount to betrayal. She had hoped that somehow the questions might open the door to some kind of lead, but now she realized that her hope was unfounded. She had underestimated the public's prurient interest in people with recognizable names. She tensed only slightly, but Michael noticed. Gently he moved her away from the microphone and, speaking over the shouts from the floor, announced that Mrs. Symington could take no more questions.

Now they were after him. "Mike, Mike. What's your interest in this? Are you personally involved?"

"Mr. Symington is an American citizen who has disappeared in London. Of course the embassy is involved. As it happens, I know the Symington family."

"What about Samantha Symington? How well do you know her?"

Michael had had enough. "Captain Hastings will be glad to answer any questions about the investigation. A flyer with a picture of Andrew Symington and contact numbers for the London Metropolitan Police and for a direct line to Mrs. Symington will be provided."

With expert skill, he maneuvered her out of the room and away from the cacophony as the reporters advanced on Hastings. They didn't speak again until they were in the car, pulling out of traffic and onto Hampstead Road, heading home.

"Don't be angry," Sam said gently, as Michael savagely honked his horn at a car pulling out in front of him. "They were just doing their job."

"I know it, and I should be used to it. But if they could just once focus on solving the problem instead of digging up dirt, the change would be refreshing."

"Look at it this way. It's the dirt that makes it a story. And if one person comes forward with information after reading the story, nothing else matters."

"You're right, of course," Michael admitted. "How come I'm the professional and you're the one who's so cool?"

"I'm not cool. I'm scared stiff. But I've got nothing to prove. I've only got one goal: to find my husband. And I'll do whatever it takes to get him back."

He wanted to say, "He's a lucky guy, your husband," but he knew that would be stupid. For all they knew, Drew Symington could be lying dead in a ditch somewhere. Still, Michael couldn't help what he felt, and when Sam talked about her husband he was overwhelmed with envy. For Sam's sake, he sincerely hoped they'd find Drew alive and well. But for his own, he knew that if they didn't, he'd be right there to comfort her.

They had met every day for the past thirteen days, sitting in the same booth. She'd stopped ordering grilled cheese sandwiches after the third day, happy to relegate the greasy concoctions to the realm of childhood memory where they belonged. But it was a quiet time of the afternoon, and nobody bothered them if they sat for a couple of hours over refilled cups of decaf, especially since they always left a very large tip, which, after arguing over who owed whom what, they had agreed to split down the middle. Sarah's days were planned around her forays to the Galleria, and now she was relieved rather than aggravated by James's continued nocturnal absences.

Their rendezvous had fallen into a convivial pattern of lively discussions and shared opinions on everything from lifestyles to literature. Even though she seldom talked about herself, Sarah felt that Ian knew her better than almost anyone else, for one simple reason. He listened to her and seemed to be interested in what she said. Under Ian's unassuming tutelage, Sarah blossomed, allowing her physical presence to make as much of a statement as her intellectual convictions.

So it was with dismay that Sarah heard Ian say, "I'm sorry, Sarah, but I can't come here anymore."

She kicked herself for not being ready, for not anticipating disappointment. But surprised or not, disappointment was the one thing she was practiced at handling.

"No problem," she said. "I understand. Do you want to leave now?"

They had just arrived. She had put on a new dress today, a simple tank that bared her arms and legs, casual but pretty. Her hair hung loose over her shoulders, and she had thought the effect was quite fetching. Not fetching enough, obviously.

Ian was already heading toward the door. "Why prolong the agony?"

She wanted to beg for two more hours of what he called agony, but she bit her lip and rose to follow him. Agony was what she would endure at home, knowing there were to be no more animated afternoons with Ian at the Galleria, just endless days of waiting for James and exchanging banalities that interested neither of them.

Outside, he paused at the door and turned to her. Hoping to preempt the apologies and excuses she'd been trained to expect, she extended her hand. "Thank you for some interesting conversations," she said, wishing she could thank him for restoring her life and implore him not to snuff it out.

He wouldn't even shake her hand. She did not understand the look of dismay on his face, and she didn't know what else to say. "I'd better be going."

She started to walk away, not looking back. He grabbed her from behind and whirled her around to face him. "Are you crazy?" he asked, genuinely baffled.

"What do you mean?" She was as confused as he was.

"Where are you going?"

"Home."

"Why?"

"Because you said you didn't want to see me anymore."

"No, I didn't. I said I didn't want to come here. To this coffee shop. It's a dump and the coffee stinks, and we sit here every day for two hours. I didn't say anything about you."

"Oh." She was quiet for a moment, joy and

embarrassment vying for top colors, joining in a blush that did them both proud. "I thought you meant . . ."

"Hello, Sarah? This is Ian. Have we been sitting across from each other for almost two weeks? Or was that someone else?"

"It was me," she said shyly.

"Well, I don't know if you noticed, but I'm addicted. I thought you were too."

She threw her arms around him. "I am," she said fervently. "I am."

"Then what made you think I'd want to end it?"

How could she explain her life as a nonentity? With him, she'd become pretty, witty, and bright. How could she tell him about crushed hopes and diminished expectations? With him, there had always been the promise of tomorrow.

She heard a sudden clap of thunder, and though the sun still shone, raindrops as huge as gum balls started to splatter around them.

"Let's get out of here," he said, grabbing her hand and making her run through the rain and onto a bus just as the door was closing. He deposited enough change for the two of them and then pushed her toward a window seat, squeezing in beside her.

"I've never been on a public bus," she said, and it took him a minute to realize she wasn't kidding.

"Well, my motto is, why take a fifty-thousand-dollar limo when you can take a one-hundred-thousand-dollar bus?"

She laughed and turned to watch the rain pelting the window as the unfamiliar streets rolled by. She didn't ask where they were going. She didn't care. It was warm and dry in the bus, and she felt as if she were inside a cocoon, safely evolving into the butterfly she was meant to be.

He was staying in a bed-and-breakfast on a tree-lined street on the border between Oakdale and Woodland Cliffs. The house was not in its prime, but it was tenderly cared for by an elderly widow. The bus deposited them a half a block away, and they ran again, hand in hand, sloshing through the puddles and choking with laughter. By the time they got to the front door, they were both soaked.

"I thought I'd get Mrs. Boggs to serve us some tea, but I hate to leave puddles in her parlor. Let's go up to my room and dry off first."

He took the stairs two at a time, and Sarah bounded after him, feeling like a young girl. The room was small, dominated by an iron-framed bed covered with a patchwork quilt. A small table stood between two stuffed chairs next to a window that looked out onto the street.

"I love it here," Sarah said guilelessly.

"Why? It's just an ordinary room."

"That's why I love it," she answered aloud. And because it's yours, she added to herself.

"Here," he said, tossing her a blue chambray work shirt and a towel. "Get dry." He pointed to the bathroom, then turned away, pulling off his shirt. Her heart tripled its beat as she glimpsed a ripple of muscle, and she quickly closed the door, afraid of what a broader view might elicit.

She slid out of her dress and threw it over the shower curtain rod. She was glad she hadn't worn a bra; she would have felt self-conscious having to hang her underwear in a strange man's bathroom. Not that Ian was strange—on the contrary. She slipped on his shirt, buttoning it slowly, noticing that the shirttails came to mid-thigh, glad she'd shaved her legs that morning. She wrapped the towel around her head and glanced at her reflection in the mirror. She couldn't stop smiling. It didn't matter that all traces of makeup had long since been washed from her face. It didn't matter that her hair was folded into a twist of terry cloth. She knew with a certainty that she had never before experienced that Ian would find her beautiful.

Sarah left the bathroom and found Ian standing before her in a pair of clean jeans and nothing else.

"You look good in my shirt," he said, eyeing her appreciatively.

"You look good without it."

"I wish you weren't married," he said, shocking himself. He hadn't meant to be so forward. He had seen how fragile she could be, and he didn't want to frighten her.

"So do I," she answered, not frightened at all.

In two steps he was beside her, and a moment later she was in his arms. They kissed, not without passion, but with tenderness, their lips gently reaching for each other's souls.

Ian pulled away first. "I didn't bring you here to . . ."

"I know."

"Sarah, I want you. Don't think I don't. But not like this. A furtive hour in a rented room until it's time for you to go home. If I started to make love to you now, I wouldn't be able to let you go."

"What if I said I'd stay?"

"Forever?"

He sounded so eager she had to laugh. "Actually I meant for the rest of the afternoon."

"Oh." Now it was his turn to be embarrassed and disappointed.

Sarah sat in one of the chairs, curling her bare legs under her. "Ian, I don't love my husband. I haven't for a long time. In fact, I don't know if I ever did."

"Why did you marry him?"

"Because it was the right thing to do and the right time to do it. I was the slow girl in a fast crowd, and I was looking for a place to belong. I thought James would give me that, but I was wrong."

Without asking, Ian pulled the towel off her head, and began to comb out the tangles in her blond hair, gently easing his way through the knots, careful not to hurt her. It was more clearly an act of love than any she had experienced in her entire marriage.

"Would you leave him?" Ian asked so quietly that he was afraid she might not hear over the beating of his heart.

"I've never had the courage to even think about it."

"Do you now?"

"Yes, but it's not so simple. Since my brother's

been banished, James has become my father's designated heir. I wouldn't just be turning my life upside down, I'd be messing with a Fortune Five Hundred company."

But Sarah knew it was more than a matter of economics. With Drew gone, the family dynamic had been upset, and she didn't know how to deal with that. On the surface, some things had remained the same. Forrest still did business, Mathilde still drank, Bethany still came to dinner. But the equilibrium had shifted, and the balancing act they had been doing their whole lives was suddenly out of kilter. Sarah had been allowed her adolescent rebellion when Drew finished college and joined the family business, as was expected. Drew had been in trouble in Europe when Sarah had been married at home, safely ensconced in the bosom of her family. There had always been an unspoken understanding between the siblings. One of them could be bad only when the other was good. And now Drew was gone. He had committed the ultimate act of defiance by marrying outside of the acceptable circles. How could Sarah even consider following in his footsteps?

"Anyway," she added, trying not to think about anything beyond how happy she was at this very moment in this very place, "aren't we being a little premature?"

"Maybe. But I don't have much time, and I want to know in advance how deeply I should get involved. Because I have a feeling that if I let myself fall in love with you, I'll be a goner for life."

She'd stopped hearing after the first sentence. "Why?" she asked, trying to keep the panic at bay. "Why don't you have much time?"

"I have to go home. I only came here to do what I had to do. I start teaching in a couple of weeks."

"Why did you come here?" Sarah asked. They'd talked of many things, but not that. After his initial reluctance, Sarah had never again mentioned his predilection for hiding in bushes. After all, that had nothing to do with her, and it wasn't any of her business. Now suddenly she felt that everything about him had something to do with her.

He put down the comb and sat in the chair opposite her. "I came to find my birth mother."

"Really?" she was shocked. Even though he had told her he was adopted, this was the last thing she would have thought of. "And did you?"

"Yes, but I never confronted her."

Sarah instantly understood. "That's what you were doing in the bushes, isn't it? Diane Myles is your mother."

Ian nodded. "I wanted to see her, see if she had a family, what she was like. I thought maybe if she seemed approachable, I'd introduce myself and ask her why she gave me up. But I never had the nerve to knock on her door."

His voice was small, and he gazed at the floor, unable to meet her eyes, like a little boy waiting to be scolded. In a second she was out of her chair and sitting on his lap, her arms around his neck, her cheek pressed against his, smelling the sweet damp scent of his hair.

"It's funny," Sarah mused. "That's why we met. Because I was afraid to knock on her door, too."

Ian smiled ruefully. "A match made in heaven."

"Yeah," Sarah added. "Do we get together, or do we get therapy?"

Ian laughed, "Does one possibility obviate the other?"

Sarah tried to get up, but he held her on his lap and kissed her. She kissed him back, then looked at her watch. Abruptly he let her go.

"Don't be angry," she pleaded. "We're having dinner at my parents' tonight. I'm going to be late."

"I'm not angry. I'm jealous."

"Don't be jealous, either. It's you I . . ." She stopped herself and went into the bathroom to get her dress to keep herself from going further.

"Sarah," Ian called after her. But she came out quickly, wearing her own clothes, and put her hand to his lips.

"Let's stop now. I think we've said enough for one day. Let's give the dust a chance to settle."

He knew she was right. They had taken each other on an emotional roller-coaster ride, and they were both exhilarated but exhausted. "Okay. Tomorrow. Here instead of the coffee shop. Same time. We can think about it all night."

He called her a taxi and kissed her good-bye, a kiss so sweet and giving that it lingered long after his lips had left hers. He was standing at the window when she turned and waved good-bye. He had put on the shirt she had worn, and it hung open over his jeans. It took all her willpower not to dismiss the cab and run back upstairs to hug his lean frame and bury her face in his tousled hair. For the first time in a long time, she couldn't wait until tomorrow.

9

Watching the setting sun turn the sky a blood orange as the cab wound its way toward Woodland Cliffs, Sarah marveled at the mystery and the miracle. In less than two weeks she had fallen in love with a virtual stranger. And not just any stranger. A stranger who happened to be the son of Diane Myles. She had a sudden vision of herself and Ian sitting in the Myles backyard with Drew and Sam while Harvey cooked hamburgers and Diane served lemonade. For a moment she wondered why she always equated paradise with a barbecue, and the thought made her laugh out loud.

"Did you say something, lady?" the cabby asked, looking at her in his rearview mirror.

"No," Sarah said, still giggling. "I'm just laughing because I'm happy." She realized only as she said it that it was true.

"It's not going to depress you if I turn on the news, is it?"

"Go ahead," Sarah said. "Nothing's going to depress me today."

She leaned back in the seat, humming to herself, not really listening. Only when she heard her own name on the radio did she suddenly become alert. "Could you turn that up a little louder?" she asked, leaning forward.

The newscaster was in the middle of his report: "His wife, Samantha, held a press conference in London earlier today, pleading for anyone with information to come forward. Drew Symington is the son of local VIP Forrest Symington, CEO of the D'Uberville Motor Company, but he is said to have been estranged from his family since he married. Scotland Yard is conducting the investigation, but as yet no clues have been discovered that might shed light on the younger Symington's disappearance. In other local . . ."

The driver was talking over the newscast. "Isn't that something? The guy starts out with all that money, and what good does it do him? He's probably lying dead in some ditch."

Sarah couldn't breathe. Her heart was beating so fast she thought it would break. "My God," she repeated to herself, over and over. "My God, my God."

The driver turned down the radio. "Are you okay, lady?" The news was never good, but it didn't usually get this kind of reaction.

Sarah managed to choke out, "I've changed my

mind. Instead of going to Crescent Drive, take me to the Belvedere estate on—"

"Shit, I know where it is," said the driver, cursing his big mouth. "That's the Symington place. Are you—"

"Please hurry," she said, cutting him off, making it clear she wasn't prepared for any further conversation.

She huddled by the door, holding her arms around herself, shaking, until he pulled up to the gates.

"Listen, lady. I'm sorry about what I said. I didn't know . . ."

She took out twenty dollars, twice as much as the figure on the meter, thrust it at him, and jumped out of the cab, slamming the door behind her. She was inside the gates and running up the winding drive before he had pulled away.

Robert opened the door for her, but Mathilde was not far behind him, talking as she approached.

"Chérie, you're late. *Ton père* and James are here already." She stopped when she saw Sarah standing at the door, disheveled and panting. *"Mais qu'est-ce que c'est?"* She scowled. "Why aren't you dressed?"

Sarah was crying. "Did you hear the news, Maman?"

"What? What is it?" Mathilde drew close to her child, alarmed.

"It's Drew," Sarah sobbed. "He's missing. It was on the news."

Sarah felt her mother stiffen. "Shh," Mathilde said, looking toward the library where her husband

and son-in-law were waiting. "Go upstairs and change. You can wear one of my dresses. Odile will help you."

"Why should I change?" Sarah knew she was screaming, but she couldn't help it. "Who gives a shit about clothes? Didn't you hear what I said? Drew is missing. Your son has disappeared."

"Arrête!" Mathilde commanded. "Stop now. I heard you. We will talk about it later."

"Did you hear me? Drew could be dead. Don't you care?"

The shouts had brought Forrest and James hurrying into the foyer.

"I thought I'd made it abundantly clear that we were not to speak that name in this house." Forrest intoned sternly.

"For God's sake, he's your son," Sarah snapped.

"He is not my son. Not anymore." There was no emotion in his face or in his voice.

Sarah was out of control, "You're sick. Do you know that? Sick!"

Forrest's expression was knitted into a dark cloud. "You're behavior is entirely inappropriate."

"My behavior? That's a laugh. Your son has disappeared somewhere across the ocean and you don't give a damn. Why? Because he married a wonderful girl he loved, but she wasn't the girl you wanted. I'm upset because something might have happened to my brother, and you're pretending he doesn't exist. Your own flesh and blood. No, Dad. It's your behavior that's inappropriate."

James watched the family disintegrate, not saying a word. This was exciting news—and useful, he was sure—but he had to play his cards very carefully. Clearly Mathilde required sympathy, but Forrest would expect support. James would have to walk the middle ground, being careful not to give away his position.

Simply put, James could not have been happier. He had feared that someday Drew would reappear on the scene and make peace with his father. If that happened, James knew it would be the end of his ambitions. Drew had never trusted him, never liked him, and James was certain that if he re-entered the bosom of his family, Drew would make sure that James was shunted aside. Now it looked as if he wouldn't ever have to face that problem.

Best of all, with his actions, Forrest was isolating himself from the rest of the family. No target was so easily accessible as the one that stood alone.

James rapidly assessed the situation. Forrest and Sarah were still glaring at each other, shaking with anger. But it was Mathilde who seemed the most fragile. Laying his hand gently on her shoulder, James offered the only comfort she was sure to take. "You're upset, Maman. Come into the library and let me pour you a drink."

"Non, merci," said Mathilde, surprising them all. "I don't want a drink. Forrest, you and James go. I will talk to Sarah."

James quickly switched gear. "Come on, sir," he put a manly arm around his father-in-law's shoulders. "I'm sorry about Sarah. I don't know what's gotten into her."

Sarah glared at her husband. "You snake . . ." she started, but one look from her mother silenced her. The look wasn't beseeching or even forbidding. It was knowing—conspiratorial, even—and Sarah suddenly understood that her mother had information to impart. Without another word of protest, she followed her mother up the palatial staircase to the inner sanctum of Mathilde's room where, even as a child, she'd been made to feel like an intruder.

The room was lined with mirrors and Sarah couldn't help but see herself as she must have looked to the impeccable Mathilde—like a ragamuffin, her face streaked with tears, her hair disheveled, her dress rumpled and still damp from the rain. For a minute she was embarrassed, feeling like a dark, dirty stain on the immaculate splendor of the white-carpeted room. She was tempted to run away, but her mother took her hand and led her to a small French Provincial settee upholstered in the palest gold brocade. Mathilde sat and indicated that Sarah should do the same. Sarah hesitated, irrationally afraid that she would leave an indelible mark for which her mother would never forgive her.

"Sit, *chouchou*," Mathilde said, startling Sarah, who hadn't been called *chouchou*, little cabbage, since she was four years old.

"Maman, what's going on?" Sarah asked, positioning herself beside her mother. "Did you know about this?"

Mathilde reached up and pushed a coil of blond hair away from Sarah's face, sweeping it behind her ear, realizing as she did it how long it had been since she'd made a gesture of affection to her only daughter, or to anyone else, for that matter.

"I knew, Sarah."

"Then why didn't you do anything about it?" Sarah was starting to cry again. She felt helplessly emotional, struggling futilely to keep from drowning in the sea of Mathilde's composure.

"I did," said Mathilde quietly, instantly stopping her daughter's tears.

"What?" asked Sarah, completely baffled now.

"I gave Samantha money and sent her to Michael Litton in London, so she could try to find Drew."

"Samantha? You mean Drew's Sam? You talked to her?"

Mathilde nodded. "She came to ask your father for help. He refused. I could not. *Mais il ne peut pas savoir,*" she hastily added. "That's why I could say nothing downstairs."

"Oh, Maman," Sarah was hugging her, "I won't say anything. Have you heard from her? Is there any news?"

"Not yet. Michael called me. He is helping. *Ne t'inquiète pas.* They will find him."

"Of course they will." Sarah paused for a minute. "Maman, would you mind if I skipped dinner? James will probably stay; he's got a lot of sucking up to do. But I couldn't face the pretense right now."

Mathilde was shocked. This was not her obedient daughter talking, the quiet one who shuffled behind them, never questioning, never demanding. She looked at Sarah. This could not just be a change brought on by an altercation with her father over her missing brother. This was a new attitude that pervaded everything about her, and Mathilde was suddenly aware that it had been happening for a couple of weeks. Sarah was dressing differently, acting differently, talking differently. Mathilde hadn't registered it before because it wasn't entirely new. It was an old Sarah, last seen before her marriage, challenging the authority of her family and insisting on living her own life, even though it wasn't a life she particularly wanted. Only now, in retrospect, did Mathilde realize that in taming Sarah, James had ineffably changed her, extinguished a spark Mathilde had not missed until this moment when it had returned.

"What's happened to you, Sarah? You are not the same."

"You're right, Maman," Sarah said, following an unprecedented urge to tell her mother the truth. "I think I've fallen in love."

"Mon Dieu," gasped Mathilde. "You are having an affair?"

"I didn't say that. I said I've fallen in love. I've only known him for two weeks, and I kissed him for the first time today. But I think I'd like to spend the rest of my life with him."

"Who is he?" asked Mathilde, afraid, but needing to know.

"Nobody you know. He's from out of town. A teacher. A wonderful person who cares about what happens to others and who treats me with respect and tenderness."

Mathilde looked at her only daughter, and suddenly she was flooded with a memory from over twenty years ago. It played so vividly in her mind it could have happened yesterday. She felt a little girl's skinny body, warm from the sun, as it hugged her own. They had been by the pool and she had told the five-year-old Sarah that she would take her to the circus in Saint-Tropez.

"I love you, Maman," the little girl had said, flinging her arms around her mother's neck. "You are always so good to me."

"And I always will be," Mathilde had answered, kissing the top of her daughter's golden head.

But she hadn't kept her promise. Her little girl had grown up, and Mathilde had barely been present, let alone good to her.

"Sarah, please listen to me, *ma chérie.*"

"Maman, if you're going to tell me that he's the wrong sort of person and that I owe it to the family to stay with James, I don't want to hear it."

"That's not what I was going to say." Mathilde stood up, almost deciding to say nothing at all. Then she looked at her daughter—Sarah as she should be, strong, eyes blazing, a mess, but beautiful, not the carefully coiffed but wilting bloom she'd become. "Does he love you?" she asked.

"I think so. We haven't talked much about it; we're still putting it together. But I feel it, you know, even without his saying he loves me. When he looks at me or touches me, I know he does."

"What about James?"

"James is a shit. He cares more about sucking up to you and Daddy than he does about me." Sarah looked at her mother defiantly, expecting a reproach. To her surprise, Mathilde was smiling. "What's so funny?" asked Sarah, baffled.

"You haven't talked this way to me since you

were twenty. It makes me feel young." The two women burst out laughing and fell into a spontaneous hug.

"Ma pauvre fille," Mathilde said, pulling away and looking at her child. "I know you have not been happy, but I don't think this is the way."

"Why? Because Ian's not from the right family? If I go with him, will you disown me like you did Drew?"

"Not me, *chérie.* Your father, perhaps. But you will always be my children. Both of you."

"Why is he so crazy, Maman?"

"Perhaps because when I married him, he was also a nobody."

"But your family stood by him. They helped him, gave him money to start off on his own."

"Maybe that is the problem. He does not like to be reminded. We gave him what he wanted, and he has never forgiven us. Do you understand?"

"Not really."

"It doesn't matter." She took her daughter's hand. "Don't do anything foolish, Sarah. At least wait until we hear from Samantha, until we know Drew is all right. I can't handle more than one crisis at a time."

"Looks like you're doing a great job," Sarah said, kissing her mother's cheek.

With her mother's blessing, Sarah left Belvedere without a word to the others, borrowing one of her mother's cars. Her own house was quiet; the staff had been dismissed early because she and James had planned to be out for dinner. She liked the house this way, quiet and empty. She thought about what it must be like to come home every day to be greeted either by loved ones or by no one at all, not to have to steel yourself before walking in the door, knowing there were expectations to be met. She wandered into the kitchen and imagined herself cooking a meal for the man she loved—probably a bad meal, since she'd never learned to cook. He would eat it anyway, until she let him off the hook and fed him kisses instead. It was too soon to believe she could live this way with Ian, but it was Ian who was making her think she could live like that at all.

By the time James came home, Sarah was asleep. She was dreaming, smiling in her sleep, and he had to resist an urge to throttle her. How dare she threaten his hard-won position with her mewling over her goddamn lost brother? He realized that, with all the time he'd been spending with Bethany, he'd been neglecting Sarah, and his absences were obviously making her excitable. He'd have to put in some work on her, too, remind her that without him her life would be pretty damn empty.

James slipped into bed beside Sarah, careful not to touch her sleeping body. It amazed him that he had once found her desirable. Of course, he had courted her for the advantages of her money and family, but he had wanted to possess her as well. Now all he dreamed of was having all the advantages and ridding himself of her and her supercilious family forever.

With Bethany he had found a way to make that happen, and to get his rocks off at the same time. In between their frequent trysts, she'd already had

several secret meetings with board members. She
had convinced them that since Drew had left the
fold, Forrest was losing it, and that James alone was
holding the company together. James never asked
her what took place at these meetings. It didn't
matter to him whether she used anatomy or ideology to get her point across, as long as she was able to
deliver the votes when he was ready to make his
move. And then, at last, he'd be the one on top, out
in front. The Symingtons would be currying his
favor the way he'd been scurrying after them.

The only reason to eat shit, he thought, is so that
you can make others eat shit later. Confident that
his time was coming, he closed his eyes and slept
like a baby.

Drew felt himself shaking. He was somewhere far
away. He was trying to get to someone just out of
reach. And he was being shaken.

"Yank, wake up," he heard Moira say, as he
forced himself back to consciousness. "You can't
keep falling asleep in the middle of your Irish
history lessons."

He stretched like a cat and, smiling lazily,
reached up to bring her mouth close enough to kiss.
"I already know all the Irish history I need to
know," he said, teasing her with his tongue. "I want
to work on something else now."

"You're a very naughty man," Moira said, delighting him with her broad Irish brogue. But she
put aside the book she had been holding and took
hold of him instead.

Moira was a quick study and, with plenty of time

to practice, she had learned a lot in the short time they'd been together. She blossomed under his tender tutelage, and it pleased him to watch her growing into her woman's frame. They made love often, deftly, and with passion, and Moira was quick to note that his amnesia didn't seem to have affected any of his more instinctual skills. He did not tell her that, in fact, when he made love to her, sometimes his ardor would elicit a different desire, a yearning for a memory he could not place. Instead, he would redouble his efforts, feeding his hunger on the intensity of her need, her love, until all would be forgotten in the climax of their mutual rapture.

Moira had persuaded Colim and Seamus to give her a chance to convert their hostage to the cause, pointing out he'd be more useful as an operative than as an unidentified corpse. They'd been left pretty much on their own after that, with Colim and Seamus moving into an old barn on the property to keep the Yank from seeing them. But Colim had warned her that she would be held responsible for delivering a willing soldier when the time came. She didn't need to be reminded of the IRA's punishment for failure or betrayal.

Lying in his arms, basking in the afterglow, she tried to divert his attention from the physical and back to the philosophical.

"If we were living in a free Ireland—" she began, trying to make it sound like a natural segue, although she was perfectly aware that it was not.

But he wouldn't let her go on. "Listen, Moira, you don't have to keep trying to brainwash me. I can't even remember my own history, let alone Ireland's. The only thing I can believe in right now is you. And if the IRA is what you believe in, then I'll accept it too."

"You will?" Moira was surprised at how easy it was. She knew that as a good soldier she should probably insist that he embrace the ideology, but she didn't care. She loved him, she wanted him alive, and she wanted him with her always. Nothing else mattered.

"Will you help us?" she asked, knowing he'd have to prove himself to Colim and Seamus.

"Well, I'm not going to blow up any innocent babies," he said glibly, "but sure, I'll fold envelopes or demonstrate or do whatever other volunteer tasks you're dishing out."

"Oh, Yank," she said, kissing him. He was naive. Without a history, he was like a child. And she realized that she could reassure him as she would a child and keep him by her side. He had not been exposed to anyone or anything since his recovery. There had been no radio, no television, no magazines, no newspapers, no visitors. She was his only source of information, his only means of protection.

"That'll be just fine," she encouraged him. "We'll just take it as it comes along."

Her answer suited him. That was what he was doing, taking it as it came along. Who he was before was almost starting to feel irrelevant. He still had dreams, felt himself reaching out to someone or something, but he never heard names, never saw faces, and the dreams always ended the same way, with frustration and sadness and the unknown remaining unreachable. Awake, he had become accustomed to the routine, spending his days with Moira, reading, talking, making love. He knew there were others on the property, and sometimes he heard their voices. But he never met them, and he and Moira left the cottage only when the others were not around. Although he had some curiosity about what went on outside his room, he was content to let Moira feed him information in small spoonfuls, as she saw fit. Because, in fact, he was aware that he had not yet recovered his full strength and wasn't ready to tackle the unknown.

Meanwhile obviously no one was looking for him or he would have heard something by now, so he was clearly no one of great importance. He even wondered if he might be better off not knowing anything about his past. Maybe he had chosen to forget it because it wasn't worth remembering. All he had was Moira. And if she had brought him back to life so that she could keep him, who had a better right?

His eyes were closed and Moira was kissing him. She had started on his mouth and was working her way down his body. He let sensation suppress thought. Thinking was too painful.

The first thing Anne did when she came home after work was turn on the telly. She didn't really watch it; she just kept it on for the sound. Standing in Victoria Station all day at the Tourist Information desk, she was surrounded by the clamor of people. While she appreciated being alone in her flat, the sudden silence was sometimes just too striking. She didn't really want company; she just didn't want to feel alone.

She didn't really pay attention to the news on BBC 1, but she was intrigued by the glimpse of a gorgeous redhead behind a bank of microphones. She'd missed most of the press conference, and it took her a minute to catch on that the woman's husband was missing and that for some reason he was on the outs with his family. It wasn't until they flashed his picture on the screen that she realized why the name Symington had sounded so familiar. The missing man was the handsome, bargain-hunting American with the platinum American Express card. She'd had a fantasy or two about him after he'd appeared at Victoria Station, so she wasn't likely to be mistaken. She grabbed a pencil and jotted down the phone number on the screen.

Anne wondered if she should bother to call. After all, she'd only seen him for ten minutes, and she had no idea where he went after he left her. Who knew what he was involved in? She might do just as well to stay out of it. On the other hand, from what she'd heard on the newscast, he'd disappeared around the time he'd come to her. She tried to block the image of his beautiful wife from her mind as she imagined what form his gratitude to her might take if they were to find him based on some tidbit of information she had given them. She called the number and left a message.

* * *

Sitting in a neighborhood trattoria with Michael, Sam was trying hard to do justice to the meal he had ordered for both of them. Sam hadn't wanted to leave the house in Hampstead, but Michael had finally convinced her that sitting and watching the telephone wouldn't make it ring. He had hoped that by taking her out of the house, he could get her to grant herself some peace, if only for an hour or two. But he could see that the two-block excursion had been a dismal failure. He told the waiter to wrap up the rest of the food in case Sam got hungry later. Then he paid the check and took her home.

When they came into the house, they were welcomed by the blinking message light on the answering machine. Sam tried not to get her hopes up. They'd had a couple of crank calls already: a man offering to take her husband's place, which Michael had shut off when the caller went into graphic detail about the things he could do for Samantha; a woman saying that she hoped the dirty American was dead and that all dirty Americans deserved to die. But this time she was gratified to hear a voice that sounded sane, with none of the stridency that seemed to go hand in hand with mad telephone callers.

"Hello . . ." There was a hesitation. "Uh . . . my name is Anne Frommer. I, uh . . . work at the British Tourist Information Center at Victoria Station. I booked a room for Andrew Symington about two weeks ago. If you want to talk to me about it, I'll be at work tomorrow at nine."

"Tomorrow?" Sam said, alarmed. "We have to wait until tomorrow?"

"I'm sorry," said Michael, feeling very guilty "I shouldn't have made you go out."

"No, it's probably good you did. Otherwise the phone wouldn't have rung at all. It's the carry-an-umbrella-and-it-won't-rain principle."

"Kind of you to say, but of course that doesn't hold in London. Everyone always carries an umbrella, and it always rains."

"Never mind," she said, putting a hand on his arm, not wanting him to feel bad. She felt bad enough for both of them. "Tomorrow will come soon enough, and then maybe, finally, we'll get our lead."

But tomorrow could not come soon enough for Sam. Michael heard her pacing the floor above him, her footsteps tracking a light circle around his ceiling. He wondered what it must feel like to have someone like Sam love you as much as she loved Drew. The thought made him feel sad for Sam and sorry for himself. Finally, realizing he wouldn't sleep as long as she was awake, he took a bottle of brandy and two glasses and went upstairs.

The night seemed endless, and Sam was happy when Michael tapped on her door.

"Am I keeping you awake?" she asked anxiously, not wanting to take advantage of his kindness.

"Of course you are, but I'm not complaining."

He poured them each a brandy and sat down on the bed, hoping she would sit beside him. When she did, casually accepting the snifter he held out to her, he tried not to focus on the hint of curve beneath the cotton robe she had tied tightly around her waist. He was here to help her, he told himself.

And if he didn't want to blow any chance of anything else that might come later, he would do well to remember that.

"Tell me about Drew," Michael said, knowing that his request was calculated to please, but also knowing that she needed to talk. "Even though our mothers are close, we haven't really seen each other since we were kids."

Grateful, Sam told Michael how she and Drew had met, laughing with him at the description of her quaking naked behind a tree, oblivious to the tantalizing effect of her imagery. She talked about how they had loved each other at first sight, if there was such a thing, then learned to hate each other in spite of it. She told him how difficult it had been for them to win back trust and affection, and how their firsthand knowledge of the fragility of love colored everything they'd done, every decision they'd made since then. As she talked, he could hear the pain and the fear and the desperation lurking at the edges of her stories. My God, how she would suffer if they didn't find Drew alive. How much help she'd need to survive.

Michael listened, making a comment now and then to keep the conversation going, but basically just letting her talk. He refilled her glass once, then took it out of her hand when she seemed to have forgotten all about it. He told her to lie down on the bed while she talked, and he sat on the edge, taking her hand but never breaching the border of supportive sympathy. And when she fell asleep in mid-sentence, he covered her with a blanket, kissed her cheek, and tiptoed out of the room, even

though he would have given anything to spend the
night beside her.

Anne saw them leaning on the British Tourist
Information desk when she arrived ten minutes
early at Victoria Station the next morning. There
was no mistaking the red hair and elegant figure: it
was the woman she had seen on the telly the night
before. Anne was unreasonably disappointed to
find that Mrs. Symington looked even better in
person.

"I was so shocked when I heard Mr. Symington
had disappeared," she said, recovering, after she
had introduced herself. "He seemed like an exceptionally nice person."

"Thank you," Sam said, meaning it. "He really
is. She emphasized the present tense as much for
herself as for the woman she was addressing.

"Can you tell us everything you remember about
him that day—no matter how trivial it might
seem?" Michael knowing how anxious Sam was,
cut the pleasantries short for her.

Wanting to impress them, Anne was most accom-
modating, even alluding to her own surprise at
being asked to help a clearly upper-crust American
find a budget establishment. She looked to Sam for
elucidation, but Sam just smiled ruefully and asked
her to go on. They were excited when she told them
she had made a reservation for him at a hotel off
Sloane Square, but crushed a moment later, when
she obligingly called the hotel, only to be informed
that Mr. Symington had never shown up and they
had released his reservation that evening.

Sam couldn't keep the tears from springing to her eyes. For a moment she had had such hope. She had imagined a reasonable explanation. Drew was in a different hotel, so sick with the flu that he couldn't read newspapers or watch television or even make a telephone call. But even as she thought it, she knew it was impossible, and Anne's call just confirmed it.

"Did you happen to notice which way he went when he left?" Sam asked, knowing it really made no difference.

"No, I'm afraid some other people were requesting my service, and by the time I had finished dealing with them, he'd closed the locker and gone."

"What locker?" Michael and Sam asked in unison.

"I was getting to that," Anne said, not wanting them to think she was stupid enough to have forgotten something significant. "I told him he couldn't check into his new hotel for another hour. He said that would be fine, and then I saw him put his suitcase in a locker."

Having watched him from behind her desk, Anne could give them a sense of the area the locker was in, although she couldn't identify the exact one. Flashing his embassy credentials, Michael was directed to the proper official, and in a matter of minutes Anne had led them to a wall of lockers, almost all of them in use. Sam stood in front of them, shaking her head as each was opened and then hastily shut again. They'd been through seven or eight, when she clutched Michael's arm. He reacted immediately, holding back the official's hand as he went to slam the door shut.

It took Sam a moment to speak. "That's it," she said, her voice sounding hollow in her own ears. "It's Drew's coat, his suitcase."

"Yes," confirmed Anne, as though it were necessary, "I noticed because not too many of my customers carry bags from Hermès." She was rather proud that she could recognize designer merchandise even without initials.

Sam reached for the coat, wanting to hold it to her face, to smell Drew's scent, but Michael held her back. "I'd better inform Captain Hastings."

"What are you looking for?" Sam asked when Hastings arrived with a flurry of assistants.

"Clues of any sort. We'll need to take these things down to headquarters and check for fingerprints, bloodstains, that sort of thing."

Michael saw Sam flinch, and put a protective arm around her shoulder, as if he could fend off bad news. For a minute she felt as though she might faint, and let herself sink into his shoulder. But a moment later she was rigidly alert again, as Hastings turned to her and asked, "Mrs. Symington, do you have any idea why your husband would go wandering about London without his wallet or identification?"

Two hours at the New Scotland Yard headquarters on Victoria Street provided no new information. Sam was instructed to catalog the contents of Drew's bag, and as far as she could ascertain, nothing was missing except the clothing Drew presumably was wearing. Almost all the money she thought he had taken was accounted for, as were his personal documents, including passport and license.

"This case doesn't quite fit the pattern," Hastings commented as Sam completed her examination of Drew's belongings.

"What pattern?" she asked.

"Usually, when a person wants to assume a new identity, he leaves all his belongings behind but takes his cash with him—although, in your husband's case, Mrs. Symington, I suppose it would be safe to assume he might have other monies with him that you were not informed of."

"No, Captain Hastings," Sam said icily, "it's not safe to assume that at all. Drew and I were being very careful with our capital. I know exactly how much money he took. And furthermore, Drew did not disappear by choice. I know that for a fact, whether you choose to believe it or not."

"I'm not trying to upset you, Mrs. Symington, but I've been in this game a long time, and so far we've found no indication of foul play. Sometimes a husband does things that his wife just can't fathom."

"Not my husband." She turned to Michael. "Can we go? I don't think we're going to accomplish anything more here this afternoon."

She looked at Hastings for confirmation. He shrugged his shoulders. "I'd like to find your husband as much as you would, Mrs. Symington."

Sam's insides sagged. It didn't pay to make enemies of the people helping you. "I know you would, Captain Hastings. Please keep trying. Don't close the book on this. I guarantee you, it's not over."

They let her take Drew's things with her, and she held them grimly on her lap all the way to Hampstead, refusing to let Michael put even the suitcase in the trunk. It wasn't until she was in the guest room alone, Drew's coat wrapped around her body, that she let herself cry.

◦✑ 10 ✑◦

It had become almost a nightly ritual. Jack would leave the union office around six and drive over to Sam's place where Melinda was house sitting. There, the two would wait for Sam's call, which usually came around seven. Even though there had been no further news since the discovery that Drew had left all his belongings in a locker at Victoria Station, Sam and Melinda usually spent half an hour on the phone, buoying up each other's spirits. When Melinda hung up, she and Jack would make dinner together, and then he'd stick around until ten or eleven, talking about Sam's situation or Melinda's health, or some new case he was litigating for the union. Somehow they never seemed to run out of things to say or the desire to say them to each other.

Jack had already started on a new pasta sauce he wanted to try on Melinda when the phone rang.

"Say hello for me," he called from the kitchen, as Melinda picked up the phone.

"Hi, sis," she said, without waiting. "Jack says hello."

"Hello back to him," said Sam. "It's nice that he's always there with you."

"Yeah, I suppose. But it's starting to make me nervous."

"Why do you say that?"

"Oh, you know, I'm afraid I'll get to rely on him too much."

"Nothing wrong with that. He's a pretty reliable guy."

"Maybe. But he's really here because he's your friend and he's afraid I won't keep him posted if he's not right here beside me when you call."

"Is that what he told you?" Sam was smiling. She knew her best friend and her sister better than they did themselves.

"No," said Melinda. "But there's one way to find out. You come on home with Drew, and we'll see if Jack still hangs around. Are you coming?"

The line was clear, and it sounded to Sam as though her sister were just around the corner. She longed to be home, to see her family, talk to her sister over a cup of coffee, get a hug, share a laugh. She felt desperately alone, and for the first time she felt deathly afraid.

"Melinda, I don't know what to do," she confessed, tears in her throat. "It's been over a week since we found his clothes and there's been nothing else."

"What does that guy at Scotland Yard say? Hastings, right?"

"Nothing. Just that the police won't close the book on this case, but since there are no signs of foul play, they have to consider it possible that Drew disappeared because he wanted to."

"God, that's so stupid. Why the hell would he want to vanish? You two were just married and more in love than any two people I've ever seen in my life."

"I know that. But Hastings keeps talking about Drew's problems with his father, and losing his money and his position at DMC. I guess I can't blame him. He doesn't know Drew. Maybe that stuff would matter to someone else."

"What about Michael?" asked Melinda, knowing her questions were useless. If anything could be done by anyone, Sam would have seen to it.

"He's been wonderful. I've almost taken over his whole life. I'm living in his house. He hardly goes to work at the embassy anymore, just stays here with me trying to come up with leads to follow. But, Melinda," Sam almost choked on her words, but forced herself to say them, "there aren't any more leads."

Melinda wished she had some magical words of comfort that would make what she had to say more palatable, but no amount of sugarcoating would sweeten this bitter pill. "Maybe," she began slowly, carefully, not wanting to upset Sam more than she was already, "maybe, in that case, you should come home for a little while."

"I can't just give up," said Sam, her anguish cutting through the distance between them.

"I'm not saying give up. I'm just saying leave the experts to work on the case for a while. Hire a private detective with the money that Drew's mother gave you; then come home. If anybody comes up with anything, you can always fly back. But I think maybe now you should be with your family."

There was a silence on the line, and Melinda waited, afraid that Sam had been offended and was going to hang up without saying anything. Then she heard a soft sniff, and she knew that Sam was crying. "Don't, Sam. The search isn't over. But you're in London all by yourself, living in somebody else's house, totally miserable, and it's not helping. So what's the point? If there was anything you could do, I'd be the first to tell you to stay. But you said yourself there isn't."

"I know," said Sam in a tearful whisper. Melinda ached to hear her big, strong sister sound so very small.

"Come home," said Melinda, more forcefully this time.

"I'll think about it," said Sam, feeling herself starting to lose control. "I've got to go now. I'll call you tomorrow." She hung up the phone quickly and burst into tears. She knew Melinda was right. She couldn't go on living in Michael's house indefinitely. Even though he never complained—quite the contrary in fact—she was aware that she had turned his life upside down. Finding someplace else to stay, isolating herself even further, would only defeat the purpose of her being in London in the first place. What choice did she have?

And yet the thought of returning to Oakdale without Drew was unbearable. She had called Mathilde several times since she'd been here, offering encouraging observations to keep her spirits up. Mathilde had thanked her profusely, kissed her over the phone, told her that she had placed her trust in her new daughter-in-law. What would she tell Drew's mother if she went home alone?

She went to the closet and took out Drew's coat, which she had carefully hung beside her own. Still crying, she put it on. The sleeves hung below her wrists and the hem touched her ankles. She pulled it close around her body and lay on the bed, her face sinking into the collar, drowning in the scent and memory of Drew.

Sam was still in the same position when Michael had quietly slipped into the room. She had fallen asleep, and she sat up with a start as he entered. She felt uncomfortable, as though she'd been caught doing something foolish, and quickly slipped out of Drew's coat.

"I must have dozed off," she said by way of explanation.

But Michael didn't need an explanation. The sounds of her sobs had reached him downstairs, and had realized it was only the second time he had heard her cry. She tried so hard to be so strong that it just made him see her as all the more vulnerable. He looked at her, her face still flushed from sleep, stained with tears, her left cheek branded with a little crease from lying on the collar of her husband's coat.

"I'm sorry," Michael apologized, feeling as though he had intruded on an intimate moment. "I thought you'd want to see this." He handed her a fax.

Sam rubbed her eyes and read aloud. "At Harrods on the day the bomb exploded, I waited on the man you are looking for. I remember him because he was expensively dressed, said he wanted to buy something special for his wife, but was willing to spend only fifty pounds, which I thought strange. He left my department approximately five minutes before the explosion occurred. I did not respond sooner because due to trauma I experienced after the explosion I took a leave of absence and went to the countryside. Going through old newspapers, I saw the picture of Mr. Symington. I am not giving you my name as I have absolutely no other information and do not wish to be further involved."

"I already checked the number on the bottom of the fax," said Michael, knowing she would ask. "It was definitely sent from Harrods."

Sam's heart was racing. She felt dizzy and confused, unable to ascertain if this was good news or bad.

"Michael," she said, needing to get the fear into the open, "you don't think . . . he could have been coming out of Harrods when the bomb went off . . . that somehow they misplaced a body and he's lying in a morgue somewhere?" She had never actually spoken of the possibility that Drew might be dead. The words alone felt like a small death inside her.

"It's possible, Sam. I'm not going to lie to you," Michael said cautiously. "I've already spoken to Hastings. He's checking all hospitals and morgues again, and he's sending men out to question everyone who was at the scene. They're also going to track down the salesperson and talk to him or her, too."

"There's another possibility, Michael." Her head was beginning to clear. Her heart had slowed, and it was telling her that this could be good news.

"There are always other possibilities."

"The IRA set that bomb. Drew could have stumbled on them somehow, and they could have taken him. They wouldn't want a witness running around loose."

"That's true, Sam. But I'm not sure that's better. The IRA can be pretty ruthless."

"But it means he's alive. If they had killed him, wouldn't the police have found the body?"

"They're looking now."

"They're not going to find it," she said with determination. "Drew is alive. I know it. I can feel it."

"I know you've always said that, Sam, but now we're dealing with more facts."

"Please, Michael, don't doubt me now. You've been on my side all along. I need you there now. I can't do this without your help."

"Do what?" She was making him nervous. Her eyes were blazing and she had somehow changed from frightened mouse to Amazon woman.

"Contact the IRA," she said.

"Whoa, now we're getting in way over our heads. Let Scotland Yard—"

"No," she cut him off. "The IRA isn't going to tell Scotland Yard anything. If they respond at all, it's going to be to a wife's plea. Whatever is said about them, these people are human; they have families."

"It's too dangerous."

She thought a minute and then, to his surprise, acquiesced. "You're right." But she didn't stop there. "It's much too risky for you. All I'm asking is that you help me get the information. Tell me how to get in touch with them, and I'll do it myself."

"Are you crazy? You could get killed." He should have known better than to think she'd give up so easily.

"You don't understand, Michael," Sam said softly. "That doesn't matter to me. Without Drew, I'm already dead."

After she hung up the phone, Melinda was too upset to eat. Jack had tried to feed her a few forkfuls from his own plate, reminding her she had to eat for two now, but it did no good.

"Both of us are upset," Melinda had responded, "and neither one of us can eat."

Jack didn't push it. He'd been keeping a close eye on Melinda, and he knew that she'd been taking good care of herself. He couldn't blame her for having no appetite tonight. She started to cry, and he pushed away his own plate, got up from the table, took her hand, and led her to the sofa. She whimpered on his shoulder for a few moments, letting him pat away her tears, then grabbed the tissue, moved to the other side of the sofa, and blew her nose.

"You're too nice, and I don't deserve it," said Melinda, still sniffling.

"What brought that on?" Jack asked, baffled. Melinda often confused him. It was part of her charm.

"You're being nice to me because you think I'm crying about Sam. And I am. She can't find Drew and she doesn't know what to do, and it's going to be awful for her to come back without him."

"Okay," said Jack, aware that things weren't getting any clearer. "I still don't see where you deserve punishment for this."

"I'm not just thinking about Sam," Melinda confessed. "I'm thinking about me, too. She's going to come home and want her apartment back, and I'm going to have to return to my parents' house, and I won't see you anymore because you'll be here with her. And that's where you should be, because she's really going to need you. But I still feel bad. I know it's really selfish and awful of me, but I can't help it."

Jack started to laugh and slid over to her side of the sofa. He had read that hormonal changes during pregnancy could cause the expectant mother to have mood swings, but Melinda was always surprising him by the degree of irrationality of which she was capable. On the other hand, she had been pregnant since he'd met her, so it occurred to him that it was possible she was like this all the time. The truth was, it enchanted him. He had never found absolute logic particularly appealing. It was one of the things that had driven him away from the law, and now that he had returned to the courtroom, the logic was the element that bored him the most. Earthbound by the union and its legal demands, Jack saw Melinda as his escape from the conventional and as an affirmation that even though he'd finally cut his ponytail, he was still the nonconformist he'd always insisted on being.

"You're laughing at me," Melinda pouted.

"That's right, I am." He turned her face toward his and kissed her forehead, her eyes, her nose, and finally, her mouth. "Do you really think that the only reason I come here every night is to find out what's going on with Sam?"

"Isn't it?"

"It's part of the reason. Thirty minutes' worth, to be exact. Then there's the rest of the night. Let's face it, you haven't cornered the market on selfishness."

"But if Sam comes back alone, and Drew never . . ." She sounded as if she might start crying again, but this time she would really be crying for Sam.

"Shhh," said Jack, pressing a comforting finger to her lips. "Even if Sam comes back, she's not going to give up on Drew. And we're going to be here with her and do everything we can to help her. And if you don't want to move back in with your parents, you can move in with me."

He hadn't meant to say that; it had just slipped

out. For a minute the statement hung in the air, unclaimed. Then Jack broke into a broad grin. It was exactly what he had meant to say, and prefacing it with a tender kiss, he repeated it. "Move in with me, Melinda. Please."

"You're crazy," Melinda said, kissing him back. "You can't want me. I'm fat and ugly, pregnant with another man's child."

"Stop it. You're blooming and beautiful, and that baby in your belly is part of you. I love you, and I love your baby."

"But you're not the father."

"The baby wouldn't have to know that," said Jack softly.

Melinda was crying again.

"What's wrong now?" asked Jack, perplexed.

"I think you're wonderful. And it took this horrible thing that happened to my sister to make me realize it. And it's awful to think that because of her tragedy, I'm—"

"Shut up and kiss me," Jack commanded gently, and Melinda obliged.

His hand traced the mound of her belly and the fullness of her breasts. She felt herself become aroused. It had been a long time since she had felt desire or desirable. "This can't be right," she said. "I'm almost seven months pregnant."

"The baby won't know a thing," Jack whispered. "I'll be very gentle." And he was.

Ian was waiting with some of Mrs. Boggs's tea when Sarah raced up the stairs to his room. "Any

news?" he asked, as she gratefully took the prof-
fered cup and sank into the chair by the window.

She had come from her mother's, as she did
every day now. Together Mathilde and Sarah kept a
vigil, waiting for word from Sam, taking comfort
from each other's presence when no word came,
taking turns talking to her when she finally called.
In just a few conversations, Sarah felt she had come
to know her sister-in-law, even though they'd never
met. Whatever their histories, the bond between
the three women was irrefutable. They all loved
Drew and wanted him home.

Sam had reported some news today, but Sarah
wasn't sure what it might mean. She and Sam had
agreed not to say anything about it to Mathilde
until they had more details, and Sarah was desperate to share the little bit of information she had
with someone who cared.

"They found out that Drew was at Harrods the
day of the bombing. Sam thinks the IRA might
have him."

Ian let out a low whistle of surprise.

"Do you think that's good or bad?" asked Sarah,
her voice filled with trepidation.

"Good," said Ian. "Definitely good."

It was what she wanted to hear, what she needed
to hear.

"That's what I thought. At least it means he's
alive."

"And between Sam and Scotland Yard, they'll get
him back," Ian pronounced with certainty.

Sarah and Ian beamed at each other. They were

both thinking, "and then . . . ," although neither one of them needed to say it aloud. They had agreed to put the issue of their own future on hold for the time being, allowing Sarah to concentrate her whole focus on Drew's disappearance. The hiatus had come partly at the request of Mathilde, but it was good for Sarah, too. She would suffer enough guilt for leaving her husband without having to deal with the current Symington family crisis. Besides, it didn't seem right to plan a lifetime of happiness while Drew was missing and those who loved him were miserable.

Ian had been more than understanding. He had spent two months in Oakdale seeking his birth mother. He wasn't about to condemn Sarah for wanting to preserve the family she'd had all her life. And in suspending the courting process for the time being, they had become fast friends, forgoing physical connection for a mental and emotional bond, confident that they were laying the foundation for a lifetime of complete bliss.

In the short time he had known her, Ian had watched Sarah change, grow from the shrinking violet to the blooming rose. He was proud to see that with his careful nurturing, she had gained a sense of self, a certainty about who she was and what she could accomplish. Ian knew that when the situation with Drew was resolved, one way or another, Sarah would choose to live with him regardless of the consequences. And, in a way, he felt unworthy. He had done nothing to match her courage, to take control of his life, as she had of hers. If she was brave enough to embrace an

unknown future, surely he could find the strength
to confront his unknown past.

He said nothing to Sarah about his plan. She
didn't stay long, because she wanted to be reach-
able in case Sam called with more news of Drew.
When she left, he kissed her tenderly and told her
that he might have news of his own when he saw her
next. And then, without giving himself time to
change his mind, he took the bus to Thayer Street.

Standing at the curb, Ian studied the house where
his mother lived. The fresh smell of new-mown
grass hung in the air, and he breathed it in, trying to
imagine what life would have been like if he had
been raised in this house. If Diane and Harvey
Myles were good people, he guessed it might not
have been so very different from being raised by
Frank and Elise Taylor, his own parents—firmly
working class and filled with the family values that
the conservative wealthy liked to talk about but
that the laboring poor actually embraced. A childhood on Thayer Street couldn't have been better
than what he had known, because as far as he was
concerned, he had had the best. So why was he
here, stalling, building up his courage to introduce
himself to the woman who had given him away?

Ian remembered a book he had once read to a
kindergarten class when he was filling in for the
school librarian. It was called *Are You My Mother?*
and it was about a duckling that hatched after his
mother had left the nest to find food. The duckling,
having no idea what a duck looked like, wandered
from place to place questioning everything he
encountered—a cow, a crane, a tugboat. "Are you

my mother?" he kept asking, until his mother finally found him and identified him as her own. The children never wondered what might have happened if the mother duck hadn't found her offspring. But Ian did, figuring if the cow had been amenable, the duckling could have been raised to eat grass and chew cud, and would never have known it was meant to swim. He had identified with the duckling in the tale, and here he was, his nerve faltering, wishing he could just hug a tree and ask, "Are you my mother?"

Ian knew that Diane Myles was home alone. He had watched her husband drive off with his bowling ball, and it was clear Harvey wasn't to be expected home for hours. He knew, from Sarah, that Melinda Myles was living at her sister's place while Sam was in London. There was a light on in the kitchen, and he could see Diane moving around, putting on the kettle. He knocked loudly on the door, momentarily drowning out the beating of his own heart.

"Who is it?" she called through the closed door, a note of concern in her voice.

"Uh . . . my name is Ian Taylor. I . . . uh . . . I'd like to talk to you."

"What about?" she asked without opening the door.

Foolishly, he hadn't expected this. Why would she open the door to a stranger at night? On the other hand, how could he shout out his purpose into the night without even seeing her face? He hesitated, knowing that the truth would only make her more nervous, then finally hit upon the one introduction that was guaranteed to get him invited inside.

"I'm a friend of Sarah Fielding. She talked to Sam today."

In an instant the door was open and Diane Myles was motioning him inside. "I talked to Sam, too," she said. "Is there something new? Did they find Drew?"

Ian shook his head, "Not that I know of."

"Then why . . . ?" Diane let the question hang in the air. Sam had told her that she was in touch with the Symingtons and had been speaking with Drew's mother and sister on a regular basis. Still, it wasn't like them to send an emissary, especially when they had nothing to report.

"Actually," Ian began carefully, "I didn't come about Sam or Drew. I . . . I need to talk to you about something more personal."

Diane looked at him quizzically. He was watching her guardedly, but he couldn't seem to peel his eyes away from her face. He seemed intense and nervous, but not frightening. In fact, he appeared to be a little afraid of her. There was something sweetly familiar about him, although she couldn't place it, and she didn't think they had never met before. His anxiety was contagious, and a small mist of apprehension was settling like a cloud above her head.

"Should I know you?" Diane asked.

Ian pondered the question. He wanted to scream, "Of course, you should. I'm your son," but instead, he stated quietly, "My name is Ian Taylor. My parents are Frank and Elise Taylor from Seattle. Does that mean anything to you?" he asked, but he could already see that it did.

Diane stared at him, mouth open in shock. "Oh, my God," she whispered, then repeated, "Oh, my God. Are you telling me that you're . . . Are you . . . ?"

He decided to help her. "I think I'm your son."

Tears streamed down her face. She reached out as if to touch his face, then held back, not sure her caress would be welcome. "Can I . . . ? Is it okay . . . ?"

He nodded, then took one hesitant step toward her. She stood on tiptoe—he was a head taller than she—and put her arms around him in an embrace so awkward and so touching that he almost began to cry himself. Over twenty-five years of love repressed, acknowledged in the instant of a clumsy embrace.

"I have thought about you and prayed for you every single day since you were born," she said, without drama, stating a simple fact.

"Why?" was all he could say, his manners forgotten, his plan to sound casual and only mildly curious abandoned. "Why did you give me up?"

Diane wasn't ready to answer that question. She was still shaking from the shock of meeting the child she had given up for adoption so long ago. She couldn't take her eyes off him. There was something of her in his eyes and around his mouth, but there was something of his father, too. He was a good-looking young man, and there was intelligence in his face. She felt unreasonably proud and ashamed at the same time.

"Would you like to come in and sit down? I know I need to."

Ian noticed that she was trembling. He had tried to anticipate his own emotions, worrying how he might feel if she said one thing or another. But he'd never really thought about what his appearance might do to her. "I'm sorry," he said, and was surprised at how sincerely he meant it. "This must be quite a shock to you. I guess I should have called or written first."

"It doesn't matter," she said quickly. "I would have still been shocked, and I would have wanted to see you. So the waiting would have just made it worse. You did the right thing."

Color flooded his face as Ian felt a surge of what he could only call foolish pride. His mother wanted to see him. She approved of what he had done. As Diane went to get them some tea, he tried to scold himself out of his idiotic state of euphoria. What did it matter what this woman thought? She had given birth to him, but she was no less a stranger. Still, he was unreservedly relieved. He had been afraid that if he appeared at her door, she might throw him out, deny him. Instead, she had embraced him, wept tears, and confirmed his most childish dream: that she had always loved him and had never forgotten him.

After she poured the tea, they made awkward small talk for a few moments.

"Do you still live in Seattle?" Diane asked.

"Yes."

"Do you like it? I hear it's a wonderful city, but it rains a lot."

"Yes, I like Seattle. Yes, it's a wonderful city. Yes, it rains a lot." Ian smiled.

Diane liked his smile, and returned it. "I guess you didn't come all this way to talk about the weather."

"To tell you the truth, I'm not a hundred percent sure why I came. I guess I just needed to know . . ."

He allowed his voice to drift off. Diane was nodding; she understood. Ian found himself liking his mother.

Diane took a deep breath. She hadn't spoken of these things in over twenty years, but he had a right to know. "This is the way it was," she stated flatly. "I was a married woman with a young child. I had an affair with a married man, and I got pregnant. My husband didn't know; the other man's wife didn't know. Nobody knew. I wanted to pretend the baby was my husband's, but the child's father wouldn't let me. He was a powerful man and he threatened all kinds of things. I don't remember exactly what anymore, but I was pretty damn scared. He wanted me to have an abortion. I couldn't do it. So when I got close to showing, I pretended I was having a nervous breakdown, went away for three months, had you, and gave you up for adoption. It was the single hardest thing I ever did in my life, and my biggest sorrow. I don't know if it was a mistake or not."

"I don't think it was," Ian said quietly. She looked at him and saw he was sincere. "I have wonderful parents. I love them dearly, and I'm afraid they spoiled me rotten."

"No," Diane spoke softly. "I can see they did a great job. I thought they would when I picked them for you. Do they know that you're here?"

"They're the ones who told me how to find you."

"Well, tell them for me that I'm forever grateful to them."

"That's funny," Ian said. "That's exactly what they said I should say to you."

They talked then, for several hours, and the time seemed to fly by. Diane wanted to know every detail of Ian's life, from as far back as he could remember. What school did he go to? Was he popular? What subjects was he good at? What did he get for his birthdays? For Christmas? Did other people know he was adopted? Did he get teased about it? Did he feel bad about it? Why did he go into teaching? Was he happy now?

Ian answered all her questions with ease and joy, and allayed all Diane's fears. He left her with no doubt that he had had a happy childhood, that he had lacked for little, and most definitely not love, that he found his life full and satisfying. And by the time they realized the hour had gotten late, and that they could never speak of a lifetime in an evening, Diane knew for certain that she had done right by her son.

"Look," she said when Ian started to make leaving motions. "I don't want to impose, but I don't want to lose you, either. Can we stay in touch?"

"Of course. I spent the whole evening talking about myself. I'd like to know about you, too. I'd like to meet your family—my half sisters, I guess."

"I'd like that, too," Diane said, but he heard the hesitation in her voice.

"Unless you'd rather not."

"Oh, no," said Diane quickly. "I want you to get to know them. They're wonderful girls—women, I mean. I still think of all of you as babies."

He smiled, pleased to have her include him with her other children.

"It's just that," she was going on, not looking at him now, "nobody knows about what happened. And I wouldn't want . . . Not so much for me anymore, but they're going through rough times of their own right now, and another scandal would be an added burden. Would you be hurt if I introduced you as a friend?"

"I'd be honored," Ian said gallantly. "That's what I'd like to be." His time with Sarah had brought him an understanding of what scandal meant in small towns like Oakdale and Woodland Cliffs. Diane had never meant him harm, and he wished none for her now. "Anyway, I could never think of anyone as my mother except Elise Taylor. But I'd like to have you as part of my life."

"Now it's my turn to feel honored," she said, sealing their bargain with a heartfelt hug.

Ian felt almost giddy. For months, apprehension had been tightening around his soul like a vise and now he was suddenly released. Sometimes the unknown was less fearsome than one expected. Like a child instantly grown up, he understood that

shadows weren't monsters; they were just shadows
He could share that knowledge with Sarah to help
her, when the time came, to face her own fears and
make her own future.

"I'd like your permission to tell just one person,"
he said to Diane as he was heading out the door.
"The woman I'm going to marry."

Diane beamed. "You're in love."

"Very much. Our situation is a little complicated, but we're going to work it out together, and I
don't want to start our relationship with any secrets
between us."

"You're right about that," Diane said fervently.
"I've learned the hard way that secrets don't do
anybody any good. They have a way of growing into
a whole lifetime of lies."

"Then it's okay?"

"Sure. Anyway, I guess it won't do anybody any
harm if someone in Seattle knows about us."

"Actually, she's not from Seattle. She's from
Woodland Cliffs. I've been in town a couple of
months, trying to get up the courage to introduce
myself to you, and she's been helping me through
it."

"Well, we still probably wouldn't know each
other. People in Oakdale don't mix much with that
crowd. What's her name?"

"Sarah Fielding."

Diane felt her heart stop, "Sarah Symington
Fielding?" she asked, knowing the answer, but
hoping for a miracle.

"Yes. I wasn't being totally honest when I said
she was just a friend. I've been keeping up on the

situation with your daughter Sam through Sarah—"

"Ian . . ." She tried to interrupt.

But Ian didn't hear. "And I want you to know I really feel for you and your family—"

"Ian!" she said louder, more ominously.

This time he heard. He looked at her.

Her face had gone a dead white.

"What's the matter?" he asked. "Are you all right?"

"You can't tell her."

"Listen," he said, thinking he understood. "You don't have to worry about Sarah. She won't say anything to anybody if I ask her not to, not even her brother. And once we're married—"

"Ian . . ." Diane interrupted again. She sounded almost angry. "You can't marry Sarah."

Ian was taken aback. Everything had gone so well in their meeting. There had been such mutual respect and affection. He hated to see it all end with an inappropriate demand.

"Why not?" he asked a little testily, hoping she'd back off.

"Because Sarah is your half sister. Forrest Symington was the married man who got me pregnant."

Diane was still talking, but Ian couldn't hear exactly what she was saying. There was a ringing in his ears, and over it he caught phrases like "sorry . . . didn't know . . . don't hate me." He wanted to run, but something was holding him back, and it took him a minute to realize it was Diane.

"I . . . have to . . . go," he said, each word as

sharp as a dagger. Instantly she dropped her hand. Liberated, he walked out the door, down the short path, and onto the sidewalk, picking up speed as he strode away from the house. He didn't slow his pace until he was several blocks beyond Thayer Street, and then he stopped, and overcome by a fierce nausea, more compelling than any he'd ever known, he leaned against a parked car and vomited.

He heard someone scream, "Get away from my car, you lousy drunk," and forced himself to move on, ignoring the cold sweat that dripped into his eyes and down the back of his neck.

"I'll be all right," he told himself out loud to keep from having to stop and be sick again. "I just have to get back to my room, pack my things, and take the next train home. Once I'm back in Seattle, I'll be all right."

✑ 11 ✑

There didn't seem to be much point in getting up. Sam lay in bed, awake but unmoving, her mind not so much drifting as being dragged from thought to thought. Michael had gone to work at the embassy. He had come in to bring her tea and say good-bye about an hour ago, but she had pretended to be asleep, and he'd left the tray on the night table beside her bed. The tea would be stone cold by now, so there was no point in getting up for that.

Sam had decided that if nothing happened by the end of the week, she would go home. It was already Thursday, and nothing had happened. She told herself she should get up and call the airlines to make a reservation, but instead, she rolled over and closed her eyes. She wanted to sleep again. Only sleep brought relief from pain, because only dreams brought her closer to Drew.

The phone was ringing. She covered her head with a pillow and decided to let the answering machine pick up. She remembered the days when she had jumped at every ring and run to answer every call. But after the flurry of activity following the revelation that Drew had been at Harrods the day of the explosion, the calls had become less frequent and more irrelevant. At least there had been no calls from the morgue. No extra bodies had been found. Although sometimes she caught herself thinking that if Drew was dead—she was sure that he was not, but *if* he was—it would be easier if they would just find his remains and be done with it. She tried to push her mind in a direction more conducive to the sweet dreams she craved.

It took Sam a minute to realize she couldn't fall asleep because the phone was still ringing. Michael always left his answering machine on, assuming that if someone was home, the telephone would be answered before the machine picked up. Incessant ringing could only mean it wasn't the primary line.

"Wrong number," screamed Sam, hurling her pillow at the phone to no effect. Now she didn't even have a pillow to muffle the sound.

Defeated, she hauled herself out of bed. "Yes?" she said, shortly into the mouthpiece, allowing the full extent of her annoyance to show.

"Sam? Are you all right?" It was Michael.

"Oh, Michael, I'm sorry. I didn't think it was you. Why are you calling on the second line?"

"Because I thought you might be sleeping, and I didn't want the machine to pick up. We have to talk."

Sam was instantly alert. "Why? Do you have news?"

"Not on the phone. Can you meet me downtown?"

"Of course, but what—"

Michael cut her off. "Not on the phone," he repeated with such emphasis that she clamped her mouth shut. "Meet me in Grosvenor Square, across from the embassy. Can you make it by noon?"

"I'll be there," Sam said, hanging up and racing to the shower before Michael could even say goodbye.

It was that London rarity, a cloudless day, and Sam was sitting on a bench in Grosvenor Square, her face lifted to the sun, by eleven-fifteen. Her hair was still wet, and she had fanned it over her shoulders to dry in the summer breeze while she waited. It was hard for passersby not to stare as the damp tendrils seemed to absorb the very essence of the sun and transform themselves into waves of copper flame. Eyes closed and shielded by dark glasses, Sam, as usual, was oblivious to the attention she commanded. But Michael, approaching from the American embassy across the street, was not, and he fervently wished that he were meeting this beautiful woman to do something other than find her husband.

Michael tried not to startle her, but Sam still jumped when he touched her arm. "Sorry," he said, by way of greeting. A drying curl had attached itself to her cheek, and he brushed it away, feeling the softness of her skin.

She smiled her thanks, but dispensed with any preliminaries, asking, "What's happened?"

It was a direct question, but it was full of expectation, not dread, and Michael marveled at her ability to keep her optimism intact. "I've spoken to a friend of a friend, and I've been able to set something up."

Without warning, Sam threw her arms around him and kissed him. "You did it! You got me a meeting with the IRA! I knew you could do it!" And she kissed him again.

It took all of Michael's self-control not to grab her and try to turn her gratitude into something more. But he knew it would do more harm than good. He looked around quickly to make sure no one had heard. She was quick to pick up on his anxiety.

"Sorry," she whispered, still smiling. "Let's just pretend we're lovers. No one will notice." She snuggled into the crook of his arm.

I'll notice, Michael thought. But he bent his head toward hers and, looking into her eyes with an ardor that was no pretense, said, "There are ground rules."

"Fine. Whatever is necessary," Sam responded eagerly.

"Okay. First of all, the IRA is an illegal organization. You are not meeting with the IRA. We don't know anyone in the IRA. You're meeting with a man who, I am told, has connections and is willing to listen to you and maybe pass on what you have to say. That's all I know. That's all you know. Do you understand?"

"Perfectly."

"When you meet this man—I don't even know his name; I was just told to call him Taoiseach, which means prime minister—you are to tell him your story, and that's all. Make no demands, no threats. Just ask for what you want and thank him for his time. When he says the meeting is over, it's over."

"But is he going to tell me where Drew is? Or if they'll let him go?"

"Sam, we don't even know if they have Drew."

"Well, then, he can tell me that, can't he?"

"I don't know what he can tell you. Whatever he says, accept it. Don't argue with him. Okay?"

"Okay," she said quietly. But he could hear she was disgruntled.

"Sam, this is no joke. You are dealing with people who kill people they don't even know. I don't want to think about what they do to people they don't like. If you don't promise me that you'll stay in line and in control, I won't take you."

"I promise," she said quickly. Sam turned to look at him. He still had his arm around her and was leaning close as if whispering sweet nothings in her ear. This time she saw the affection in his eyes, and the concern. "Don't worry about me. I can take care of myself."

"It's me I'm worried about," he joked. "If anything happens to you, I'll be out of a job."

He was kidding, but Sam knew it was true. Michael was putting his career on the line for her. "Thank you, Michael," she whispered, resting her cheek against his for a moment. "I'll never forget you."

Michael smiled and said nothing. He was hoping with all of his heart that she would never forget him. If this contact didn't come through, he didn't think Sam would ever find her husband. He knew that would be a crushing blow for her, and for her sake he prayed that's not what would happen. But if it did . . . if it did . . .

Colim looked at Moira skeptically when she announced that the Yank wanted to join the IRA.

Moira tried to mask her worry with contrived enthusiasm, "He really wants to do this. I think he should be given the chance."

Seamus was more vocal. "You're a fucking idiot, you know that, Moira? He doesn't even know who the fuck he is and you expect us to believe he's committed to the Irish cause? All he's committed to is fucking you. We should have killed him when we had the chance. We still can," he added, scowling at her.

"All you're committed to is being a homicidal asshole," Moira responded angrily.

"Shut up, the both of you," Colim said, putting an end to the argument. "The truth is, neither one of you is exactly a soldier of the cross. But times are hard and we're not as choosy as we used to be. If the Yank is willing to go into battle with us, I'm not going to be the one to say no."

"You're right," said Seamus. "We can always use a good man for a suicide mission."

Moira glared at him, but spoke only to Colim. "We're always complaining there aren't enough of us. And if he works with me, I guarantee you, he'll always be loyal. At least he's not coming to us with any preconceived notions."

"You know this decision is not up to me, Moira. Take it up with a higher authority."

"London?" she asked nervously. She had known the situation would come to this, though she had hoped for Colim's enthusiastic support to carry her through. But from the way he was talking, she suspected that she would be on her own. She squared her shoulders. The Yank was hers, and she would not be intimidated into letting him go. "Fine, I'll take him to London. Once they meet him, they'll see that he's an asset, even though you cretins can't seem to catch on so quick."

She turned to go back to the house, but Colim stopped her at the door. "I can't let you go alone, Moira."

Moira's heart surged. Colim was going to come through for her after all. If he favored letting the Yank in, there'd be no argument. "That's great, Colim. With you standing up for him—"

"Not me," Colim interrupted. "I'm under orders not to leave this place. Seamus will take you."

"Seamus? What good will he do me?" She was upset. "He'll just shoot off his foul mouth and stir up trouble."

"Just see to it I don't have a reason to shoot you or your lover boy," Seamus grinned.

"I'd just as soon go alone, if it's all the same to you," Moira said coolly.

"It's not all the same to me," Colim replied brusquely. "You'll go with Seamus or not at all."

Moira got the picture: they didn't trust her. She opened her mouth to say something, but then thought better of it. She could start an argument, but she couldn't win it. She could lie to them but not to herself. She had dreamed of taking off into the countryside with her Yank and disappearing, getting him a new name and papers, flying somewhere south—maybe to the coast of Algarve, where it wasn't too expensive—living in a little cottage by the sea, and raising a family together. She was tired of fighting this war, avenging those already dead, and paving the way for those yet to die. She wanted to reaffirm life, and if she couldn't do it for all of Ireland, why not for just one of its citizens: herself. But dreams were merely a diversion. Reality, at least for a soldier of the IRA, offered no escape. And Seamus would be with them to make sure of that.

"Guess what, Yank? We're going to London," Moira said cheerfully, belying the sense of foreboding she was beginning to feel about the entire enterprise.

He raised his eyes quizzically but said nothing. His heart was beating faster, and he wasn't sure if that was because of excitement or fear. He hadn't left the confines of the farm or seen another soul since he had regained consciousness to find himself in Moira's bed. After the initial panic at not knowing who he was, he had suppressed his curiosity. Instinctively working on the presumption that a watched pot would never boil, he had ignored his apprehension, hoping that as he regained his physical strength, his memory would follow unaided.

Gradually, under Moira's careful ministrations, his body had healed. But his memory had not returned. Sometimes he suspected that Moira encouraged his amnesia, fearing that she would lose him if he regained his identity. Sometimes he pushed back the memories himself, because with them came searing pain and an anxiety for the unidentified entity that was lost in his past, and that pain was so overwhelming that he felt crushed by it. When he was stronger, he told himself, never mentioning it to Moira, he would work it all out. In the meantime he'd allowed his jailer to become his lover, although he knew that her purpose was to defeat his. Going to London meant he was to be released from his prison but stripped of his cocoon. If he was ever going to get stronger, it would have to be now.

"Are we going alone?" he tried to sound casual.

Moira looked at him. She wondered if he'd been thinking the same thing she'd been thinking. Was he looking for an opportunity to escape—for the two of them, or just for himself? She loved him, but she could not know him any more than he knew himself. And though he returned her passion, he had no more to give than what they had together. That was enough for her, but she never knew if it would suffice for him. Perhaps it was just as well that Seamus would be with them, and she would not need to put it to the test just yet.

"Seamus is driving us," she said, as though it were just a courtesy.

"Are we going for any particular reason?"

"Yes." There was no point in lying. "To see about getting your status changed from hostage to soldier."

"So I'm going to be inducted into the army, is that it?" he said with more joviality than he felt.

"Something like that." She smiled.

"And if I'm turned down?"

"Why should you be?" She wasn't going to face that possibility.

"Oh, I don't know. Maybe I'll fail the physical."

She put her arms around him and kissed him, teasing, "That would be impossible. I'll be your reference."

He kissed her back, then pulled away. "Okay, let's say I'm accepted as one of the gang. Will there ever be any chance for us to live a normal life?"

Moira's heart sang. He was talking about a future for the two of them. "What exactly do you mean by 'normal'?"

"Normal. In a house where we're allowed to go out and see the neighbors. Where we can go shopping and go to movies. Where I can find a job and earn some money and—"

"The IRA will take care of us. We won't starve."

"That's not the point. I don't mind sharing your politics if that's what you need. After all, you've done a lot for me. But I can't go on this way indefinitely. I need to go to a doctor, to find out what's wrong with me and why I can't remember anything from before. I'm happy with you, Moira, don't get me wrong. But I might have a family."

Moira started guiltily, remembering the wedding

ring she'd slipped off his finger when she'd first laid him out in this room she'd come to think of as their haven. "If you had anybody who cared about you, don't you think we'd have heard something by now?"

"How? We don't have a radio, we don't get newspapers. We have no contact with the outside world. How would we have heard?"

"I'm sorry, Yank. We did have a radio when we first got here, and we read all the accounts of the explosion. Believe me, we were looking for someone to claim you. In that whole first week, there was nothing. How long would it take for someone who loved you to notice you were missing? Personally, I couldn't make it through a day without you."

She sounded close to tears, and he put his arms around her. He knew she must be right. If there were people to whom he was connected in his past, they could not have cared for him very much. Perhaps he had done something shameful that had caused his alienation. As Moira clung to him tightly, he began to feel that perhaps she was right. Perhaps his past didn't matter. He might not *have* a past, but at least he had a future. And at the moment, he wasn't about to jeopardize that.

"All right, Moira," he whispered in her ear. "We'll go to London, and I'll make them like me. Then we'll figure out what we're going to do with the rest of our lives. How does that sound?"

"Wonderful," she said fervently, kissing his eyes, his nose, his lips. "That sounds just right."

And, for the moment, he thought so too.

* * *

Something doesn't look right, Sarah thought to herself as she pulled into her own driveway.

She had stopped in to see her mother at Belvedere on her way home from Ian's, certain that James, as usual, wouldn't be home for hours. There had been no further word from Sam, but both Mathilde and Sarah were optimistic, feeling somehow that they were getting closer to finding Drew. Even if it was just an illusion, they shared it greedily for an hour, like dieting women stuffing themselves on cream cakes while no one was looking. And when Mathilde had asked about Sarah's friend, she had told her mother honestly that as soon as Drew came home, she was going to leave James and go with Ian. Mathilde had remained silent for a moment, and then, to Sarah's shocked delight, she had hugged her daughter and sworn to help her in any way she could. She had limited control over Forrest's reactions, Mathilde warned, but she would not make the same mistake twice. Sarah had left her mother, aware that some major breakthrough had been achieved. For the first time in her life, Mathilde d'Uberville was thinking not about what was proper, but about what was good.

Now, as Sarah parked her car in front of the house, her good cheer was replaced by a sense of foreboding. As she pressed the bell and waited for the maid to answer, she suddenly realized what was different: all the lights were on. Usually, when she came home in the evening, the outside lights were gleaming, but her frugal staff, in spite of her admonitions, kept the house inside dark until the masters had returned. Tonight the entire house was ablaze. It could only mean one thing: James was home.

Sarah relaxed. She didn't relish the prospect of seeing James, but he no longer intimidated her as he once had. Being with Ian had empowered her, given her back a strong sense of self that would not be cowed by her imperious husband. She was prepared to ignore him or fight him, whichever he wanted. What she was not prepared for was the table for two, set romantically with flowers and candles, in front of the library doors opening onto the garden. And the sight of James smiling at her from the patio, holding open his arms and saying, "Darling, where have you been?"

Sarah hesitated for a moment before joining him. "What's all this?" she asked, trying to act nonchalant, keeping the dread at bay.

Drawing her into his arms, he began, "I've been working so hard, and it's been such a long time since you and I . . ."

Sarah stopped listening. He was lying already. She recognized the unctuous tone he used whenever he felt the need to invent excuses. Usually it had to do with pleasing her parents; she had no idea why he was directing it toward her tonight. She caught phrases: "just the two of us . . . romantic evening . . . want to be with you . . ."

"Stop," she said, deciding she'd had enough. "This is ridiculous."

"What?" James was taken aback. He'd noticed she'd been acting a little different lately, not waiting up for him, not asking questions, not wheedling for more time together. He'd assumed it was just because he had made himself unavailable, preoccupied as he was with Bethany and his plans for the hostile takeover of his father-in-law's business. But he knew that no matter how withdrawn his wife became, if he showed her a little attention, she'd soon be lapping at his hand like a love-starved puppy. Only tonight she wasn't lapping, she was barking.

"James, let's end this pretense. You don't want to spend a romantic evening with me any more than I do with you."

"What are you talking about?" James was getting nervous. Sarah had been angry with him before, but she'd never been this blunt. He could deal with her whining but not with this calculated honesty, which they'd managed to avoid for six years of marriage.

"I may be silent, but I'm not stupid. Do you think I don't know you sleep with other women?"

James felt as if he'd been broadsided. He was spinning, and he needed to regain control. What would he do with an unruly hound? A slap on the nose to show who had power, but not too hard, not hard enough to make the dog turn on him.

"If you were more of a woman," he said quietly, "I wouldn't need anyone else. I'm giving you another chance. I think you deserve it."

She was looking at him, saying nothing. James liked this approach. Crushing, but at the same time, giving. He was pleased that he had been able to bring her down with just a gentle tug on the rug beneath her.

He decided to be even more generous. "I'm not

saying that our trouble hasn't been my fault, too," he went on. "I could have been more understanding about your deficiencies. That's why I'm willing to help you now. Together, we can—"

He didn't see it coming until it was too late: her open palm made stinging contact with the side of his face, and her nails left little red half-moon grooves in his cheek.

"You bitch!" he screamed, grabbing her wrist and wrenching it away from him. He had to hold himself back from punching her; she still owned stock that he needed. "I should—"

"Don't," she said, her voice icy, betraying much less than he had. "Don't threaten me. Don't lecture me. Don't even talk to me. I'm leaving you, James. I'll come back tomorrow to get some of my things. Try not to be here."

"You can't leave me!" he shouted. He was losing control again. He couldn't let her go. He called on other forces. "Do you think your father will let you get away with this?"

"Fuck my father and fuck you!" she said almost gaily as she walked out the door.

James was tempted to run after her, to drag her back into the house and to . . . to what? He needed to think, to calm down and figure things out. Obviously she had found herself a boyfriend somewhere. He almost laughed out loud, imagining Sarah and some little wimp reading poetry to each other under the stars. That was about as hot as she got. What did he care? He didn't want her; he just wanted her shares in DMC. And with her pitiful insurrection, James thought, she just might have delivered them right into his hands.

He picked up the phone and dialed. It rang for a long time before Bethany finally answered. "What were you doing? Playing with yourself?" James asked by way of greeting.

"I don't need to," Bethany said, her voice husky.

"What does that mean?"

"You figure it out." She wanted to make him jealous. If he was going to spend the night with Sarah the mouse, she would let him know what he was missing. Bethany knew they needed Sarah on their side if James was to be successful. With some well-placed pillow talk, she'd managed to turn quite a number of board members against Forrest. But James would still need Sarah's shares to carry him over the top. Even so, it wouldn't hurt to remind him that DMC wasn't the only prize. There was Bethany as well.

"Are you alone?" he asked, getting her drift.

"I am now."

"So am I," said James, and listened to Bethany's silence. He had surprised her, as he intended.

"I thought you were going to woo your wife tonight," Bethany said. She didn't like surprises, and her displeasure showed, which pleased him all the more.

"So did I. But she didn't want to be wooed. She says she's leaving me."

"Shit."

"Why, Bethany, I thought you'd be happy," James teased. He felt his sense of humor returning.

He had a fresh scheme all figured out. "Don't you want me all to yourself?"

"Of course I do, James darling," Bethany said carefully, beginning to realize there were rules in this game. "But we had a plan. You were supposed to take control of her daddy's company before you lost control of your wife."

"Oh, I haven't lost control. On the contrary. See, the way it stands now, Sarah wants something only I can give her: a divorce. I don't think she'll let a few lousy shares of D'Uberville stock stand in the way of her freedom. Do you?"

"You could be right." Bethany was smiling again, James could hear it in her voice.

"I know I'm right. So why don't you come over here and suck my dick?"

"Charming as ever, dear, sweet James," she said, knowing, as he did, that sarcasm not withstanding, she'd do whatever he asked. "But are you sure that's wise?"

"Sarah won't be back until tomorrow. And I'm as hard as a brick just thinking about what life will be like when I take over the company."

"I think you mean 'we,' darling, don't you?"

"I'm not forgetting, baby. We're a team." And she was good pussy. He could figure out what to do with her later.

"I'll be there," she said, knowing where her strength lay, but at the same time aware, as James was not, that all her cards were not between her legs.

* * *

They had talked about it before, and it hadn't done any good. But Melinda wanted to talk about it again.

"Tell me about the rabbits, Lenny," she began, and was rewarded with a laugh.

"Okay, you know Steinbeck, so you can't be all bad. But no, I will not move with you to Los Angeles," said Jack, kissing her on the nose to soften his words.

"I just don't understand you, Jack. I mean, your father has this great firm out there. He handles all these famous people, he really wants you to be in business with him so you could handle all these famous people, and you choose to stay in this one-horse town and work for the union."

"I don't want to handle famous people. I just want to handle you," he said, pulling her down on the sofa to prove it.

"But we could have such a good life out there."

"You don't have a life in L.A.; you have a lifestyle."

"Well, I want it."

"It's a terrible place to raise children. It's filled with conspicuous consumers who teach your kids to be shallow and materialistic."

"So what happened to you?"

"I escaped. But I'm not taking any chances with my baby."

"It's not your baby," Melinda pointed out unnecessarily, as she hoisted herself up.

He pulled her down again, with a little more force than he had intended. "Don't say that. You're my baby, and this kid in your belly is my baby, and nobody's ever going to know different."

"I hate you," she said, and he knew she meant she loved him.

It was the only bone of contention between them. Ever since Jack had told her about his Beverly Hills upbringing and the pressure Horace Bader put on his son to join the family firm, she had been on his case.

Jack understood Melinda's need to get away. Oakdale was a factory town, and she carried in her own body the evidence that the factory's ugly tentacles could engulf a person's entire life. He didn't blame her for wanting to leave behind the grimy chimneys and the grim reminders of what the D'Uberville Motor Company had done to her and her family. He had offered compromise. They could move elsewhere in the state, maybe buy a farm. He had no compunction about giving up the practice of law for a second, and final, time.

But that hadn't satisfied her. "What about New York, then?" she had responded. "There are a lot of opportunities there."

"For whom? You or me?"

"How about for both of us? There are lots of classy law firms there. You'd make a lot more than they pay you at the union."

"I'm not a member of the New York State Bar."

"Big deal. You're a genius. You could take the test. You'd ace it for sure."

"Thanks, but no thanks."

"Why not?"

"Because New York is worse than L.A. for children. And I don't want to work for a classy law firm. If I did, I would have stayed with my father."

"Okay. That's my point. Let's just go to L.A., then."

"I am not moving back to L.A."

They were back to square one, and Melinda was beginning to despair. She did love Jack, as much as he loved her. He was smart, kind, and generous to a fault. He had not only accepted her in her plight but had made it his own and turned it into no problem at all. And as if a man who looked like a Greek god needed enhancement, he was an extravagant and highly skilled lover who clearly adored women, and her above them all. Melinda would gladly have lived with Jack forever. But not in Oakdale or any hick town like it.

"Well, too bad. Because I'm not going to waste my life in some backwater burg having babies and getting fat."

"I can think of worse things, but nobody's asking you to do that. We could find a nice college town, you could go back to school, get a profession if you want."

"I don't need to go to college to become a movie star."

"Oh, please. Not that again." He wished he had lied and told her he had been raised in Oshkosh. He had known it was a mistake the minute he mentioned L.A. and she breathed, "Hollywood," with such awe that he'd had to keep himself from laughing. It had touched him to realize that a life devoid of romance had warped her thinking as surely as malnutrition distorted the body of a child.

He had tried to explain that the glamour depicted in magazines was carefully orchestrated by a phalanx of publicists, makeup artists, and media flacks and that being a recognized "personality" was (a) not easily accomplished and (b) highly overrated. But his explanations hadn't done any good.

"Look at Demi Moore; she's had babies. I can get back into shape in no time. And if we were in L.A.—"

"Melinda," he interrupted, "it takes more than a good body to be a movie star."

She gave him a hard look. He shook his head, understanding. She expected him to be honest. "Okay, so not always. But even if you look great, stardom won't necessarily happen for you. There are a lot of great-looking women in Hollywood, all going after the same thing, and most of them don't get it. And they don't have babies at home to worry about."

"Damn it. The stupid, fucking baby again." She pointed at her belly as though she were fingering a criminal in a lineup. "You care more about this baby than you do about me."

"I didn't say that." He could see the fight was getting uglier than usual, and he wanted to end it. He got up to leave.

But Melinda wasn't finished. "You want to live in some rural hole because you think big cities are bad for children. Well, I was raised in a small town and look where it got me—pregnant, without a job, a man, or a future."

"Thank you very much," he said sardonically, reminding himself that hormonal changes in pregnancy made some women very volatile. "I think I should go now. You can calm down, and maybe we can talk about this another time. In fact, I'm sure we will."

He went to kiss her, his hand automatically lingering on her belly as it did so often these days. She pulled away angrily. She had been trying to hurt him, and already he was forgiving her. He was so damn good, he wouldn't even let her be bad.

"I'll call you tomorrow," he said, blowing her a kiss as he headed out the door and down the stairs.

"Don't bother!" she shouted, following him out. "I hate you," she said for the second time that evening, meaning it this time. "And I hate this baby. I wish it were dead. I should have had an abortion when I had the chance. I'm giving it up for adoption as soon as it's born. Do you hear me?" she hollered after him as he hurried down the four flights of stairs. "Then you won't have me or the baby." She leaned over the railing on the top landing, demanding a response. "Do you hear me?"

Jack heard a crack. He looked up and screamed "No!" and for a split second Melinda thought he was answering her question. And then she was screaming too, as she realized her feet had left the floor and she was falling, fast and far. By the time they both stopped screaming, Melinda was lying at Jack's feet, facedown, four floors below.

❧ 12 ❧

Melinda felt the loss before she saw it. Her eyes were closed, but she was awake. There was pain, but it seemed to be all over her body; she couldn't tell where it generated from. She was lying on her back, her body covered. She tried to move her hand. It hurt, but it responded to her unspoken command. Gingerly she passed her palm over her torso. And then she knew. There was no mound to scale, just a flat plain of bruised skin. The baby was gone.

A tear squeezed from the corner of her eye. A hand brushed it away, not her hand. Someone whispered to her from very far away. "Melinda? Melinda? Can you hear me?"

She recognized Jack's voice as he repeated her name. She wanted to stay far away, but she was coming closer to him. She tried to push herself back down into the space where she had been, distant and alone, but he wouldn't let her. He kept talking, "Come on, sweetheart. Open your eyes. Talk to me."

Melinda opened her eyes. She was in a hospital bed. Jack smiled at her gently from overhead. "I didn't mean it," she said. "I didn't want my baby dead." And then she began to cry.

Jack held her. "I know that. It's okay. It's not your fault," he murmured.

But she would have none of his comfort. "Yes, it is. I said those awful things. I made it happen. This is my punishment."

"Stop it," he said firmly. "What happened was an accident. You do not make things happen by saying them. I upset you. You were angry; you were mouthing off. There are no thought police among the gods that come and strike you down whenever you say something you don't mean. That's just superstition and stupidity."

"I shouldn't have—"

But he interrupted her. "A lot of things shouldn't have been done and shouldn't have been said. But that has nothing to do with your accident. Things happen. I don't know why. But I know you didn't fall because you willed it to happen. So stop blaming yourself."

She looked at him, forlorn. "Who can I blame?" she asked, but he had no answer.

"Maybe the baby just wasn't meant to be," was all he could say.

He had the grace not to say "It's all for the best," but she thought that was what he was thinking. She wondered what the dead baby thought. Maybe it *was* for the best. Maybe she wouldn't have been a fit mother. Maybe her baby's soul would be reborn into a family who deserved a child, to a mother who didn't curse her own flesh and blood.

"We can have more babies," Jack was saying, *"Our* babies."

But not *this* baby, Melinda thought, and just shook her head no.

Jack misunderstood. "Yes, you can. You're okay. Actually, the baby saved your life. Because of the way you landed, you were protected . . ." He didn't go on. She didn't need to hear the gory details.

Her mother came into the room. Jack moved over, making space for Diane beside Melinda's bed.

"I know it's hard," Diane said, "but at least you're all right. I was so scared for you, pumpkin. Dad, too. But you're okay and that's all that counts."

It wasn't all that counted to Melinda. She seemed to be the only one who cared that the baby was dead. And she was the one who had cursed it. Everyone else seemed happy just to have her alive. Melinda wished she were dead.

A nurse came in and took her blood pressure and temperature. She smiled a lot and chatted pleasantly with Jack and Diane.

"You just need a little rest, and we'll have you out of here in no time," she told Melinda as she jabbed a needle into her arm.

Melinda said nothing as she felt herself merciful-

ly drifting into sleep. She was in no hurry. She felt
that she had nowhere to go now and nothing to do.
She was a void, empty of thoughts, of plans, empty
of baby.

The lights were off on Mrs. Boggs's porch, and
the front door was locked. Sarah knew there were
house rules—among them, no visitors after hours
—but there was no question of her going away. She
looked up and saw a light in Ian's window. She
could see his shadow moving around behind the
lowered blind. For a minute she thought about
throwing pebbles at his window to get his attention,
but she wasn't that good a shot. There was always
the chance she'd hit someone else's window, if she
made contact at all, or even break something. She
was better off taking her chances with Mrs. Boggs.

Sarah's hand hovered over the bell as she realized how nervous she was. She had just walked out
on her husband, faced possible disownment by her
father, and decided to pick up and follow a virtual
stranger, albeit a stranger she loved, all the way to
Seattle, but she was afraid to face Mrs. Boggs.
Laughing out loud, she rang the bell.

"I'm really sorry," she apologized profusely
when the landlady opened the door. "I know it's
against the rules, but I have to see Ian. It's an
emergency."

"Oh, dear. I hope nothing's wrong," Mrs. Boggs
said, solicitous as usual.

Sarah smiled, reminding herself she was going to
have to stop being so fearful and start trusting that
good things could happen to her.

"No, no, nothing's wrong," she assured Mrs. Boggs. "In fact, I have good news. It's a . . . a happy emergency." She knew she was babbling, but she didn't care. Reality was starting to hit her with full force: she was free, she was in love, and for the first time in her life she was going to do exactly what she wanted to do. No one could stop her.

"Well, you'd better go on up, then." Mrs. Boggs smiled.

Sarah beamed back, then raced up the stairs, understanding the infectious quality of joy, and anticipating the delight of sharing it with the man she loved.

She didn't even think to knock. Bursting into the room, she found Ian as she'd seen him when she'd first realized she wanted this man—wearing only his jeans, his chest bare, the skin taut over rippling muscles. He was standing by the bed, and with an exuberant leap across the room, she pounced on him, pushing him backwards onto the quilt.

"I'm yours," she said, laughing. "I'm yours, I'm yours, I'm yours," and began to cover his face and body with kisses, expressing her desire as she had never done before.

It took a moment for the shock to register on Ian, and then it kicked in with a vengeance. Summoning his strength, he lashed out, pushing her away, shouting, "Get off me," with the strangled cry of an animal under siege.

Sarah fell back against the iron headboard, not hurt but dazed. A knot of dread, the seed of the fearfulness that she had forcefully jettisoned at the door, took root in the pit of her stomach and began to spread its familiar tentacles through her body. She was dismayed to find she almost welcomed it. Passivity seemed so comfortable, so much more natural to her.

"What's wrong? What did I do?" she asked, not quite cowering, but ready.

Ian looked at her. He had never felt such yearning and such revulsion at the same moment. He longed to take her in his arms, to tell her she had done nothing wrong, that he loved her, that he wanted her, but he stopped himself. The very thought was enough to call up deeper reservoirs of revulsion. She is your sister, he silently castigated himself. And if you love her, you will let her go without making her feel ashamed, without telling her the truth.

"Jeez." Ian laughed, as though she'd played a joke on him. "You sure surprised me. I just wasn't expecting you, that's all." He got up from the bed and put on his shirt, as though it was no big deal, just something he was going to do anyway.

"Sorry," said Sarah, watching him, wary. "I was so excited, I wanted to share my good news with you."

"Oh, yeah? What? Did they find Drew?" He tried to sound as if Drew's safety mattered as much right now as it had before.

"No. I left James." It sounded hollow, stupid, not such good news at all.

"Really?" said Ian, confirming Sarah's assessment. "Do you think that was a good idea?"

"We *did* talk about it," Sarah said, letting her annoyance show. Why was he acting as if she was feeding him unprocessed data?

"Yeah, I know. Of course, we did." Ian felt awful. He knew he was undermining every bit of confidence she had tenaciously amassed, and that pained him as much as it did her. "But you said you weren't going to leave James until after Drew was found."

"Tonight just seemed like the right time. He was trying to con me into a romantic dinner because he wanted something—probably from my father—and then he blamed me when I saw through his scheme. I just couldn't spend one more minute listening to him put me down and puff himself up. Walking out seemed right."

She sounded close to tears, and Ian desperately wanted to comfort her. But he couldn't, not in the way he knew would work best. Turning his back, he walked over to the window and pretended to study the moon.

"Look, if it seemed right, it probably was. But maybe you shouldn't have come here. This could just complicate things for you. Maybe you should go to your parents. You said your mother was sympathetic. She can help get you through this."

Sarah was looking around the room. She had stopped listening. "You're packing," she said, her consternation apparent. "Why are you packing?"

"Uh . . . I have to go back to Seattle. You knew that."

"But not yet. School doesn't start for another couple of weeks. I was going to go with you."

"Well, I don't know if that's such a good idea—I mean, on such short notice. You've got things to straighten out here, and I got a call from my principal. There are things I have to do before the semester begins. It's no big deal."

Ian knew he sounded callous, but he didn't know how to change that. He had meant to write her a letter before he left, a long, gentle, kind letter, telling her how special she was and how much she had meant to him. But he couldn't say those things in person, not without her expecting him to hold her, not without him wanting to.

"When are you going?" Sarah's voice was dead, and he knew how miserably he was failing her.

"Tomorrow."

"When were you going to tell me?"

"I was going to leave you a note. It happened so suddenly, and I couldn't very well call your house."

"No, of course not. Anyway, it doesn't matter. I'm here now and I know."

Ian nodded. He wanted to scream: You don't know anything. You don't know that I love you. And that it's killing me to leave you. That I can't tell you why I have to go because I'm afraid you might make me stay. And that it might kill you if I did. Sarah, my sister, my love, you don't know anything.

She was moving toward the door. "I guess I'd better go." She turned to him. "So this is good-bye."

"For now," he said.

"For now," she responded, but it sounded like forever.

"Where are you going? To your parents?" he asked, hoping.

"No, I'll just go home."

He couldn't stop himself. "Listen, Sarah. Don't do that. Don't go back and take his abuse. You're a beautiful, vibrant, loving woman. James is a bloodsucker. He'll put you back in that coffin of a marriage, and you won't come out alive. Get out while you can."

He wasn't touching her, but Sarah felt him connecting. She looked into his eyes and saw a reflection of her own, filled with pain, longing, need, love, confusion. For a visceral moment, she knew she had not been wrong.

"Ian . . ." she began, but he heard what she did not say, and turned away. She lost her nerve. "I've got to go."

"You deserve better than James," Ian said, keeping his eyes averted.

"I thought I deserved you," Sarah answered quietly. And when he turned back, she was gone.

In the car, driving around Woodland Cliffs, trying to decide if she really should go home, Sarah wondered why she wasn't crying. She figured this must be like being in an accident. At first you went into shock, and you couldn't even tell if you were bleeding. She knew she was bleeding. She just didn't know yet if her wounds were fatal.

Something had happened that she didn't understand, and she sensed that if she tried to work it out right now, a gallon of novocaine wouldn't numb her pain. There would be time for that later on.

Years of desolation to figure out what made it so hard for someone to love and to keep her.

She cruised through the neighborhood, trying to sort out her thoughts. She'd left James pretty definitively, but that didn't mean she couldn't go back. After all, she was still her parents' child; they still owned all the cars, so she still had something James wanted. James would certainly be mean to her, but she couldn't be hurt much worse than she'd been hurt tonight. And in her state of shock, which at the moment was beginning to seem like an advantage, she would hardly feel a thing.

Bethany heard the car first. James realized something was wrong only when her head stopped moving in his lap.

"Don't stop, baby," he whimpered. But at the slam of the car door, the complaint died in his throat, and pushing Bethany's head away, he jumped up and ran to the window.

"Shit, shit, shit, shit," he said, as he grabbed Bethany's arm and started pulling her toward the terrace. "It's Sarah. Get out."

"You said she'd be gone all night," Bethany hissed.

"I was wrong. She's back. Get out."

"I'm naked, for God's sake." Bethany was furious. She wouldn't have minded if Sarah had walked in on them. She could have handled that scene with aplomb. But James wanted her to hide, and that put her in an awkward position, and she hated feeling awkward.

"Shit, I almost forgot. Your clothes." He started

grabbing things, stuffing them into her arms, never releasing his grip on her as he shoved her outside onto the balcony, two stories above the English rock garden.

"What am I supposed to do out here?"

"Get dressed and shut up. I'll get rid of Sarah, and then you can sneak out."

Bethany had always liked cheap thrills, sex with a risk. But this was tawdry. There was a difference. "James, I am not—" James tightened his grip. "Ouch!" she wailed. "You're hurting me."

"I will really hurt you if you don't shut up. Don't ruin everything for me, Bethany. I've put six years into this marriage and I'm not going to screw it up for a lousy blow job."

"Lousy?" she protested, but he had already shut the French doors, slid the dead bolt in place, and drawn the curtains.

James was in bed reading the *Wall Street Journal* when Sarah came into the bedroom. He didn't lower the paper. "Back so soon? Did your lover boy have a change of heart?"

"I know you're going to have to torment me over this, James. But not tonight, okay? I'm tired."

"I could have told you, Sarah. Even poets don't want to live on poetry forever. Every man wants a real woman."

It didn't matter what he said; she wasn't listening. "I'm just going to get some pajamas and sleep in the guest room."

"You don't have to do that. I'm still your husband. Let's just say you owe me one." He'd been upset when she came back, but now he liked the way things were turning out. She was giving him a chance to be magnanimous. He could forgive her tomorrow and get her to sign over the stock. Maybe if he played his cards right, he could even get her to finish what Bethany had started.

He waited for her to respond, but she wasn't saying anything. He lowered the newspaper a half inch, just to see what game she was playing. Then he dropped it. She was standing in front of him, a pair of red and black lace bikini underpants hanging on her finger, swinging back and forth in front of his eyes.

The best defense is a good offense, he told himself, refusing to panic.

"Why are you waving your underpants in my face?" he asked her, no hint of nerves in his voice.

"They're not mine."

"Really? Well, they're not mine." He guffawed and went back to reading the paper, as if the question had been answered.

She ripped the newspaper out of his hands and hurled it onto the floor, then threw the panties in his face. "Get this straight, James. I don't care who you fuck as long as it's not me and as long as it's not in my house. I'm going to the guest room. Get her out of here, and make sure she doesn't come back."

"You're crazy, you know that?" he shouted, running after her. "There's nobody here, but anybody who knows you wouldn't blame me if there was."

"That's it, James. I've had it. I am not a piece of

dirt and I won't be treated like one any longer. By you or by anybody. Get a divorce lawyer. You're going to need one."

When Sarah closed the door to the guest room and James heard the lock turn, he rushed back to the bedroom balcony. Bethany was dressed and waiting. "You stupid bitch," James greeted her, throwing the offending panties at her. "Sarah found these. Now the shit has really hit the fan."

"What's your problem?" Bethany said calmly, slipping her panties on under her dress. "I'm glad I got these back. They're my favorites."

"Don't you get it? She's going to give me trouble because of you."

Bethany did get it. She'd had plenty of time to think, standing on the balcony. It was clear that James was not capable of handling a crisis. Maybe she had bet on the wrong horse. But there was still time to play another race. "No, James. Because of *you.* She doesn't even know who I am. And I can't imagine you're going to want to tell her."

The appointment had been set for eleven, and they'd left before eight, plenty of time to get to London without speeding or calling attention to themselves in other ways. But they'd only gone about two miles in the last half hour, they were still a good forty-five minutes from central London, and it was already eleven-fifteen.

"Can't we get off this road?" Moira asked nervously, staring at her watch and peering over the seat into the traffic ahead.

"Yeah. I can crash through the fence and plow

across the field. Nobody will notice." Seamus was just as anxious as Moira, and it didn't make him any pleasanter to be with.

Moira looked at the Yank, sitting beside her in the backseat, and shrugged, trying to give him a reassuring smile. She didn't want him to be upset. He still had to impress the Taoiseach, and showing up a couple of hours late wasn't going to make the task any easier for him.

"Look," he said, trying to break the tension, "there's something going on just over that hill."

"Shit," said Seamus, spotting the flashing red lights of a police car. He leaned down, pulled an Uzi from beneath the seat, and placed it beside him, his hand resting on it for comfort.

Moira went ballistic. "Are you crazy? What the hell do you think you're going to do with that thing? Put it away!"

She tried to reach for it, but Seamus slapped her hand away. "If this is a roadblock, I'm not stopping. We'll shoot our way through."

"They'll kill us," she said unceremoniously, knowing it was true.

"We all got to go sometime. I'd rather die fighting than hanging in a British prison."

Moira felt the Yank taking hold of her hand. She leaned against the seat beside him, and he pulled her close, into the crook of his arm. "Don't argue with him," he whispered in her ear. "It will only aggravate him and make him more volatile."

Moira nodded and rested her head against his shoulder. She felt safe. She had rescued a wounded bird, and he'd turned into an eagle to protect her.

Once he was accepted into the Republican ranks, they could get married. They'd find a way to distance themselves, maybe get posted to another country and live a normal life, as he had said. But not America. She didn't want him to ever go back to America. He was hers now. He couldn't ever go back.

Helping Moira gave him comfort. He needed no past reference to know the woman in his arms needed him. None of the rest of it really made sense. He had agreed to this interview for her sake, but even without memory, he had recovered enough to recognize that the political arena was alien to him. He did not belong here, in this country, in this morass. But until he could figure out where he did belong, it would suffice. To take off alone, an aimless, wandering drifter who didn't even know his name, held no appeal. He doubted he would be allowed to do that even if he wanted to. At least Moira gave him a purpose. He could question everything else, but he didn't have to question her love.

The car inched closer to the flashing lights, and he could discern a buzz of activity. "Put away your gun, Seamus," he said. "It's just an accident. Nobody's after you."

Seamus gave him a dirty look in the rearview mirror, and he had the feeling that the Irishman would have relished a little bloodshed. But the gun was returned to its hiding place, and he could feel Moira relax against him.

"We're going to be over two hours late for our

appointment. Are you sure that'll be all right? Should we stop and call or something?" he asked.

"No." Moira was adamant. She didn't want to give anyone the opportunity to turn them away. "Let's just go. He'll see us."

By one o'clock Michael Litton had parked his car in front of the nondescript building where the Taoiseach held court. They were an hour early, but Sam had been so agitated that he'd agreed to leave the house just to keep her from throwing things against the wall. At the fish and chips place on the corner he'd bought them each a cup of tea, which they sipped from Styrofoam cups.

"If they want a ransom, I'll pay it," Sam said, breaking the silence.

"We don't even know if the IRA has him."

"Well, if they do and they want a ransom, I don't want to involve the police. I'll just get in touch with Mathilde, and we'll pay it and get him back. I've already discussed it with her."

"Don't do this, Sam," Michael said gently. "Don't anticipate. It'll just make it harder if you're disappointed."

He was trying to be kind, Sam knew. Michael was invariably kind. But he did not believe the way she believed. Drew was alive and she was going to get him back. There might be obstacles, but in the end, she would not be disappointed.

"How much more time?" she asked.

"About forty minutes. I don't think we should show up early."

"No, you're right. I'm just going to get out and stretch my legs."

She leaned against the car, sipping the tea, gazing around her, trying to keep her mind on anything except what might transpire in the next hour. She'd already been through that dozens of times with dozens of scenarios, and she knew Michael was right. Anticipation served no purpose.

There was some moderate activity on the street, and she watched, without really seeing, as people went in and out of the shops on the ground floor or called to each other from the fire escapes outside the windows of the residential second story. This was a blue-collar area, clean and well kept. She watched as a car slowed, looking for a parking space, and smiled, knowing that she and Michael had snagged the last spot. Half a block ahead, the driver gave up and double-parked. A man and a woman emerged from the backseat and started walking back in her direction on the sidewalk opposite.

"Hey, Sam, listen to this," Michael was calling to her from the open window of the car. He had the radio on, and she could hear the voice of the BBC announcer, but nothing registered. She dropped her cup. Hot tea splashed on her feet and legs, but she felt nothing.

"Drew!" she screamed, and suddenly she was running toward him. "Drew! Drew!"

Moira saw her coming toward them and for a minute thought they were observing a well-dressed maniac. It wasn't until the Yank stiffened, stopping dead in his tracks, staring at the beautiful woman with the flaming red hair, that she understood.

"Oh, my God!" she gasped, grabbing his arm. "Get back to the car. Come on. We've got to get out of here!" She was pulling him, and she was grateful that he seemed too stunned to resist. He kept looking back toward the woman running after them, and Moira could see from his face that something was happening in his mind, but at least he was coming with her.

She opened the car door and pushed him onto the seat, scrambling in behind him. "Drive!" she shouted to Seamus. "Go. Go. Go."

"What's happened?" asked Seamus, but her urgency was not lost on him, and he had already turned on the ignition.

"It's a trap. It's someone who knows him or something. I don't know. But we can't stay here."

"What do you want me to do?" If he couldn't shoot his way out, Seamus was at a loss.

"Just drive. Go back to the country. I'll work out a plan with Colim."

She looked at the Yank—Drew. He was looking out the rear window and shaking. She followed his eyes. The redheaded woman had been joined by a man. They were running the way the woman had come. Moira prayed it was over.

"Yank?" she said softly. She would not use that other name. "Are you all right?"

He shook his head no and covered his face with his hands. He had said nothing from the moment the woman had appeared. Moira tried to catch her breath, and fervently hoped that what had just happened was simply a bizarre incident with no relevance. But hoping would not make it so. She knew her Yank was Drew and was somehow connected to that woman, and now he knew it, too.

Drew. The name hovered above him like a hawk waiting to settle. He felt himself drowning in stimuli—names, words, images, demanding recognition, coming at him as though a sluice that had been closed too long had suddenly and carelessly been opened, and now threatened flood where there had once been famine. He struggled to surface, afraid of being sucked into an undertow of eternal forgetfulness. He shut his eyes tightly and forced himself to stop gasping, to breathe in and out, in and out. Gradually his heart slowed, and the panic abated. And then memory settled over him like a mantle, sure and comfortable, familiar and recognized. Drew. He was Drew Symington. Andrew Symington of Woodland Cliffs. And the woman who had called his name was his wife.

"Of course I'm sure!" Sam screamed at Michael when he came running after her. "I know my husband."

"Why didn't he say anything? Why didn't he come to you?"

"I don't know. Maybe he's been drugged. I don't know. We have to follow them. We can't let him get away."

They ran back to Michael's car and managed to keep the battered Vauxhall in sight, even though it had a good head start.

"Call Hastings," Michael said to Sam, handing her the car phone as he drove.

She got the captain on the phone and put him on the speaker.

"What the hell were you doing parked out there anyway?" Hastings wanted to know.

"It doesn't matter at this point, Bruce," Michael said, giving her a quick look. "Mrs. Symington saw her husband. He was hustled into a black Vauxhall, looks to be maybe six or seven years old. I couldn't get the license number but it's heading past Euston now, toward Camden High Street, and my guess is they're going for the A1."

"Okay. I'm putting a bulletin out. We'll find them. You'd better drop back. They could be armed and dangerous."

Michael looked at Sam. She was vigorously shaking her head and mouthing "no."

"Maybe I'd better just keep the car in sight for the time being, in case your men don't pick it up right away. I'm staying far enough back not to be a threat."

"Just until I've got a confirmed tail on it. Then you're out. Do you understand me?"

"Yes, boss," Michael said, and rang off.

"Michael, you've been absolutely wonderful to me, and I'll never be able to repay you," Sam said quietly, after Hastings had hung up, "but if you purposely lose sight of that car, I will never speak to you again as long as I live."

"I had a feeling you might feel that way," he said, with good grace. He concentrated on the drive, on the road, on the Vauxhall two cars ahead. It was better than focusing on what his heart was telling him: they were finding Drew, and he was losing Sam.

By the time they were on the A1, passing through Cambridgeshire, there were four unmarked cars on the trail. Michael had recognized them from Hastings's description, and allowed them to pass, so he and Sam were fifth in line behind the Vauxhall. Since Michael had promised Hastings they'd quit the convoy, they'd stopped communicating with police headquarters, and so were left to follow and assume that Scotland Yard knew what they were doing.

"I don't understand why they don't just pull them over," Sam fretted. She was trying to stay calm, but the long drive was taking its toll.

"As Hastings said, they could be armed. If the police try to stop the Vauxhall, anything could happen. Once they get where they're going, it will be a lot easier to take them by surprise."

Sam nodded. He was right, but that didn't help. She wanted Drew beside her now. In her arms now. Safe at home now. She tried to pray. She couldn't even think.

At Tuxford, an hour and a half out of London, something happened. The black Vauxhall pulled into a service station. The first unmarked car continued on the A1.

"Oh, my God, they didn't see," gasped Sam, even as the second unmarked car turned off the highway and onto the station ramp.

"They saw," said Michael quietly, slowing. "Two

of the cars are going into the station. The other two are probably circling around."

"Pull in, pull in, pull in," shouted Sam, as if her urgency alone could command Michael. "Please," she begged, when he hesitated and the car behind him gave him an angry honk.

"Okay," he said, not sure he was doing the right thing, but unable to bear either her wrath or her pain. "I'm going to park by the rest stop. But stay in the car. No matter what happens, you stay in the car until it's all over."

The three of them had driven in silence halfway to the Lake District. Drew leaned forward, his head buried in his arms, letting remembrance flow over him. He knew who he was, where he was, and what had happened. He just didn't know what to do about it. Where there had been confusion, there was now only fear.

"Talk to me, Yank," Moira had finally said, unable to stand his silence any longer. "Are you feeling all right?"

She had given him the idea then, and he'd looked up and seen the sign for the Tuxford service area. "I'm sorry, Moira," he answered, partly telling the truth and partly stalling for time. "Something is happening to me, and it's making me feel sick. Can we stop for a minute?"

She looked at him, and saw something she did not recognize in his eyes. But he took her hand and put it to his lips, and said, "Help me," and she could not refuse.

"Pull into that petrol station," she said to Seamus, as though it had been her idea.

"Why? I've still got half a tank."

"Yank's got to go to the loo. You can fill up now and we won't have to stop later."

Seamus shrugged. It made no difference to him. The entire trip to London had made no difference to him, and no sense, either. He pulled up at the pumps and stopped the car. Immediately, Drew opened the door and got out.

"Go with him," Seamus told Moira. "And if you're not back in five minutes, I'm coming after the two of you."

"Put it back," she said in disgust as he fingered the Uzi for emphasis. "Where the hell are we going to go?" But she was just as happy to follow her man.

From the door of the men's room, Moira could see it happening. There were eight of them, moving two by two, converging from the four corners of the service station. She could not see weapons, but she was sure they had them. Oblivious, Seamus drummed his fingers on the steering wheel, while he waited for the attendant. Her first instinct was to shout a warning. She wasn't sure if it was fear of surrender or hope of survival that kept her mouth clamped shut. She slipped into the men's room and closed the door behind her.

Standing at a urinal, Drew saw her over his shoulder and smiled, having fully expected her to follow him. "You're in the wrong room, lady," he teased, but stopped when he saw her ashen face.

Quickly he zipped himself up and came to her, afraid she might faint and fall before he reached her. "What is it? What's the matter?"

"They're here." Her throat was dry and her voice cracked.

"Who?"

"I don't know."

They heard the gunfire then, the *rat-a-tat* of the Uzi and then *blam-blam-blam* in response. There were shouts, a scream, words exchanged that they could not make out between the bursts of shelling. The machine gun seemed to get louder, as though it were right outside the door, and then the door was flung open and Seamus was inside with them, still shooting, shrieking a string of unintelligible invective over every blast.

In the second that the door had remained open, Drew had seen her. She had jumped from a car at the rest stop and was trying to run toward him. A man had leaped from the car after her and was struggling to pull her back.

Seamus crouched at the door, inching it open every few seconds to deliver another round of bullets. The noise was deafening.

"Sam!" Drew shouted, but wasn't sure if he spoke aloud.

Moira pulled at his arm. "There's a window in back," she whispered, her mouth right in his ear. "Seamus is too busy to notice. We can get out. Get away."

He shook her off. "I can't, Moira. I have to go out there."

Seamus heard him. "Stay where you are. No one's going anywhere, understand me?" and let off another barrage for emphasis.

"Who is she?" Moira asked bitterly. She had seen her, too, the woman from the street, the woman who had called him Drew. She had followed them, brought danger to them.

"My wife," he said simply, but from the way he said it, he might as well have said his life.

"God damn. This is happening because of you and your fucking Yank." Seamus was foaming at the mouth. "He got us into this, he'll get us out." He grabbed Drew around the neck and held the gun to his ribs. "Let's go."

"What are you doing?" Moira cried.

"He's a hostage, isn't he? I'm going to use him as a fucking hostage." He moved to the door. "Walk out in front of me, Yank."

"Let him go. They could kill him," Moira's pitch was rising. She was on the verge of hysteria.

"Yeah, well, if he doesn't do what I say, *I'll* kill him."

Seamus nudged Drew forward with the gun. "Open the door, Moira," he said. She hesitated, knowing what she would have to do. "Open the fucking door," he screeched.

And she did—throwing it open and leaping across the threshold in one herculean hurdle that knocked Drew to the floor and left Seamus tripping over him.

The response was instantaneous: a barrage of gunfire, a cacophony of screams, shouts, pounding footsteps. Drew somersaulted, cradling his head to protect it from the pebbled asphalt, in a fetal crouch rolling for his life. In another instant the noise abruptly ended, and he came to rest, huddled in an eerie silence that frightened him almost as much as the clamor.

He looked up and saw men rushing toward him, their hands reaching out. They were asking him questions. Was he hurt? Was he all right? He couldn't answer. A simple yes or no seemed insufficient, anything more complex, futile. Then she was on her knees beside him, her arms around him. It was the only answer he needed. "Sam," he whispered, crying into her glorious flaming hair. "Sam."

Sam was crying, too, and repeating his name, holding him, kissing him. He was paler, thinner, weaker, but it was Drew. After a moment he pulled away. "I have to . . ." he said, and she understood and let him go.

He passed Seamus's body, a cloth thrown unceremoniously over his face, guarded even in death by a detective with a gun. A few feet to the left lay Moira. Someone had covered her with a jacket, but he could see the blood leaking onto the ground beneath her. He could hear the sirens approaching in the distance, but from the faces of the people around her, he understood the ambulance would come too late. The others moved away when he came near.

"Moira," he said, bending his head to hers. "Can you hear me?"

She opened her eyes and smiled. "Do you know who you are now, Yank?"

He nodded and placed his arm under her head as a cushion. "Andrew Symington at your service. But everyone calls me Drew."

"It doesn't matter," she whispered. "You'll always be my Yank. At least in my mind."

"In my mind, too, Moira," he said, kissing the top of her head. "I'll always be your Yank."

✑ 13 ✑

The return of Samantha and Andrew Symington turned into a giant media event. The discovery that an American citizen had been held hostage by the IRA was newsworthy in itself, but when that citizen was Andrew Symington, it became the lead story on every broadcast and in every newspaper in Oakdale and Woodland Cliffs. Hours before their plane was expected, a battery of lights was already being set up, with the networks vying for the best vantage points and staking out their territories.

Even Forrest, regardless of his personal feelings, had been forced to show up at the airport by the public approbation of his only son and daughter-in-law. Profits at DMC had been down slightly in the first two quarters of the year, and some free media coverage was highly welcome. To add to his problems, he'd had a disquieting visit the day before

285

from Drew's ex-fiancée, Bethany Havenhurst, who had informed him that his son-in-law, James Fielding, was trying to engineer a hostile takeover. She'd been a little cryptic about how she knew so much about the plan, but her data had been unequivocal, and he'd had to admit that he owed her one. Forrest had confronted James and fired him on the spot. James, of course, had threatened legal action, but in the face of the irrefutable evidence, denial was impossible, and any action would have been futile.

The only real flak Forrest expected was from his daughter. But to his surprise, when Sarah was informed of the course of events, she offered a reprisal of her own. She intended to divorce her husband as soon as possible, and all she asked of her father was that he hire a top lawyer for her to make sure that James got as little as possible. Given the circumstances and the potential for scandal, it appeared prudent to milk every bit of good publicity from Drew's return. And Forrest Symington was nothing if not a prudent man.

Dodging requests for interviews and microphones thrust in her face for spontaneous comments, Sarah waited with her parents at the airport. Unwilling to focus on the shambles she had made of her own life, she concentrated on anticipation of Drew's arrival and was rewarded with a few rays of joy shining through the clouds of distress. She watched, bemused, as Mathilde held court, playing the charming grande dame with several of the anchormen, and Forrest, surrounded as usual by sycophants in three-piece suits, "handled" things.

Preferring to remain in the background, Sarah

maneuvered herself away from the maelstrom, but still she felt that she was being watched. At first she assumed that someone in the pack of journalists was scrutinizing the sister of the hostage. But the farther she drifted from the vortex of the media operation, the more intensely she felt a presence engaging her. Finally, whirling around in annoyance, she saw Ian standing on the far side of a tour group from Japan, a bag slung over his shoulder. He was looking at her with eyes so full of love and longing that his gaze deepened over the distance and cut through all interference between them.

For a moment their eyes locked, and it was as though they were in the same space, breathing the same air, sharing one heart. But then she took a single step forward, and he turned away, melting into the ever-moving crowd. Sarah felt her soul shattering. She forgot where she was and why she was there. All she knew was that she had been frightened into losing so much that she could not allow herself to be intimidated again. If she was going down, let it be in flames. This time she would not bail out.

"Ian!" She called his name, running after him, weaving her way through the travelers, bumping into suitcases, muttering apologies, but never stopping, never even slowing down. She knew he heard her and pretended not to, but still she pursued him. She had seen his eyes, loving points of light that offered hope of a safe landing on a bumpy runway, and that was enough.

He had to stop at the gate for his flight to Seattle, and she caught up with him there.

"Don't run away from me," she said quietly.

He didn't deny that that was what he had been doing. "It's too hard, Sarah," was all he said.

"What? What's too hard?"

"Everything," he answered, then changed the subject. "I heard about your brother on the news. It's really great. At least something good is happening for you."

"Other good things are happening, too," Sarah replied. "James is out of my house, out of my father's company, and out of my life."

"That's wonderful," Ian said, and Sarah knew he meant it.

"So why can't I go with you?"

This was what he had been afraid of. "Look, it wouldn't work—"

"No," she interrupted him. "Don't lie to me. Not you. I know we love each other. I know it would work. We both do."

"It can't," was all he could say. They announced that passengers could now board the plane. "I have to go," he said.

"I won't let you," Sarah answered. "I may not be able to stop you from getting on this plane, but I'll come after you. I've learned a lesson from Sam and Drew: you can get what you want, not just what you're supposed to have."

He gave a sardonic laugh, "Well, you're definitely not supposed to have me."

"Why not?" she asked angrily, insisting on an answer. "You can go, but you owe me the truth."

Ian looked at Sarah, confronting him, blocking

his passage, her eyes blazing, daring him to contradict her. This was not the fragile woman he had found cowering in a booth at the Cozy Corner. She had changed. He had helped to change her. But, he realized, his part was over. He flattered himself if he thought that anything he said or did now would turn her back into the victim she had been. She was right. He owed her an answer.

"You know I came here to meet my birth mother."

"Diane Myles, I know. What does she have to do with us?"

"I finally got the nerve to go see her. She told me who my father is."

"That's interesting, but what—"

"My father is Forrest Symington," Ian announced before he lost his courage.

Sarah felt her knees give way. She didn't know what she had been expecting, but not this. "That's not possible," she whispered as Ian caught her arm and led her to a chair.

"It's a secret, but it's the truth. He doesn't know about me. He thinks I was aborted."

"What can we do about it?" Her voice was full of desperation. She knew she wasn't being logical, but it seemed unreasonable to just give up the greatest —the only—love of her life.

"Sarah," he spoke her name like an invocation, "we can't help what we feel, but we can't act on it either. We are brother and sister."

The final call for the flight to Seattle was announced.

"I have to go," said Ian.

"You do love me, don't you?" Sarah said, making it sound more like a proclamation than a petition.

"As much as you love me," Ian answered, allowing himself, just this one final time, to touch her face.

"Write to me," she whispered, covering his hand with hers. "We can stay in touch. We can get over this other stuff and still be family, maybe see each other sometimes."

"We can try," he said, not knowing if they could succeed, but knowing that no matter where he was, Sarah, his sister, his love, would remain with him forever.

Sarah waited until Ian's plane had gone, and then she wandered back to Arrivals. She felt dislocated, forbidden to think about life with Ian, unable to think about life without him. For the first time since arriving at the airport to await her brother's return, she was grateful to be thrown back into the media circus.

The milling crowd had grown, and Sarah saw that Sam's family and friends had arrived and had congregated at the opposite end of the room from the Symingtons. Ignoring her father's stern gaze, Sarah approached Diane Myles and greeted her warmly. There were introductions—to Harvey Myles, to Melinda, Sam's sister, and to her friend Jack Bader. They shared a few moments of euphoria, cheering each other with trite but heartfelt expressions of joy at the prodigals' anticipated return. Then she moved back to her own camp, leaving them to revel in the comfort of their own familiar happiness.

"She seems nice enough," Harvey commented to no one in particular after Sarah had gone. "It's amazing that a bastard like old Symington managed to end up with a couple of decent kids."

"Don't start, okay, Harvey?" Diane warned. "Everybody showed up for Sam and Drew, and today that's all that counts."

Even Melinda had checked herself out of the hospital to be there. Diane had tried to tell her it wasn't necessary, but Melinda had insisted, and the doctor had agreed, providing she stayed off her feet as much as possible. Diane looked at the row of seats where Jack had parked himself with her younger daughter. Melinda had made up carefully, to compensate for her pallor, and though she looked exceptionally beautiful, there was a sadness in her young face that hadn't been there before. But there was a new strength as well, that showed beneath the frailty of her mending body, and Diane had a feeling that Melinda would recover far more quickly than expected.

Sitting in the airport waiting area, Jack's arm resting protectively, possessively, around her shoulders, Melinda was indeed beginning to feel a new strength. In the hospital bed she had felt vulnerable, incapable of dispensing with the past or proceeding with the future. Jack had been with her every day, planning for the two of them what she could not consider alone. He had been a comfort to her, but his presence had been enervating, inducing a lethargy that made any effort to reconsider her life fruitless. Here it was different.

The sight of Forrest Symington, providing sound bites for the evening news, had galvanized her thinking. He had studiously ignored her, but she had caught the flicker in his eye when she crossed his path, had seen the almost imperceptible double take as she walked by without acknowledging his presence. She was glad for the effort she had put into her appearance, even though her ostensible purpose in going to the trouble of looking good was to keep from scaring her sister. But here, in the airport, she had to admit to herself that she'd expected Forrest to be here, and if not him, then his wife, and she had wanted to make an impression. It still mattered.

Watching Forrest operate his family unit and manipulate the press, Melinda both detested and envied him. He had ruined so many and gained so much, it hardly seemed fair. His power had given him leave to wreak havoc and be rewarded. His abuses disgusted her, and yet seeing him suddenly clarified for her what it was she needed: the license to be as self-centered as ambition required.

If she'd had the baby, things might have been different. But there was no baby anymore. There was just the desire to show him, to show them all, that she could do better, command more attention, make more money, be more famous than anyone else in this stupid small pond. If success required a certain carelessness toward the feelings of others, so be it. She could have the power.

"Jack," she said, the tenderness in her voice

belying the strength of her conviction, "after Sam and Drew get settled again, I'm going away."

"I think that's a good idea, honey. I'll take some time off from the union. We can both get away."

"I'm not talking about a vacation, Jack."

"What are you talking about?"

"About moving to Hollywood."

Jack rolled his eyes. "Not that again. I thought after what happened—"

"Don't," she interrupted. "I know what happened, and I know how awful it was. I know it better than you do. But that doesn't change the fact that I hate this town."

"Okay. I understand that. I've always agreed to go somewhere else."

"Jack, I'm going to Hollywood. There's no reason anymore for me not to."

He stopped short and looked at her for a long time.

Melinda averted her eyes. She knew she had hurt him. She hadn't wanted to, but it had been necessary.

"The fact that I won't go there isn't reason enough?" he asked, forcing her to say it.

"No," she answered, her voice shaking a little, but her determination unwavering. "Not anymore."

"I see." He paused, seeming to weigh his words. "What exactly do you think you're going to do out there? Become a movie star?"

"Yes," she answered, trying to ignore the tone of derision, but hurt that he would use it with her, even though she understood it might be necessary for both of them to inflict more wounds before this was over.

"Listen to me, Melinda." He was being earnest now; there was no hint of sarcasm or condescension in his voice. "I love you. There's no denying you're beautiful, and you probably could do whatever you set your mind to. But I've been in Hollywood. It's full of other beautiful women who are just as ambitious, just as determined as you. And I'm telling you that in the end, when the ambition swallows them and the determination takes over their lives, they can get pretty ugly. Please believe me. It's not a wonderful life."

They were interrupted by one of the newsmen. Having spotted Melinda, he'd approached and was asking for a comment. How did the family feel? Were they excited? Had they been afraid for her sister, concerned that she might not return, with or without her husband?

Jack saw Melinda toss her hair and instinctively turn her face into the light. "We never doubted Sam," she pronounced, managing to convey loyalty, fear, and belief in one breath. "We don't give up easily in our family," he heard her say. And in that instant he understood that Melinda could listen to him talk all night, but she would never hear what he was saying. And in that instant, in his mind, he kissed her good-bye and wished her luck.

On the plane, Sam and Drew watched the lights of the city spread out beneath them. The United States Air Force had kindly provided them with transit, and except for an occasional visit from the copilot to see how they were doing, they had been alone for the six hours of the flight.

It was time they sorely needed. There had been a barrage of media attention, a few days of debriefing for Drew, a sad and silent trip to South Armagh for Moira's funeral, and no time for themselves to say the things that had remained unsaid for the months they'd been apart.

Sam could see how difficult the ordeal had been —and continued to be—for Drew. She longed to comfort him, but it was hard to find the right words. She could not tell a man who had just recovered his memory that he should try to forget what happened to him. And, seeing him as he stood alone at Moira's freshly covered grave, tears coursing down his cheeks, she herself could not forget that something profound, irrevocable, had happened to the man who was her husband. From now on, and forever, there would be a part of him she could not share.

"I can't talk about it now," he told her, when she asked him, in the most general terms, what had taken place. "I don't know if I'll ever be able to."

She fell silent, understanding, but hurt nonetheless, and he saw it.

"I love you, Sam," he said, taking her hand. "Me, Drew. That wasn't me in that cabin in England. It was some guy called Yank, whom I didn't really know and never will."

"He was the one Moira loved, wasn't he?" she asked softly.

"Yes. She saved his life. *My* life. Twice. And now

she's dead, and I can't repay her. The worst part is, I know that if she had lived, I would only have hurt her. There would never have been a happy ending for Moira."

"Because there is a happy ending for us."

They fell silent. Sam turned to Drew and took his face in her hands. Saying nothing, she kissed his forehead, his eyes, his nose, his cheeks, remapping the territory that had once been hers. With each press of her lips, she felt him release a little more, as though a gate, long closed, were slowly being unlocked. And when, finally, her mouth was on his, and his arms moved to encircle her, she felt the gate burst open, the last barricade between them gone.

"Welcome home, my love," she said, smiling, but unable to stop the tears from rolling down her cheeks.

Gently he brushed them away with the back of his hand. "I will never, ever, leave you again," he said fervently, and then he kissed her for a long, long time.

A subtle cough made them separate, and they found the copilot, eyes discreetly focused somewhere above their heads, smiling and waiting. "Sorry, folks," he said when he heard them laughing and knew it was safe to look again. "We're about five minutes off the ground, and the tower tells me you've got a welcoming committee about the size of Kansas down there. TV crews and all. I thought I'd better warn you."

Drew shook his head in rueful good humor. "Get knocked on the head, forget who you are, end up in a shoot-out, and suddenly everyone wants to know you."

"Hey, I got to admit," the copilot said, laughing, "the pilot and I were considering making you sign over your movie rights to us before we landed, but we figured if we didn't get yours, we could always buy them from some guy who knew you in the third grade."

"Does this mean I have to comb my hair?" Sam joked after he had gone back to the cockpit.

Drew looked at her. Her makeup had long since worn off, and copper curls spilled haphazardly around her face. She looked radiant. "You don't have to do anything to be beautiful. You just are," he said, not complimenting her, just telling the truth.

"It's because I have you back. If I could figure out a way to package bliss instead of blusher, I'd have the market cornered."

The plane bumped down and slowed to a smooth stop. Looking out the window, they could see that barricades had been set up to keep well-wishers and press from spilling onto the runway. Camera lights had already been turned on and were illuminating the night sky like a Hollywood set.

"Are you ready for this, Mrs. Symington?" Drew asked Sam, as they stood up and stretched.

"Just hold my hand and I'm ready for anything," Sam answered. "How about you?"

Andrew Symington looked at his wife. Now that he remembered every detail of their life together, he felt amazed and frightened to think it might have been lost forever. More importantly, looking into her eyes, he recalled not only the past but saw the future as well. Although he'd never admitted it to Sam, he'd been worried before, wondering how they would make it, if they could survive the stern reality of a life programmed for hardship. But they'd been through far worse than he could ever have imagined, and here they were, intact. No matter what happened to them from now on, it could only get better.

Drew took Sam's hand and clutched it tightly. "Ready," he said.

POCKET BOOKS
PROUDLY ANNOUNCES
THE LAST TITLE IN OUR
SUMMER OF LOVE TRILOGY

TO LOVE AND TO CHERISH

LEAH LAIMAN

Coming in Paperback
from Pocket Books
mid-July 1994

The following is a preview of
To Love and to Cherish . . .

There was no introduction. One minute Phil Donahue was standing in the audience, rustling his papers, putting on his jacket, and the next minute they were on the air.

"This man, Andrew Symington," Phil said, with heavy emphasis, "was born into one of the richest families in this country. The Symingtons. Have you heard of them? The D'Uberville Motor Company?" he asked the audience. There were murmurs of assent. He plowed on, quieting them with his words.

"This woman, Samantha Myles Symington, Drew's beautiful wife, was blue-collar all the way. She was an assembly-line worker in his family's auto factory. So was her father. So was her mother. Drew and Samantha met, they fell in love, they got married. A fairy tale? I don't think so. Tell us what happened."

Phil bounded toward the stage, pointing at Drew. The camera moved in close. Sam smiled at her husband and squeezed his hand. The audience saw and seemed to approve.

"Well, first, my father disowned me." He tried to go on, but Phil was there.

"Completely? Cut off? No more money?"

"Not a red cent," Drew said sweetly.

"How did you feel about that?" Phil was addressing Sam now. "You married a prince, you got a pauper."

"It didn't bother me," said Sam. "My financial position didn't change; Drew's did. I married for love, not money."

The audience applauded. Drew and Sam smiled at each other again. They were making friends.

"Okay, I buy that," Donahue was back to Drew again. "What happened next?"

"Well, briefly, I went to London to try to raise money so Sam and I could start our own business, and I got caught in a bombing at Harrods."

There was a collective gasp in the studio.

"Wait," Phil admonished. "It gets even better."

"I was wounded," Drew continued, "and taken captive by the members of the IRA who had engineered the attack. My injury caused me to have amnesia, so I ended up staying with my captors in their hideout until Sam came and rescued me a few months later."

"Unbelievable, isn't it?" Phil asked, and the audience applauded in response.

"You almost became one of them, didn't you?" Phil queried earnestly.

"Yes, but not out of conviction," Drew answered carefully.

Phil paused and checked his notes. He looked at the audience, then back at Drew and Sam. He took a breath and paused for dramatic effect. "There was a woman, wasn't there?"

Drew looked at Sam. She took his hand.

Phil wasn't ready to let him answer yet. "She was a beautiful young revolutionary, a woman who loved you, who saved your life and tried to recruit you into the IRA. Isn't that so?" The question sounded like an accusation, and Phil bounded toward the stage, as if ready for a fight.

"Yes," answered Drew simply. There wasn't anything to fight about. "It was a woman."

"Did you sleep with her?"

"I beg your pardon?" Drew was taken aback. He'd expected his story to be sensationalized, but not quite like this.

Phil looked at the audience and shrugged his shoulders, raising his eyebrows as if to ask what they thought. "That's what we all want to know, isn't it?" He tried to sound sheepish, as if he were just a pawn of the audience's will, but there was no mistaking the gloating in his voice as the audience broke into applause and laughter.

"I don't see that it's relevant," said Drew quietly, holding Sam's hand a little more tightly. There were groans of disapproval from the audience.

"Let's see," Phil consulted his notes again, as if he hadn't planned the interview down to the last detail, as if this were just a spontaneous investigation into an interesting enigma. "You're injured by a bomb, planted by the IRA. You stumble into the arms of one of the terrorists, a gorgeous young woman, who manages to notice that you're not so bad looking yourself." Again eyebrows raised to audience, more laughter and applause.

"So she decides to save you instead of just letting you die there, as some other less fortunate people did. She takes you to her hideout, nurses you back to health. What I'm getting at is, *to what purpose?* You don't expect us to believe she just wanted to help the cause?"

"Well, Phil," said Drew calmly, refusing to be caught up in the animation of a titillated crowd, "I hate to ascribe motivation to someone who can't speak for herself . . ."

"Why not?" Phil was almost on top of him. "Because she wouldn't admit to the affair she had with you? Because it would embarrass you, and I guess, the young women as well?"

"No," said Drew, his voice quiet, measured. "Because she's dead."

There was a burst of laughter, then silence. It had sounded like a joke, but it wasn't a joke. There were whispers and nervous titters as Phil looked at his notes. He wasn't as prepared as he thought he was. He tried another approach.

"Okay, now let me get this straight." He was looking at the audience, but it was clear that he was addressing Drew. Phil knew how to work that camera. "You marry this woman, who is not only gorgeous . . ." Catcalls and whistles came from the audience as Sam smiled and lowered her head demurely. "No, I mean it," Phil said. "She's gorgeous. And if I got this right, she's also some kind of automotive genius." He turned to Sam. "You've invented some kind of gizmo that's going to make driving as we know it obsolete. Is that right?"

Sam laughed charmingly. "Not exactly. It's an energy-saving pollution-control device that could be manufactured quite cheaply and easily implemented into current models."

Phil raised his hand to Sam, cuing the audience to applause. "As I said. Gorgeous and some kind of genius. She goes into a war-torn country to save you"—he was back to Drew—"risking her own life, if I'm not mistaken. And because of her, your family, your very, very rich family, I have to add here"—pause for effect—*"disowns* you." Deep groans from the audience, a commiserating rumble. "Does this make sense?" Phil went on gratuitously.

"It doesn't make sense to me," Drew said without artifice. "Sam is the most wonderful person I've ever met, and as far as I'm concerned, by keeping her out of their lives, they have lost much more than I ever could."

"Beautifully spoken," Phil said approvingly as the audience applauded wildly.

When they'd quieted, Sam got her turn to speak. "You have to understand that the Symingtons feel they have a position in society to maintain, and I was an assembly-line worker in their auto factory when I met Drew. It's hard for them to adjust."

"Very charitable," said Phil. "Have you tried to get them to change their minds? Has there been any contact?"

He turned to Drew, but it was Sam who answered, and the camera quickly shifted focus. "When Drew was missing, both his mother and his sister helped me. I know they would like to normalize relations. But Forrest Symington is a very controlling man. You don't buck his authority unless you're ready to face the consequences. You can see what happened to Drew."

"Exactly. You're out of the family home, out of the family business." He bounded off stage and into the audience, crouching low as he thrust the microphone into the face of a heavyset woman who was standing in the aisle.

"First I want to say that I think you two are just great. You're like real American heroes," she began.

Phil pulled the microphone away, "What's your question?" He pushed it back in her face, his head lowered.

"Well, if your family cut you off, what are you going to do now?"

Drew and Sam smiled at each other. This was what they had been waiting for: the reason they had agreed to appear on television and expose themselves and their lives. "We're starting over again on our own," said Drew. "My father did it, with my mother's money, of course," he went on, and was rewarded with genuine laughter.

Sam picked up where he left off, a well-orchestrated duet. "We've got my invention and Drew's knowledge of the business side of the automotive industry. After all, he's worked for his father for his entire adult life. I know how cars are built; he knows how cars are sold. I think we make a pretty solid team."

"And what are you going to use for money? Dreams are free, but reality takes cash, am I right?" said Phil, rubbing his fingers together.

Drew laughed. "That's the hardest question you've asked so far, Phil," he said, trying to convey warmth and camaraderie. "The truth is, we have no idea. We'll have to go out and raise money, and we're determined to do it."

The audience applauded. Phil beamed. "I feel a lot of love in this studio today," he said, allowing himself a moment of sentimentality. And though it was corny, it was true. "You're a brave and beautiful couple, and you deserve to make it."

Phil was saying good-bye and telling the audience what to expect on tomorrow's show. Sam and Drew looked at each other and grinned.

"Did we make fools of ourselves?" asked Drew.

"Do we care?" answered Sam.

Sarah hung up three times before she finally had the courage to speak. Ian recognized her voice after her first hello.

"I had a feeling it might be you," Ian said.

"Why?"

"I don't know. I guess because I wanted it to be."

They were both silent for a few seconds, feeling each other's presence over the distance.

"Ian . . ." Sarah finally spoke, relishing the feel of his name on her tongue. "I have a favor to ask you."

"If I can do it, I'll do it," he said without hesitation.

"Come back to Woodland Cliffs."

She heard him groan, as if she had somehow

managed to physically punch him through the telephone wires.

"What good would that do?" he asked, with evident pain. "It wouldn't make our lives any easier."

"I'm not asking you to come back for me," she said quickly. "I mean, I want to see you, but you're right. Life won't be any easier. I want you to go after my father."

There was a moment of stunned silence. "How do you mean that?"

"Sue him. File a paternity suit. Go public if you have to. Make him recognize you as his son."

"Why? I don't want his money."

"I know that. But that's where he lives. If you threaten his finances, you threaten his position. If you threaten his position, you threaten his control. And if his control is threatened, maybe he'll stop acting like such an asshole."

"Drew?"

Sarah knew Ian would understand. "Sam and Drew are having a terrible time. Their factory burned down, and they can't raise money to start over. Sam is working as a mechanic, and Drew can't even find a job. My father could help, but he won't. I think you're the only one who could scare him into changing."

"Even if I came back and sued him, how would that make him reconsider the way he's treating your brother?"

"He might agree to set up a trust fund for Drew in exchange for your backing off. I mean, if you were willing to give up your own claims . . ." Sarah faltered. She knew what she was asking. Ian could stand to make a fortune by pressing his own legitimate rights. But she also knew, with dead certainty, that he would never even consider taking up the issue for personal gain.

"I see," Ian said, and as she had expected, there was relief in his voice.

"Will you do it?"

"Sarah . . ." His voice was hoarse. "If I come back, and we see each other . . ." He broke off, then started again. "I think about you all the time. And I'm having trouble thinking of you as my sister."

"I know. It's the same for me."

"What are we going to do about it?"

"What can we do?" She flushed with pleasure to know the desire was still there; then, fast on its heels, came the shame. "Let's try not to think about it," she said quickly. "Let's just try to help Drew and see what happens. Can't we do that?" It was as much supplication as inquiry, and Ian could not be immune to her need.

"What about your mother—and mine? If I went public about Forrest being my father, it would affect them as much as me. I don't think Diane Myles has ever even told anyone she gave a child up for adoption."

"If they agree, would you come?"

"I don't know. Let's both think about it. I couldn't leave during school, anyway. By the time the term is over, you may not feel the same way. You may not want me to come after all."

She wanted to shout, "Not a minute of a single day goes by when I don't want you to come." But she knew a statement like that would just terrify them both. "Think about it," was all she said, and she knew Ian would understand everything else.

The traffic was stopped. Melinda Myles, dressed in a diaphanous white dress, walked down the Paseo Montejo toward the Plaza Mayor in downtown Mérida, her chestnut hair stirring around her shoulders by the tropical breeze.

"Qué linda," someone in the crowd whispered, as people pressed forward against the wooden sawhorse barriers to see what was happening.

"Cut and print," Prescott Wills called out. "Let's go to the next setup."

Melinda abruptly stopped her walk in mid-step and turned back toward the Casa del Balam hotel, where the small American movie crew was staying. The sawhorses were moved, but the passersby still milled around, smiling and nodding at the Americans who had become minor celebrities in the Mexican city. Melinda returned their smiles, exchanging a few words with the few brave souls who approached her and spoke to her in halting English. She had come to love these people. Like so many others, Melinda had become inured to the image of Mexican immigrants in the United States—the "wetback," the dishwasher, the migrant worker— that she had forgotten that some of these people were descended from Mayan princes. Here in the Yucatán peninsula it was easy to discern the heritage in these noble faces.

"It's going to take us a while to set up in the plaza," Prescott said, taking her arm solicitously. "Why don't you wait inside where it's cooler? We'll call you when we need you."

"Okay," she agreed. "What about you? Can't you take a break?"

"Not right now," he said, distracted for a moment by some activity on the street. "But don't worry. I'm an old hand at making movies. I know the first rule for any good director is to sit down every chance you get."

Melinda laughed, gave his hand a discreet squeeze, and headed into the hotel. Sitting at a small wrought-iron table in the courtyard of the Casa del Balam, shaded by palm trees and hibiscus, she was tempted to pinch herself to see if she was dreaming. On the other hand, if she was, she had no desire to wake up.

Things happen, she reminded herself, as she often did. And this time they had happened quickly. She and Prescott had been lovers for a week when he told her that he had a script he'd wanted to do for five years but had never felt he had the strength. He wanted her to star in it.

At first, though it was an answered prayer, she was hesitant. "You don't have to do this," she'd said, wondering if she was crazy. "I'm not sleeping with you so I can get a part."

"And I'm not giving you a part so you'll sleep with me," had been his only answer before he handed her a script.

After she'd read it, she stopped arguing. She had no doubt that the role was perfect for her, and no fear that she couldn't perform it, especially with Prescott to guide her. They had moved quickly after that. When the studio that had come to life on the profits of all of Prescott's other films refused to advance him the full budget he needed, contending, without shame, that he was old and hadn't had a hit in several years, Prescott had mortgaged his house in Malibu and made up the shortfall. Knowing how tight the budget was, Melinda had insisted on working for scale, and they'd begun casting. The only extravagance that Prescott had insisted on was a well-known male lead for Melinda. She had been excited when she heard that David Burns had accepted the part. She hadn't actually seen any of his films, but he was being touted as the hot new Hollywood leading man, one who could actually act as well as look good on-screen.

Prescott had invited him to the house in Malibu so they could all discuss the script together, and when he walked out onto the deck where Melinda was nervously waiting to be introduced, they had both burst into whoops of laughter that ended in a bear hug.

"Do you two know each other?" Prescott asked, bewildered.

Wiping tears from her eyes, Melinda had nodded. "Let me introduce you. This is Dave Bernbaum. He used to be a limo driver in New York. He told me he was going to become a famous actor, but I didn't know he was going to become David Burns."

"Looks like we've both come up in the world," said David, echoing her joy.

"And a very small world it is." Prescott smiled, generously excusing himself so they could have time to catch up. They never did get to read the script that day. But Melinda told Dave everything that had brought her to the house in Malibu and the verge of a new career, and Dave reciprocated with his own Horatio Alger tale. By the time they were through, it was as though they'd been friends forever, and both of them were certain that from that point on, they would be.

Prescott took them all to Mexico to shoot the film down and dirty, knowing the falling peso would make the meager dollars go twice as far. The crew was skeletal, and everyone who could did double duty, working long hours for little pay. But they all knew the work was good.

Agreeing to be discreet, Melinda and Prescott had taken separate rooms, but in fact, both of them were putting all their energies into the film, and there was little left over for anything but a few hours of well-earned sleep at the end of the day. They'd shoot from sunup to sundown, watch rushes from the week before, which had been hand-carried to a lab in the States and back, and then Prescott would work with the editor deep into the night. Melinda warned him not to overdo it, but he was driven.

"This is my swan song," he said. "You made it happen. I just have to make it right."

In the end, he was making it perfect.

"Senorita Myles?" The desk clerk had approached quietly, startling her. Melinda gave him a dazzling smile. Like almost everyone in Mérida, he claimed to be a direct descendant of Moctezuma II, and as with all the rest, Melinda saw no reason to doubt it.

"What is it, Guillermo?"

"You have a call from the United States."

She hurried to the phone near the front desk. She had told her roommate back home, Lily, that she would leave the number of the hotel in Mérida on the message tape of her answering machine, and Lily had promised to call.

"Hi," she said, assuming it was Lily.

"Melinda!" Diane's voice was full of anger and relief. "Where are you? We got this number off your answering machine."

"Mom! I'm in Mexico. I'm making a movie. Is everything all right?"

"Dad and I are fine. Sam could be better."

"Why? What happened?" Melinda felt bad. She had meant to phone home before she left Los Angeles, but the truth was, she had forgotten. Her life was moving so quickly that she couldn't quite keep up with it.

"There's been a fire. Their new plant was destroyed. Sam and Drew are just wiped out."

"Oh, no," Melinda cried, feeling even worse. She had spoken to her sister while the factory was being renovated. Sam had been so excited, so optimistic. Melinda hadn't felt secure enough to mention Prescott, but she'd joked that if they both kept on the way they were going, they'd be meeting for vacations in Saint-Tropez pretty soon.

"Things have been really tough for them. Do you

think you might get home for a while? It would really boost Sam's spirits."

"I can't, Mom," Melinda tried to explain, knowing her mother would probably not understand. "I'm in the middle of this movie. I can't just leave. It's being directed by Prescott Wills."

Even Diane had heard of him. "Isn't he dead?" she asked.

"No, Mom. He's not dead. He's directing a movie with me in it. It's really good. And I've got the starring role."

Diane sounded happy for her. Just because one of her daughters was troubled didn't mean she couldn't enjoy the good fortune of the other one. "That's wonderful, dear. It's the break you've been waiting for, isn't it?"

"Mom," Melinda said, feeling both the strangeness and the certainty of her words as she spoke them. "I think this film is going to make me famous. And if it does, I'll be able to do a lot more for Sam than I could if I just came now to hold her hand."

The assistant director had stuck his head in the door, and was motioning for her to come. "I've got to go, Mom. Tell Sam I'll call her as soon as I get a chance. It's pretty remote where we are, and the phones don't work all the time."

Prescott came looking for her just as she was hanging up. "We need you, Melinda. David is already in place." Then he noticed her face. "Is everything all right?"

"I just talked to my mother. My sister's having some trouble back home. I feel bad."

He put his arm around her. "Do you want me to wrap for the day?"

She kissed him gently on the cheek. This was an important scene, logistically difficult, and one they'd planned for several days. It would cost him thousands of extra dollars to stop shooting for her, yet he offered to do so without hesitation. It was enough that he offered.

"I'm okay. Let's go to work."

Things happen, she reminded herself, and you do whatever you have to do to realize your dream.

Look for

TO LOVE AND TO CHERISH

Wherever Paperback Books Are Sold.